DIVE INTO A SOLID WALL OF FIRE—
and come out where? That depends on if
you get it right. You dive into the sun and one
way or the other you are no longer in this
universe. You are either destroyed or you
go Elsewhere. As far as the universe is
concerned, you cease to exist.

Only if you are fast enough will you live
to see the other side.

Maya was determined to see the other
side, determined to become part of the
Queen's Squadron.

A tick from now, it will all be over.

Maya took a quick final read.

Decided. Point of no return. Execute.
Slam the accelerator. Dive speed! Into
the sun at near the speed of light, a dive
that would either force her through . . .
or destroy her.

ROC BRINGS THE FUTURE TO YOU

THE
QUEEN'S
SQUADRON

by
R. M. Meluch

A ROC BOOK

ROC
Published by the Penguin Group
Penguin Books USA Inc., 375 Hudson Street,
New York, New York 10014, U.S.A.
Penguin Books Ltd, 27 Wrights Lane,
London W8 5TZ, England
Penguin Books Australia Ltd, Ringwood,
Victoria, Australia
Penguin Books Canada Ltd, 10 Alcorn Avenue,
Toronto, Ontario, Canada M4V 3B2
Penguin Books (N.Z.) Ltd, 182–190 Wairau Road,
Auckland 10, New Zealand

Penguin Books Ltd, Registered Offices:
Harmondsworth, Middlesex, England

First published by Roc, an imprint of New American Library,
a division of Penguin Books USA Inc.

First Printing, July, 1992
10 9 8 7 6 5 4 3 2 1

 REGISTERED TRADEMARK—MARCA REGISTRADA

Printed in the United States of America

NOTE

Though Empirese and other Vikhen languages are linguistic outgrowths of the Indo-European language family of Earth, certain parallels are missing in English, making for imprecise translation. English has no third person singular non-gender specific pronoun. Therefore the translator has followed the precedent of English's close relative German in using the third person plural pronoun as third person singular non-gender specific pronoun, as is also common in the English demotic. You will find in the manuscript *they, them* and *their* used where strictly *he, him* and *his* would be employed. This is intentional on the part of the translator and should be left uncorrected.

> Office of Historical Records
> Court of Queen Isis III
> Anno Domini 5899
> Year 12 Second Eta Cassiopeian Empire

PROLOGUE

What is Götterdämmerung?

The master of this little chamber of horrors—at least the highest ranking being that Paul saw—was called Penetanguishene, a name which made him think of penitentiaries and anguish though it had nothing to do with either. But it had to do with shipwrecks, and a shipwreck was how Paul and his crew came to be under the Rhaltcaptain Penetanguishene's interrogation.

A quiet dignified mortal, the Rhaltcaptain did not enjoy his work as his assistants did, but he was efficient. Efficiency was a byword of the Vikrhalt, the immortal Empire.

"Do you know what is the plan codenamed Götterdämmerung?" Penetanguishene singled Paul out directly this time.

"No," said Paul as if the question were absurd.

The dark eyes widened ever so slightly, a ripple of expression on the interrogator's smooth face. "Tell me how the Telegonians mean to kill the gods."

"Wait a minute, I said no."

"No you didn't."

Bluffing. Had to be bluffing. No one, not even his four crewmembers, knew that Paul had that kind of clearance to know Götterdämmerung. The Rhaltcaptain was bluffing. And damn good at it. No wonder he was in charge of the interrogation center.

He looked as if he ought to be too young for this, but the eyes were as old as a sphinx's and his containment inhuman, so that Paul wondered if he were not an immortal after all. He was attractive enough. All immortals were beautiful, with or without a facemaker's art.

"Look," said Paul. "I am responsible for my crew. I *swear* if you let them go, I will tell you what I know."

Penetanguishene moved in to face him. As if asking him to repeat an insult, he said very quietly, in almost a whisper, "You swear that?"

"Yes," said Paul, paling. He knew that once his crew was out of harm's way he could expect no mercy for himself. This place was famous for what it could do to a human. But it was the best hand he could play. "Let them go. I'll tell you whatever I know. I swear it on my honor." He thought he sounded quite sincere.

Paul had heard of truthsayers, doubted their existence, and never thought he would find himself in a situation to be lying to one.

Penetanguishene moved back, motioned with his head for the guards to move. They were enormous Neanderthal-looking cloned creatures. They stepped wide of the knot of five prisoners. Paul was about to exhale in relief, thinking they were being released, when Penetanguishene produced from beneath his black jacket a primitive pistol, aimed at arm's length, head turned away, and shot Paul's lieutenant.

A loud crack stabbed Paul's eardrums. Something spattered him and he shut his eyes against the sudden spray. Beside him the lieutenant's body hit the floor with a thud. The bullet imbedded itself in the wall where one of the guards had been standing before Penetanguishene had motioned him back.

Paul opened his eyes. Brains. Those were brains sticking to him. He cried out without any conscious thought of doing so, "My God!"

Penetanguishene gestured to a guard to clean the lieutenant's vomit off his shoe.

The Rhaltcaptain was perfectly groomed, clean, and Paul could tell up close, scented. Paul watched the guard cleaning his shiny black shoe and regarded the neat little figure as an obscene monster. Paul's mouth stayed open in disbelief, shock.

Penetanguishene spoke quietly, his deep aristocratic voice charged with anger and contempt, "How simple do you think I am? Have you fallen to your own propaganda? 'Stupid Rhalt toy soldier.' Is that what you think? Your *honor*. I see what that is worth. Now. *I* promise *you*—and my word is worth a great deal more than yours—I will let them," he gestured with the antique pistol to Paul's three surviving crewmembers, "go free, when you tell me what I need to know. Otherwise their deaths will be much much less painless than his, and yours, past speaking. *I* promise."

Paul began to shake. The spattered brains drying on his face itched. He could not bring himself to wipe them off as if they were debris. He said with naked honesty, "There is more at stake here than four lives. I will never betray my home. And it's New Earth, not Telegonia; you may as well get used to that. Let them go. They know nothing." He didn't swear this time. He now believed that Penetanguishene knew the truth when he heard it.

Penetanguishene bid his guards take all the prisoners back to their cells to think it over. "And him," he pointed at the corpse. "With him." He nodded toward Paul.

The ceiling was too low to allow him to stand at full height, the walls too close for him to lie at full length, and Paul was not a tall man. He ripped the cover off the bare mattress which was the only furnishing in the cramped cubicle, and he wrapped Lieutenant Bristol's body in it, crying, hating the son of a bitch who had done this, blaming himself for inviting it. The lie had been a serious miscalculation. Hadn't he heard somewhere about truthsayers? Stupid. Stupid. Had he expected some lenience just because he was a fellow mortal? That man was a fellow nothing. Paul had nothing in common with that *thing*. An officer of the Rhalt. A mortal dedicated to immortals. Paul hadn't really credited it, as he had not credited the existence of truthsayers. He was beginning to believe he had just met one. Stupid misstep simply because he'd been too stubborn to credit what defied *his* idea of what was logical and likely.

I am worse than an ass, because I am in a position to do so much harm.

Penetanguishene was shrewd, insightful, and he was a monster. The galaxy didn't tell tales about the interrogation center Kobandrid Rog for nothing. How could Paul have been so stupid? He had badly underestimated the situation, the man; and now a crewman was dead. So fast. No time to retreat or regret. Bam. That ghastly old weapon, the lieutenant's life sprayed on him. *O God, Bristol, I am sorry.*

Hate hate hate that trim little Rhaltcaptain.

And swore by Bristol's soul and by all he believed in, he would never, never betray his country.

If the immortals found the secret of Götterdämmerung, it would not be from Paul Strand. The immortals were going down. Check and mate. He would not tell.

To my grave, to my living hell, never.

God, who art in heaven and not on Eta Cassiopeia IV, how have we come to this?

PART ONE

THE IMMORTAL EMPIRE

*To whom belongs a world? To those who were
here first or to those who will be here last?*
            —Marchale in communique to
                Telegonia (New Earth)
                advising against the name change.

Aithar Colony
Submember Vikrhalt
Vikhinden protectorate
16 February 5232
XIX. 22. 1779 Empire

I.

The child came as silently as a shadow. Humans were never so light-footed, so the unwary domestic did not hear or see this one until he was directly over its shoulder. The domestic jerked up to its hind feet, wiped dirt off its forepaws. "I—Mistress lost a coin," he explained.

The child's smooth brow knit solemnly. He looked up at the furry face. "Simshit," he said matter-of-factly.

The domestic slapped him so hard the child reeled against the garden wall. And other humans dropped their garden tools and came running.

"What are you doing!"

The simian pulled on its fur in discomfiture. It was insanity to strike a master—for so they called the human colonials, both immortal and mortal, no matter how low born.

The simian Aithran natives were subordinate even to the human cubs. One did well to keep that in mind always.

And this one was the pup of a rather high one in the human pack. Insanity.

The domestic glanced round at all the accusing eyes, knew it was about to be beaten, said, "I . . . I did it because he used bad words."

"That's a lie too," said the boy.

The domestic stared fearfully. Muscles contracted at the corners of its eyes so they became quite square and wide. *Beast. Little beast!*

The human groundskeeper, Tovrai, saw right away what was happening here. The monstrous little boy had the Sight. Everyone knew he carried it in the blood from both sides, but the trait did not usually surface until adolescence, if it ever did. Here he was, seven standard years old, with eyes like eternity. No wonder the domestic had hit him. Tovrai would like to hit him himself. He patted the domestic's shoulder. "I know. I know. Stop cowering. Children should be taught these things."

The child started to object. Tovrai cut him off with a hiss, "And if you know what's good for you, you'll keep your mouth shut about what you think you know."

And that, Penetanguishene recognized, of all things said that morning, was earnest truth.

The domestics. The term was not only descriptive of their duties. The creatures were almost a breed apart. Apart from what dwelled outside the wall.

As different as lap dogs from wolves.

Those Aithrans who served the human caretakers were a paler, suspicious, boot-licking breed who lived in terror of those who dwelled without.

The human masters themselves were wary of the untamed Aithrans. And Father had bid Penetanguishene never to venture beyond the wall. Journeys outside the wall were by armored vehicle on a beaten track in daylight. Or better yet, by VTOL. The planet Aithar was one of those which stood on the borders of the Empire where things distorted and monsters dwelled.

Penetanguishene stood on the perimeter wall and watched the mysterious shadows which shifted in the world outside. He could pick out the ones which belonged to living things from those of swaying boughs which played with what small light filtered through the dense canopy of the surrounding jungle.

He had never seen a wild Aithran, only their shadows, moving darker in the darkness. You never saw wild Aithrans.

Then, this day, with no warning or purpose, one suddenly stepped out into the open space at the foot of the wall, straightened on its hind legs and stared back at him.

It met the boy's gaze, absolutely defiant, as if to say: Why are you watching us? I shall watch you.

Their stares locked and neither would back down or drop his eyes. It had become a dare.

The creature stood erect with a a savage dignity that could be called majesty. It was a darker hue than any sim that Penetanguishene had ever seen, with a thicker pelt, and its furry hair thickened and silvered to became a mane at its neck. Onyx eyes were brilliant. Their gaze held until a domestic from within the wall saw the child up on the parapet and it screeched like a clarion bird.

Penetanguishene glanced back over his shoulder in irritation. By the time he turned back, the wild Aithran was gone, not a bent twig or trembling leaf— or moving shadow—to say which way he had gone.

Penetanguishene headed back on the long wooded path to the house. As he neared, he heard a voice raising, a man yelling at a domestic. "Later! *Nakik!* You see, I know that word." He said it as if this were a surprising and prodigious feat, the mastery of one alien word. After all, he need not know any.

He was a low strata human, so he was coarse. From such as these Penetanguishene learned all the expletives. These people used them every time they spoke. And they were eager, those at the bottom, to lord over someone even lower down than themselves.

"Do you understand *nakik,* you *stooop*id sim?"

The domestic responded in his native tongue, over-convinced of the man's knowledge.

The man cut him off. "No, don't toss that subhuman jabbercrap at me. I know your important word. It's *all* later, isn't it? Well, let me teach you some good Empirese, sim. *Now.* It means you clean the swales *now*, and I'll tell you when you can go home: *nakik*. That's when!"

The sim shuffled off to his task.

Hell of it was, Penetanguishene, who was at an age to learn languages, was picking up that "nakik" was not precisely "later." Usually it meant later, but varying degrees of later, which infuriated the human overlords. "Nakik" meant closer to "in time," or, better, "in its own time," because the Aithrans believed such a thing existed for all endeavors and events which were meant to take place, and a thing's nakik was set by Nature.

The word "hurry" which humans used so often to them, did not translate except as a vague sacrilege.

Penetanguishene remembered once a human asked an Aithran, "Nakik is tomorrow?"

"Yes."

"But the day after tomorrow is nakik."

"Yes."

"Ten years from now is nakik. The whole fucking thing is nakik to you isn't it!"

"Yes, yes, yes. You do understand!" the Aithran said joyfully, just before the human batted him head over heels down an embankment.

The Empire was precise. Tomorrow meant the day after this one. And as Aithar was part of the Vikhinden Empire, the natives had best learn to live with it.

As the garden woods thinned, the North House did not so much come into view as it loomed.

The House of the Stairs, the Aithrans called it. There were no stairs in native houses. The simian Aithrans clambered from floor to floor in their own tree dwellings.

The Rhaltgovernor Agamemnon's home on Aithar, the North House, was a huge timber structure of cathedral ceilings and labyrinthine passages and graceful stairways. The imported wood—the imported *trees*—had been a much criticized extravagance. Even the soil around the North House had to be imported in order to grow the alien trees. Phytotoxins in the native soil would not support the outland growth. The imported dirt unsettled the domestics who called it "dead earth." The sim whom Penetanguishene had caught digging had been testing how deep ran the alien stuff. Evidently no one had told him how deep an oak puts down its roots.

The infamous stairs of North House extended outside and arched even into the ornamental gardens which isolated it from its native surroundings. The walled grounds enclosed an oasis of familiarity for the governor on the alien world—a monument of arrogance because the Aithrans did not understand homesickness and no one bothered to explain it to them. In Agamemnon's house you would never know you were on the planet Aithar.

Agamemnon had hesitated in accepting the position of governor on the colonial outpost.

"Aithar will be important in coming years because of its strategic location," he was told. Aithar's sun commanded a stargate by which allies of Telegonia, especially Earth, had access to the Empire's homeworld of Eta Cassiopeia A IV.

"Ah yes, its strategic location, as you so quaintly put it, is exactly why I should turn it down." That and the fact that his wife would murder him if he transplanted her and the child one more time.

"Xenophobia hardly becomes an ambassador."

"I am not an ambassador," said Agamemnon. "Don't insult me."

But in the end, Agamemnon took the post because most of the Empire's *vondesi*, the so-called truthsayers, had settled here, and there was comfort in numbers, especially when most other people would not talk to one for fear he was reading their minds.

The vondesi were the newest and most feared citizens of the Empire. New, because they had been imported a scant thousand years ago by the immortal Marchale. Feared, because they had an unerring truth-sense which they passed down to their progeny as a dominant trait.

Since the purge of 500 years ago, the vondesi had begun clustering together. Most of them now dwelled on the outpost Aithar. So Agamemnon's family moved yet again.

"For the last time," said Elizabeth.

The child had been uprooted and transplanted so many times to so many worlds by the time he was seven standard years, had seen so many different kinds of beings parade through his father's reception halls, that the marvellous seemed mundane, and he took the astounding as a matter of course. He did not even notice when he started hearing lies. It was as natural as seeing colors, and he did not notice that he hadn't been doing it all along.

When Penetanguishene entered the house today he sensed something was wrong. Odd to see his parents so agitated. He could sense it in their quickened steps and hushed rapid conversations.

Finaliy Penetanguishene spoke out of turn and asked Mother what was wrong.

"Nothing. It's all right."

He stared at her in shock. She stared back, then suddenly all the stern lines melted from her face; her mouth dropped open and out came a cry. "O my God. O my God." And she caught him to her. She held him, sobbing. "You're too young."

You protected a child with lies. How could she shield him from the harsh world if she could not tell comforting lies? It wasn't fair. And worse, there were enemies to those who saw too much.

She channeled her dread into anger and accusation. "It's all the world-hopping. I know it."

There would be a fight about it tonight. She and father.

Elizabeth pulled back from the embrace and knelt so she faced her son. "Don't let anyone know."

"Know what?"

"That you can hear their lies."

"Can't everyone?"

"No. And don't let anyone know that you can. It's our secret."

"They know already."

"Who does?"

"Tovrai. And a domestic."

"The sim doesn't matter. Everything they say is a lie. Tovrai. I shall take care of him. Don't let anyone else know."

"How?" He couldn't very well *lie* about it. It was silly. He could hear it.

"Say nothing. If anyone asks you directly, say nothing at all. Keep silent. You have my permission—my order. Unless it's an immortal. Immortals are our lords and protectors. You must never deceive them. Anyone else, you do as I say."

"Yes, ehre."

After that, Tovrai was not seen again on the grounds, and Penetanguishene was too young to be told what had become of him except that Tovrai would never ever repeat anything he knew to anyone ever again. Mother promised. She was Rhalt. She could make people go away.

Penetanguishene padded silently down the cold stone steps, then ran across the lush carpets which could mute even a heavy man's footsteps, through rooms hung with rich tapestries which swallowed all sound. He tip-toed across the foyer of native marble that was red as dried blood. He pushed open the huge wooden door only wide enough to allow him to eel through. He guided it shut as slowly as he dared, then ducked behind the crimson and blue arras of his father's room of state.

Whatever the terrible thing was, it was not in here yet. It must be something hideous. He had never before been forbidden to watch his father receive ambassadors from other nations, provided he made no sound. "Unspeakable animals," was the phrase he caught concerning these latest visitors.

"Unspeakable animals" was a term to delight a seven-year-old boy's heart. No matter the sanction, Penetanguishene had to see.

He shifted uncomfortably. It was cold behind the arras. The stone wall held a perpetual night chill. The carpet did not reach to the wall, and so he was forced to stand barefoot on unwarmed marble. He would not be able to move once the ambassadors came in. He would just have to suffer in stillness. He resolved himself to it. He knew already in this life it was his station to do things he did not want to do.

He found a good place from which to watch. There was a hole which had been burned in the arras by a jewel-laden lady with a cigarette. Penetanguishene was the only one who noticed it happen or could see the hole in the intricately patterned fabric. It looked like part of the design. The lady had been with the Sebastionique ambassador, but was not his wife or his aide. Father said it had been an insult to bring her here. Mother said she was wicked but would not explain what made her wicked—maybe because she had burned a hole in the tapestry with her burning weeds, but somehow he doubted it.

Mother made her entrance dressed at the height of EtaCassiopeian fashion, which made her look pretty. Mother looked pretty in anything, but when she wore things imported from the capital of the Empire, she moved like a different person.

Today she had traded the loathed shimmering Aithran garments for a full skirt and tight bodice of deep blue velvet edged with white lace and pearls. On her sleek black hair she wore a blue Juliet cap edged in pearls. She seemed excited about the ambassadors though Mother abhorred hideous things. Both she and Agamemnon painted blue crosses on the backs of their hands to let these liars know who they were talking to.

Penetanguishene's heartbeat stepped up in anticipation of what would follow Mother into the room.

He had talked to fish the size of a man, to clawed shaggy beings which needed masks to breathe Aithar's air, to things that stank so horribly that the whole house needed to be fumigated after they were gone. He had seen a creature kill itself here. Now he wanted to see the unseeable.

But it must not have come. The ambassadors came and left, nothing terrible to see, or even interesting really, except when Mother got angry and said loudly, "*Yes*, I hear that you believe what you say, but you are only a mouth! I want to hear the person who told you what to say say that!"

They said something about selling out. What were they selling?

Bored and taken by a damp chill, Penetanguishene sneaked back to his room and crawled stiffly into bed. Later he heard his mother and father coming up the stairs, voices set in fighting tone. The sound had become familiar of late.

Penetanguishene curled up in the blankets, feeling the cold grown into him. He could not understand what had been forbidden.

They were only Earth men.

When Penetanguishene awoke, the jungle was thrumming; the sound engulfed the oasis that was within the wall, the whole outside world become an organism rejecting a foreign body.

Someone said they were killing the gods.

The boy could not comprehend when he heard it, how something deathless could die, how everything he held true could be wrong when he knew he had not been lied to. They were killing the gods.

It was still dark outside. He got up, went down one of the long staircases to where he saw a light.

Mother was still dressed from the evening before, in blue velvet and pearls, but her black hair was loose and uncombed, and her eyes were shadowed indigo underneath. She had not slept.

She came running into the chamber where Father was dressing to go out. "Are we safe here?"

She had to shout over the roaring tattoo of the jungle. The house itself rocked on its foundations. Father's voice was always harsh when talking to her. "Of course. We're remote here, and they know no gods live here."

"I know we're bloody remote here!" Mother shrilled after him as he strode out across the enclosure toward the hangars.

That was when they heard the breaking of doors from the rear of the house.

Mother slammed the inside doors that stood between them and the sound. She cried back over her shoulder, "Agamemnon!"

To Penetanguishene's bewilderment, he saw her pull off her single child ring and hurl it out the garden window. Like watching himself being torn from her. He could not even ask why.

She moved a big jewel-encrusted decorative ring into its place.

She ran to the outside doors, screeched toward the hangars. "Agamemnon!"

Dark things were spilling over the enclosure wall. Things dropped down from the roof. Gray, clawed hands reached inside. Elizabeth slammed the doors on them, pushed them out, locked the doors.

The interior wooden doors behind her bowed.

The wood splintered, crashed in, and suddenly the room was full of simians. Gray spidery hands tore at Penetanguishene. Mother wrenched him out of their grasping fingers, tearing them off like coiling vines. She lifted him to the garden window ledge and screamed, "Run!"

He jumped. He was across the grounds and over the wall before he realized she was not behind him and all that crashing was his.

He saw an airship go over. Father. He must have taken Mother out. That was why she was not here.

Behind him sounded crackling fire and screams the like of which he had never imagined in his nightmares.

He stared back at the wall. A barrier crossed. He hadn't even intended to cross it. Suddenly he was on the other side.

The jungle pulsed beneath his feet. They had roused the jungle.

The jungle sang, reverberated with the hunters' beat. The ground tremored. Echo trees spread the sound, their boughs swaying.

Mother said *Run*.

He pulsed with the trees, moved with them along the undulant ground.

Penetanguishene was an adaptable child with an ear for music. All children of the Rhalt were taught to dance. He picked up the rhythm and moved through the resounding jungle undetected, becoming part of it. That this should be done seemed only natural.

He danced and swayed forward, sometimes on all fours, keeping with the primal pounding ancient rhythm. It wasn't difficult.

Savage blood beat roared in his head.

Not to join them was to give off the vibration of a sick and wounded or aged thing. Predators moved in on the sick, the wounded, the aged.

The outland.

He saw some adults stumble over the wall. They insisted on maintaining their awkward upright one-foot-in-front-of-the-other gait. Clumsy with learned stiltedness they progressed, stumbled, fell. And from the dark wood came a growling. In rhythm.

Claws seized and rent. Teeth and hair flew off in tufts.

Penetanguishene ran.

When the world was still again, hard-shod human feet clicked on blood-colored marble, paused at the remains of the woman.

A second set of footsteps with a less certain stride joined the first, looked round. "Wow," he said, impressed with the havoc. He looked down. "The vondesi?"

"Check her hands."

The subordinate crouched, turned over the woman's hands. They were blue-crossed—she was a vondesi all right—but she wore no plain gold rings. The searchers had not found any child bodies in the house. But children hide. The woman's lack of gold rings revealed that there were none who might have escaped detection.

"Damn thorough, these sims." The overseer nodded. "Damn thorough."

"Want these rings, ehremat? They're beauties."

"Do I strike you as a common thief?"

The other shrugged. "I wouldn't have thought thieving as bad as murder."

"Do you know what the worst crime of all is?"

The other indicated no, grinning, intrigued.

"It is talking too much." The leader drew his sidearm and silenced him forever.

Agamemnon's ship orbited Aithar until help arrived.

Help was suspect. The first ships on the scene belonged to the Vikrhalt's undeclared enemy, the Telegonians.

The free mortal nation Telegonia shared a homeworld with the immortal Empire's premier nation, Vikhinde. Shared. Like two bears in a bottle.

Funny how fast the Telegonian ships found a Vikhinden disaster. First a minesweeper, then a carrier. Both arrived before the Empire's Queen's Squadron, so they must have been lurking very nearby. They said they were here to help. This was not the time to challenge them. Agamemnon took any port in a storm, and he docked with the Telegonian carrier.

"You live at the North House?" his savior asked, a grim foreboding in his voice.

Agamemnon lifted his chin affirmative.

"It's a mess, sir. Don't go back. There's no one there."

"I have a wife and child."

"There's a woman there. She looks like she could've been Rhalt. What do blue crosses mean?"

"It means . . . It means." He lifted his own hands, presented the thin indigo crosses outward. "Elizabeth."

"She didn't make it. And nobody found a child." Then, trying to soften that, he said, "Perhaps your kid ran into the jungle."

"No one can survive in the Aithran jungle," said Agamemnon.

Shaking and crying and retching, Captain Paul Strand shoveled through bones and human ash. It had to be done by hand in case there was actually someone still alive here at the spaceport. Not that the natives had left any other equipment intact to work with.

Paul's ship had answered the distress call first. It struck him odd when the signal first came over the com. A general distress call was odd enough coming from the Empire—the Vikrhalt liked to keep its problems to itself—but this was not from a ship in trouble. It was a whole planet. Aithar Colony calling any ship anywhere.

When he arrived he no longer thought it odd and he did not hesitate to act. Aithar was not his country's colony, but that did not matter. These people were in trouble—and the Vikhindens were *people* even if their immortal overlords were not. Paul did not wait for orders. If this was interference, so be it. If his decision was the wrong one, well, it was only Paul's career at stake. These people needed *help*.

The Aithran spaceport New Hope was an abattoir. Paul had come down with twenty-five men and women, and sent his ship roaring over the terrain, chasing wing over the native mutineers who had no idea that Paul had with him only one ship and twenty-five crew members. It sounded like the entire Telegonian fleet had landed at New Hope Port. And the simians scampered away. They were done here anyway. They melted back into the thrumming jungle which quieted suddenly to pre-storm stillness.

With the simians run off, the next tasks were fighting fires and searching for survivors, afraid you'd find one.

Here were Aithar's colonial lords, hung out like a vast field of scarecrows, impaled on stakes to watch over a crop of blooded rubble. Charred pits of bone, smelling of fuel and flesh, smoldered here and there. The Aithrans hadn't been burning the dead, one could be sure, not to judge from the sides of the pits which were scored with clawing fingernails' gouges. The simians knew that humans could not climb well. Must have been great sport.

Paul wiped his face of sweat, tears, and ashen dust. A sudden crackling bang like furious thunder made him look up.

A wide-spaced eschelon of long wicked-looking airspace ships, glowing red-white, razored through the sky. Each carried two enormous underwing engines bigger than its ship's fuselage, glowing so brightly you could not not precisely see them.

The nearest of Paul's crew gathered around him.

"Shit, look at them."

"Yeah, *look* at them."

"Know what thems are?"

"Now you see 'em, now you don't."

"Uh huh."

"Thems are c ships."

"Almighty."

The Queen's Squadron.

They were gone now, only their glowing trail persisting in the sky like burning wounds. Then barely perceptible, pale vapor trails ghosted down from where the c ships had been.

"Oh oh. Here we go."

Kingsmen.

Paul returned to his digging. Kuran lurched over to him, dragging her shovel with her. She wiped her nose with the back of her beefy hand. "Ah . . . Cap'n? Should we, ah . . . go?"

"No." Paul put down his shovel, sifted out a bone, carefully laid it aside, continued digging. "Let the Empire find us at rescue, not fleeing the scene."

Bristol took Kuran's side. Pale ash had turned his dark face gray. "The Empire will be talking provocation. As if we did this somehow."

"As if we would provoke the Vikrhalt while *that* rules the spaceways." Paul pointed at the Queen's Squadron's burnt path across the heavens. Then he agreed with his two crewmembers, "Still I have the uncomfortable feeling of having just picked up a smoking gun at a murder site as the lawful owners come marching home."

"Lawful owners," Kuran snorted. "Seems to me the lawful owners of this planet did this."

"Belay that opinion till we get out of here alive, 'kay?"

"I'm with you, Cap'n."

Paul's crew returned to their posts. On an after-thought Paul called after one, "Hey, Bristol." He bounced a pebble off Bristol's springy-haired head. Bristol turned. "Anyone else of ours here?"

"Fleet carrier *Brandten* just came in, bit ago."

"I mean any of *ours*." The *Brandten* was Space Fleet. By "ours" Paul meant Army.

"No."

"Oh joy. We're surrounded by fascists and idiots."

"Which is which?"

"I've called the Vikhens lots of things, but not idiots. Get back to it. Maybe someone's alive under this shit."

The portly Kuran minced away on Army-booted feet, carrying her shovel daintily, and pointing with a stubby finger toward the vapor trails. "And maybe that's my fairy godmother come to give me a pretty dress so I can go to the ball and Prince fucking Charming will sweep me off my little feet."

Paul returned to his task, disheartened. She was right. It was hopeless.

Hours later in the reeking afternoon, someone called his name. Paul looked up, wiped his face with the inside of his collar. He saw a uniform. At last someone of real authority, even if she was from the Space Fleet. "Captain Strand!"

Paul jabbed his shovel into the ground, tried to

make his uniform presentable. Not possible. He reported, saluted. "Captain Strand, ma'am."

The officer from the Space Fleet carrier was also called Captain, but in the Fleet that rank was considerably higher than Paul's lowly Army commission.

With the *Brandten*'s captain was a Telegonian ambassador, a dark, sleek, handsome man with a trim dark beard and brilliant blue eyes. A peacemaker. Rather late for that, Paul thought.

Both the captain and the ambassador were flanked by a small cadre of Kingsmen. There were not many of them, but the Empire did not need many to do what they had to do. There were some pretty big boys there. You never saw them if they didn't want you to. These were making their presence known. Heavily muscled arms crossed over massive chests. They all had bulging thighs no normal cut of trousers could contain. But for all their bulk they moved like sealions in water. For stealth, agility and swiftness they could out-sim the sims. These were the bad boys of the Vikrhalt.

They were all looking Paul over critically. What they saw was a short, rumpled, unimpressive young man with a bad complexion. Dirty light brown hair was matted to his scalp. There was a ribbon for valor on his jacket. He was twenty years old. Green brown eyes returned the scrutiny with a frank gaze without a trace of inferiority.

"Captain Paul Strand, is it?" said the captain of the carrier. "This is Ambassador Vreeland Forgil. You tell him what he wants to know." Which was to say, you can talk in front of the Kingsmen, but make it good.

The ambassador said, "This is remarkable. How fast you got this under control." He sounded disappointed. Perhaps he had wanted to quell the riot himself, for Vreeland Forgil had made his name by putting out political fires. Or maybe he'd thought this one an impossible task. Or maybe he was having trouble matching the man with the feat.

Paul had put down the riot, true enough, but fast? Paul did not consider what he'd done fast. They had lost everyone. They. Not Telegonia—it wasn't Telegonia's colony. But Paul could not help thinking of the Telegonians and the Vikhindens as a *we* against the inhuman savages of Aithar. Not fast enough. Though he had done it before the inhumanly swift Queen's Squadron could get here. For whatever the hell that counted.

"Yes, sir."

"Captain, who else did you have at your disposal?"

"Else? It's just us, sir. The *Everglade*."

"How many personnel?"

"Twenty-five, sir."

"Brigades?"

"People, sir. Twenty-five people. Including me."

There was a loudly silent exchange of glances. Some of the Kingsmen exchanged signals. The captain of the carrier looked like she'd just been asked to swallow a buffalo.

"*Twenty-five?* At last report this planet was in full storm chaos. The forest itself was tearing people apart."

How had this unkempt little Army captain put down the blood frenzy? When the Aithran forest scented blood, these things went on for days, for weeks, like a forest fire.

"The *Everglade*," said the Fleet captain. "That's a destroyer?"

"Uh, no, ma'am. Minesweeper."

"You put down a planet-wide rout with a *minesweeper*?"

"Uh . . ." The shock was catching up with Paul now that it was over. He wiped his running nose. A smear of soot streaked the back of his hand. He looked across the grisly scarecrow field. "Uh. We made a lot of noise."

He hadn't fired a shot. He'd taken the *Everglade* speeding at treetop level across the land, its in-atmosphere engines bellowing. The tumultuous sound overwhelmed the pulsing jungle. Vegetable instinct mistook the impotent roar for a coming hurricane, and the jungle shrank to utter stillness, shut against the fury that did not come.

Paul hadn't known what he was doing, that the trees would do that. He'd only thought to scare the sims.

The fleet captain and the ambassador looked apprehensively to the Kingsmen. These could be big trouble. But oddly they believed Paul. *The peacemaker*, thought Paul, *must feel like a spare part without us sniping at each other*.

One of the Kingsmen pointed at Paul. "You."

"Yeah."

The guerrilla soldier drew very close so he could look straight down at Paul. He waited an intimidating moment in which Paul supposed he was to make appropriate comparisons of their size and strength, then said, "What started this?"

"Hell if I know," said Paul. "I just found it."

"You beat the Queen's Squadron here."

"I was in the neighborhood."

"It's not your neighborhood."

"I was sweeping the Aithar Gate for Vikhinden litter."

The Fleet captain and the ambassador inhaled sharply, held their breath. Paul was accusing the Empire of laying mines. The ambassador was about to speak when the Kingsman offered Paul an instant commission in the Empire's service.

"No thanks," said Paul. "I can't do that."

"We're all on the same side, you know."

He meant that Telegonia would be annexed to the Empire sooner or later.

Paul shook his head a Telegonian no. The Kingsmen withdrew. When they were gone, Paul's own side clustered around him. Officers were talking promotion, decoration. Paul, who had steadily been feeling very, very sick, suddenly excused himself, whipped up a salute and ran to throw up, careful not to do it in one of the smoldering pits.

Then from across the spaceport he heard a woman shouting, "I got a live one!"

It was Kuran. She came lumbering across the rubble, carrying a child. "He's scratched up, but he don't look too godawful."

"Where was he?" said Ambassador Forgil.

"He came out of the fucking *jungle*. Sorry, sir. Says, 'I beg your pardon, ehre, is this New Hope Port?' "

The child was a handsome boy, an odd look fixed on his face, sober, wide-eyed. "Mother," he said in perfect Rhalt-accented baby-pitched voice.

"She's *gone*, kid," Kuran said with more savageness than she'd intended, and the boy whimpered. Kuran became a giant mass of thumbs as she tried to comfort the child, who never escalated beyond a whimper. Paul found himself wishing he would let out a great scream. It would be more appropriate than that sober, wise stare.

Paul returned to his loathesome task, wondering why *he* hadn't been able to find a sign of life in these charred heaps. Something to ease the horror.

The ambassador reached for the child. Kuran bundled him into his arms.

Small hands circled and clasped behind Forgil's neck. The ambassador was tall, strong-voiced, clean-smelling, handsome, and in uniform. The child of the Empire trusted a crisp uniform. Penetanguishene held tight.

"Who are your parents, child?"

"Mother," said the boy.

Forgil touched the little one's dark hair, prodded him gently for sign of injury, unfastened and turned over each of his little hands which were sliced by sharp leaves. "Look what they've done to themselves," he said sadly to the officers around him. "Immortals are so high-handed. This was inevitable. Unfortunately the wrath that was meant for them spilled over on these human innocents who were no part of it."

Penetanguishene refastened his arms round the man's neck, wondering why he was lying. Everything the man said was a lie.

* * *

When Penetanguishene was reunited with his father, the first thing the boy asked was where was Mother.

"Gone away." It sounded like half an answer. Father said he would talk about it later. That was a lie.

They were on shipboard, a big one. This was an Empire vessel, Penetanguishene could tell from its cleanliness and perfect order. The free mortal ships, especially the Telegonian ones, tended to shabbiness and strong odors.

Father was busy exchanging angry words with other men, other lordly men of the Rhalt, the Empire's highest mortal class.

Someone made reference to Agamemnon's rescue by Telegonians.

"Telegonian rescue!" Agamemnon exploded. "Telegonian instigation! The sims didn't think this up themselves. The free mortal world-nations want the stargate. That's obvious. They used the native imbeciles to do their dirty work."

The others lifted chins in reluctant concurrence. "It does smell strongly of an outside hand."

"Who has possession of the planet at this moment?"

"We have withdrawn. There is a moratorium on it just now. With any luck it will stay that way. The Telegonians have more people and ships on hand."

"Who do we have?"

"The Queen's Squadron, full strength."

"That should be more than sufficient to reclaim what is ours."

"No, you don't really understand the logistics involved here. The Queen's Squadron numbers eight ships and we need them elsewhere. Their virtue is their speed, not their firepower. They are a first strike weapon, not something one uses in pitched battle. Once the forces are gathered, their advantage is cut. They are agile but short-winded fighters."

"If we had more of them—"

"The risk of one falling into Telegonian hands increases. With only one c ship in Telegonian hands, our fortresses become open to them. No. The numbers must stay limited. Free mortals must never travel faster than light, except by means of the stargates. We keep our high cards few in number and play them very wisely. Open war is never wise, no matter what you are holding."

Agamemnon could not understand how the Rhalt-controller could be saying this. "But you used to be a general."

"Yes, you ought to keep that in mind."

"You would just give up Aithar to the Telegonians?"

"Of course not. The Telegonians are grasping hyenas. Their Ambassador Forgil is the only voice of reason in the whole lot. He is the only reason the free mortals haven't horded into Aithar wholesale. Negotiations must now see that the Telegonians agree to make Aithar off limits to both sides and keep their vultures out."

"Oh fine!" said Agamemnon. He did not mean fine. "They will agree not to touch what is not theirs. What a magnanimous concession!"

"Since when have Telegonians ever conceded anything at all? We got that much from them. You can't expect them to admit their guilt."

"And why not?"

"Please don't start reasoning like them. We are lucky to get out of this without a war."

"We have one now."

"No, we do not."

"After what they did? If that is not an act of war, what is?"

"It is. But don't be surprised if the immortals decide to settle peacefully. The Empire is not going to be eager to enter her first war with the free mortals, no matter what the cost or provocation. Fortunately for the free mortals their insurrection failed to kill any immortals. They will most likely be spared the full wrath of the Vikrhalt. The free mortals are likely to wage a ghastly dirty war. I doubt anything less than a direct declared attack could draw us out."

"The Vikrhalt cannot be thinking of making peace with those monsters. We'll have to settle with them sooner or later—and violently. That is all those death-lovers understand."

"I'm afraid so."

"Why hasn't the Vikrhalt annexed Telegonia long before now?"

"Hindsight."

"Lack of foresight."

"We thought they could govern themselves. I sometimes think the Empire is too big. As you see." He motioned to the planet Aithar in the viewer. "One's hold becomes tenuous at the edges."

"Yes, it is too big! You will get me off your tenuous frontier! I am tired of being shunted off to war zones!"

The Rhaltcontroller lifted his head in agreement. "You are too valuable to be left at the front, ehre."

"How did I become valuable all of a sudden?"

"By virtue of being rare. You are the last vondesi we have, unless your son develops the Sight, but we won't know that for years yet."

The pause stretched, snapped. Agamemnon's voice broke. "There were three hundred and forty-two vondesi on Aithar."

"The rest were caught in the melee. We should never have let you cluster like that. It is only you now, ehre."

"Tell me you are sorry."

"Me personally? What? And lie to a vondesi?"

"I thought so."

"Nobody loves your kind, and you know it. The Vikrhalt however needs you and sincerely regrets the loss."

And when the order came through, Agamemnon was posted to EtaCas.

At last!

"Come along, son. We are going home."

Penetanguishene followed silently. He distrusted his father and was afraid to ask why he'd run, why he'd left Mother. The boy had figured out what had happened to her. He had seen enough of the others.

But he obeyed. Always an obedient child—it was the way of the Rhalt—obedience became imperative now. If there was a ghost of a thought in his head that he could have done other than he'd been told, then that meant he had abandoned Mother to save himself. He must be obedient no matter what. Otherwise he'd had a choice and he'd let her die.

Why Father had left, he was sure he did not know. No one had ordered Agamemnon to run.

Penetanguishene went with him now. The ship took them to the heart of the immortal Empire, EtaCas. The homeworld.

Home. A place he'd never been.

ETA CASSIOPEIA

binary.   eccentricity .5   period 479 Earth years mean separation   72 a.u.

periastron: 36 a.u.   apastron: 108 a.u.

Star	Eta Cassiopeia A	Eta Cassiopeia B
Stellar type	GOV	dMO
magnitude	+4.5	+8.3
luminosity	1.2 Sol	.04 Sol
diameter	.8 Sol	.5 Sol

ETA CASSIOPEIAN PLANETARY SYSTEM

Planet	Distance from primary
1	.39 a.u.
2	.67 a.u.
3	.95 a.u.
4	1.12 a.u. EtaCas
5	2.63 a.u.
6	4.48 a.u.
7	8.96 a.u.
(8)	18 a.u. (mean) asteroids
(9)	(35 a.u.) extinct 2905 B.C.
10	72 a.u. (star) ηCasB

ηCassiopeia A IV
popular name EtaCas (adj. Eta Cassiopeian)

radius 6952 km
mass 7.77 x 10^{24} kg
gravitation 1.09 Earth
mean density 5.5 g/cm^3
*atmospheric composition N 77% 0 22% Ar .9%
CO^2 .05%

* dry air (water vapor 0–5%)
pressure at S/L 20 psi
irradiation from ηCasA .96 (1 = irradiation to Earth
from Sol)
period 1.13 Earth year (= 499.12 local days)
rotational period 19 hrs 58 min 5 sec (= 16 ηCassio-
peian hours)
inclination of axis 21 degrees (22 degrees Empire)
flattening 1/200
satellites 3   Stheno   9 km in diameter
                Euryale   7 km
                Medusa*   15 km
                     *retrograde

EtaCas, the heart of the Empire, was a middle-
weight planet with three inconsequential boulders for
moons. Its suns were red and golden. At periastron
the suns were as close together as Neptune was to Sol.
At apastron they were three times as far apart. The
light of the companion star was so feeble that it had
no more glory in the night sky than the nearest planet.
Its mass served only to perturb the planets' orbits near
periastron, and gave the soothsayers extra business.
The second star's influence was so tenuous that, were
the first star not there, the planet EtaCas would slip
away from the system entirely. All the havoc that it
might have wreaked had been done eons ago when
the companion star devoured the outer two planets.
Since then, the only violence in the system was between nations.

The Eta Cassiopeian star system had no direct stargate from Earth or any other free mortal world. Free mortals traveled at exclusively sublight speeds, and so were dependent on stargates to bridge the interstellar distances. Immortals claimed the fourth planet of the Eta Cassiopeian system, EtaCas, as their native world. Earth immigrants called that an obvious lie, for evidence of humanoid habitation did not go back before the first human colony—besides the fact that the salinity of immortal blood was exactly like Terrans and altogether wrong for natives of a fresh water world. The free mortals accused the immortals of creating a history and rearranging science to fit the foundation of their empire.

The immortals claimed that their kind sprang originally from EtaCas, abandoned the planet during the cataclysms which claimed the outer worlds, and migrated to Earth where they suffered persecution as sorcerers, demons, zombies and vampires, even as they tried to blend into the various cultures.

Finally, in Earth's star age, the immortals returned home where they could live by their own rules. They called their nation on EtaCas Vikhinde, around which they built their empire.

The subjects of the wide-reaching Vikhinden Empire were mostly mortals, a carefully and strictly tended, mostly contented flock.

Free mortals lived on EtaCas only by the grace and tolerance of the Vikrhalt.

The free mortals on EtaCas had organized themselves into two independent nations: Sebastionique, which the immortals considered a good neighbor; and Telegonia, the farthest thing from it.

Following the Empire's loss of its planetary colony Aithar, which ruled the stargate linking Earth and EtaCas, the free mortal nation Telegonia had the appalling insolence and bad timing to rename itself New Earth.

Not everyone was convinced that war was inevitable. Though both sides were certain that the other was making it terribly likely.

*If you think that mortality is what makes life so
precious, you are dead wrong. When death is
not inevitable it becomes a horror past imagining.*
　　　　　　　　　　—Marchale
　　　　　　　　　　　in open address
　　　　　　　　　　　to the free
　　　　　　　　　　　mortals.

Beltava, Vikhinde
EtaCas
5 January 5238
VII. 15. 1785

II.

Ashata hated finding a new facemaker. Her look
had become so much a part of her identity that she
became dependent on the man or woman who crafted
it. It distressed her when they grew old or died, for
they were always mortals. Immortals did not do such
work. Trusting herself to a new one always filled her
with apprehension.

"There," said the latest. "I've altered the nose a
bit—"

You WHAT? A bolt of profound fear quickly turned
to anger. Ashata barely heard the man continue.

"I can change it back if you don't care for it. I've
blunted the tip. The aesthetics are better."

Ashata fought to control a trembling that had seized
her from inside. Something bubbled and vibrated like
boiling blood and plucked strings in her midriff. She
said in crisp crescendo, "Who are you to question my
specifications and my *aesthetics?*"

"I am an artist."

Horror. An artist surgeon. What more ghastly con-
cept was there? Of all the abominations, a man who

carved people—and immortals—and considered himself an artist.

"I am not a canvas," said Ashata. She took out her immortal's disk and set it quite deliberately and in plain sight to execution-mode. She slapped it on the table within reach. "Give me a mirror."

The opaque walls around them transformed into mirrors. The facemaker stepped back.

It was best to double-check the entire work. Facemakers did the whole, saving the most delicate, the face, for last. Ashata ordered extensive changes to the look which her genes decided belonged to her.

She slipped off her robe and stood rigid, breath held.

She looked to the nose first. The pointed nose had been squared. It was still angular and very narrow, the way she ordered it, but now blunted, making a better line with the rest of her delicately chiseled face.

I like it.

She let out her breath, calming as she re-checked the rest of her body. She was petite, white, delicate and hard as a china doll, her hair blond as a child's, her eyes pale crystalline blue. The nose made her less severe without taking away the angularity she liked. "I like it. Change my specs."

The facemaker was not relieved; he had never been worried. The mortal was arrogantly certain of himself. He recorded what he had done for future reference and programmed it into his instruments.

"You will never be so high-handed again," said Ashata, slipping into her light blue robe.

"It would be easily corrected," the facemaker said blithely.

"That is not the point. That is like telling a mortal with ruined hair that it will grow back. The violence is done. The trust is gone." She took up her disk. "Here. I shall pay you now. There's a bonus in it for you."

The disk was still set to execution-mode when she pressed it to his palm, hard. Her unique impulses activated the custom programmed controls.

He twitched twice in dying. Perhaps the disk needed recharging. Or maybe she had been over-using it.

She stepped over the body, taking with her the file containing the instructions for her new nose, as she went to collect her clothes.

So violated and threatened. She shuddered in her vulnerability. He deserved to die. He had seemed so trustworthy. She watched herself in the mirror as she dressed, comforted by the sight of her self renewed.

The only problem with being immortal was that none of these pretty changes lasted. Alterations needed to be upkept. This last cosmetic work ought to last the rest of the year and maybe another doublevant. Then . . . Ashata hated finding a new facemaker.

Ashata was young for an immortal. That in itself was an embarrassment. They never admitted their ages. To do that would be to acknowledge something as ignoble as a birth. It was something of an obscenity, reproduction. And they hated to be traced, plotted, or bound by finite dates. They preferred to think of their lives as open-ended in either direction—except for Marchale who was old and proud to say he had been fathered by a rivergod—or so said the maiden who gave him birth on the Trojan plain 7000 years ago. On the mechanics of that miracle he was rather vague, and truth was, he didn't know. Some immortals claimed to have been born on EtaCas thousands of years before that, but no free mortal believed them— though the place, not the time, was the sticking point.

No one knew the immortals' lifespan, only that none had ever died of old age. They died of assassination or accident, but not of age.

To look at, they all seemed to be between nineteen and thirty-five standard.

Ashata was a young one, a scant thousand years old. But she was already mortally bored and sick to death of life.

Feeling hunted, she retreated to the Vikrhalt's fortress Valhalla. The place was off-world, of legendary remoteness, and secret. The mortals liked to guess at it, and had as many locations for Valhalla as they had for Atlantis.

Valhalla was in fact less remote than it was inconvenient. By interstellar measures it was in the backyard of both Earth and EtaCas. The position of its nearest stargate—twenty-nine light hours from the planet—made the approach arduous.

It was a long journey to Valhalla without a c ship. Ashata plugged into a dream machine to kill the time. She woke worse than before, restless and hungry for something to happen, stirred by the dreams only to be confronted by a gray reality.

At last her ship entered the secret world's murky atmosphere and descended into Valhalla's isolated dome of light.

Valhalla's spires glistened in the eternal light in defiance of the naturally desolate world.

Ashata went to the Autumn Quarter. Its brisk scents assailed her from the tall woods. A shimmering rope of a waterfall sprayed trembling leaves of red, green and gold with a cool mist on its way down. Bright leaves spiraled from the tower trees' high canopy, down the crevasse to float on the sky-colored water. Shafts of light filtered through the fluttering laceflowers woven on their climbing vines.

Ashata found Kveta pouring nectar for Marchale in the rose arbor. Kveta smiled in welcome and filled another long fluted glass for Ashata. Ashata sat with them under the rose lights.

Kveta had her hair arranged in a wildly curled mass entwined with flowers and pastel ribbons. "How pretty," said Ashata.

"It's ridiculous," said Kveta, sweetly comical. "I'm afraid to move my head or they'll all fall out, and I have become possessed of an uncontrollable desire to shake myself like a wet dog." And saying so, she did, sending flower petals flying everywhere. "Ah, there. That's much better." Her hair was all undone. She picked up a fallen blossom. "Back to the drawing board."

Her best friend and life companion Marchale watched her with a beatific smile. Marchale called Kveta his wife because it endeared the couple to the Empire's mortal subjects though it provoked gossip among their own kind. One had no choice but to suspect that they did other mortal things which were too obscene to think about. But they had been together for a good part of forever and Ashata wondered how they stood it.

Marchale picked up a fallen blossom and handed it back to his companion. "It was pretty while it lasted."

Ashata told them about her ordeal with the facemaker and what she had done.

Marchale lifted a brow. "Was that necessary?"

Ashata blinked crystal blue eyes, startled. That was the last remark she expected. She expected sympathy.

Marchale's tone had been benign; still, what he said was criticism. "What do you mean?" said Ashata, trying to keep the stridency from her voice, for her throat had tightened.

"Really, such a big price for such a small infraction."

"Small infrac—!" She choked. "What am I worth? That—that—*selqarth* played with my face! They are tinkering with *me*. What about *me*?"

"You look quite well, my dear," said Marchale.

"Very pretty," said Kveta.

Ashata pushed away her glass and stood. "Don't get up." She picked up a flower, tossed it to Kveta. "You looked like a bird's nest anyway." She stalked from the arbor, through the pale bluestone arch. By the time she reached the wide curved steps that led through the shimmer trees, she was running.

What in hell would Marchale and Kveta know of facemakers anyway? The only alterations those two ever made were superficial; they indulged in the conceit of *aging* themselves. They said it bred respect and authority and affection among the mortal subjects.

So she had stepped on a mortal worm and snuffed him out. So what? Why did Marchale object? It was not his business. And how had he made her feel so bad about it? *Why do I feel this way? It's my affair entirely. It was just a mortal. I was wronged. Why do I feel like the villain here?*

Enemies waited everywhere, mortals played with her face, and no one cared! Why couldn't he see the horror in that?

Her white face burned scarlet. Shame and anger fed one off the other and redoubled back on her. He made her feel bad for her lack of mercy.

Well, I am *merciless and it's none of your business!*

Hated him. Hated his magnanimity. No one ever stepped on Marchale, so he could afford to be magnanimous.

Marchale was an active ruler and he kept many personal pets. He liked caring for things. It was all Ashata could do to take care of herself.

She hated him for his life companion. There was no one Ashata could tolerate near her—not that anyone wanted to be there. As if this was somehow her fault. She was not tolerant enough. Well, it was not her fault that everyone around her was an ass.

Yet the feeling crept in sometimes that if she were only more sure of herself she could put up with these toads. Buried deep in the back of her mind she recognized Marchale's tolerance for secure strength.

She hated him for it.

Ashata ran to the edge of the world.

As she drew near, a chill mist began as a whisper and grew thicker and colder, until she came to the cliff. She stood at the brink and looked out.

Ice floes jammed up in jagged heaps near the shore which was wrapped in a fog so thick that the light no longer pierced through. From the cliff top Ashata could not see 20 meters out. The end of the breakwall was gone and beyond that was no water, no sky, no horizon, only a thick blank gray-blue murky nothing.

At the bottom of the cliff, in the twilight interface between here and nothing, the beach was a wintery shade of brown sand. On Ashata's back, Valhalla's artificial sun felt warm. On her face the cold swirled up from the half-frozen water. Its chill surrounded her and raised her white flesh rough all over.

Down below, where the light disappeared, white broken floes waited in a kind of suspension, without waves or wind, as if the whole scene had paused and even time did not exist.

A flight of stone steps led down the steep weedy embankment. Ashata had the odd sense that if she went down there she would never come back.

Suddenly out of the horizonless dark exploded a crack and a roaring, a glowing white-red flash, and fiery wings that streaked off the frozen sea. They gashed the sky, and the wounded heavens bellowed. The concussion boxed Ashata's ears. Stinging mist whipped around her. The ice floes groaned and rocked. Billowing heat roiled within the cold sea wind, dragging up a blast of sand. The spongy cliff boomed under Ashata. She fell and gripped the grassy weeds.

Next someone was picking her up and setting her on her feet. A mortal. A great wall of a man, muscled like a horse, dressed in battle fatigues of turbid green. He was one of the Empire's elite forces called Kingsmen.

"Are you hurt?"

Ashata pointed after the offending ships. "I want them dead!"

"No you don't, ehremat. Those are ours and we're under attack."

Ashata's already fair face blanched to the color of the ice. No one could hit Valhalla. No one could find it. "It's impossible."

"Ehremat, you'd do me a big damn favor if you took shelter."

The Kingsman's big hands closed round her waist and he picked her up and moved her to one side as a herd of armed brutes stormed over the cliff. He set her down and went with them.

Ashata was struck by his youth—baby young in immortal terms—and full of animal energy and that brute sexuality of which they were so embarrassingly proud. He radiated energy and life.

Ashata descended the gritty stone steps, clinging to the cold metal rail the whole way down to where the Kingsmen had gone. The world shook and reverberated in deep convulsions. It was only when she found the Kingsmen that she realized that all the noise and all the flashing was outgoing fire.

The pack of soldiers moved with a prowling swagger as they wielded the enormous emplaced guns that had sprung from the base of the cliff like things jut up during an earthquake. The sky was on fire and the mortal faces glowed with it.

She was in the way. She knew it, but too bad for them. She was their reason for being.

She looked over the massive shoulder of one crouching at a computer sight. "Did you get them?"

"Let you know."

She looked at a bank of monitors. "I don't see anything."

"You won't for twenty-nine hours. They're out there."

"What do you mean? Why don't you get them?"

"I mean they're way out there, ehremat. Twenty-nine light hours. They're just coming through the gate. They don't even know we're shooting at them yet."

So casual the way he talked to her, even with the honorific. And she wasn't slowing up what he was doing, as if talking to her demanded all the attention of chewing gum.

Ilu, they were cocky. In the midst of a life-and-death firefight, they loved it. They were so close to the lower beasts.

"If they are twenty-nine light hours away, how do you even know they're there to begin with?"

"Resonator, ehremat. Got off a warning before the invaders took one out." There were two resonators at the stargate, one here at Valhalla, touchy, vastly expensive things.

The Kingsman glanced at a monitor. "*Hei,* there goes the other one."

"There goes the other what?" Ashata cried.

He acted as if he hadn't heard her, shouted to the others, "The bastards knocked both eyes out, boys. Fire at will. Fire everywhere. Just keep your damned tweeters on for the birds."

Ashata crossed her arms, fingers digging into her sides. "If these weapons only shoot at the speed of light, it will take twenty-nine hours for them to find a target you can't even aim at."

"Twenty-nine minus the speed of the invader," said the Kingsman.

"How diffuse is all this at that distance?"

"Pretty damned diffuse, ehremat."

"Then they have all the room in the world to evade. What is all this good for?"

They grinned and shrugged. One looked at the fire-scored sky and said definitively, "It's pretty."

Then one touched the com in his ear as if listening. He said, "Ah, that's it. They're dead, thank you. Cease fire, boys. Birds in the area."

"You got them!" said Ashata.

"C ships, ehremat." He patted a monitor. "Gonna show up on here in twenty-nine hours. Ancient history."

On one of the monitors appeared the ships which Ashata had wanted dead, doing victory spins and looking, if machines could express emotion, insufferably pleased with themselves. They buzzed the recorder which fed this monitor, making the image shake.

One of the Kingsmen told Ashata, "Turn on your phone to the military band, ehremat."

As she activated the com in her ear, she overheard two other Kingsmen muttering, "Can she pick that up?"

"Immortals can tune into anything they damn well want to."

On her phone, Ashata could hear "the birds." They were notoriously voluble, the c ship pilots. They filled the emptiness of the Elsewhere with cheery chatter like sparrows. A flock of sociable loners. The c ships were one-person fighters, and the pilot of each was its captain.

"Hello hello. Anyone at Valhalla. This is Queen's Knight. Queen's Squadron victorious. For the Queen. For honor. Come in Valhalla."

"Hi hi, smart bastards. I am Kingsman 3."

"I am sorry for your mother."

"Status out there, Queen's Squadron."

"Make bad ships all gone."

"Save anything for question asking?"

"You mean those were unidents?"

"That's a yes."

A drawling voice: "Queen's Castle to Squadron, did anyone notice if we left any crumbs back there?"

A woman's voice: "Not one. Spaced 'em."

"Hello hello. This is Queen's Knight. Valhalla, you'll have to make due with the pictures when they get here."

"Queen's Castle to Queen's Knight. Race, are they saying we don't know who to go after for this?"

"Kingsman 3 to Queen's Squadron. Don't go after anyone. It didn't happen."

A chorus: "Huh?"

The Kingsman explained, "Best guess is the Vikrhalt will pretend we were never hit. If we don't say anything, then whoever sent them will just have an expedition that disappeared through stargate 49 and they won't know their fighters found Valhalla."

"Queen's Knight to one calling himself Kingsman 3. You can't be a Kingsmen. You have a brain."

"Ahem. Brain to brainless ones, there's an immortal down here who wants you dead."

There was a sober pause. The Queen's Knight said, "Really?"

"I have interceded on your behalf."

"I owe you my life?"

"That's right, ace."

"What do you think my life is worth?"

"Not a piece of pig snot."

"Just so I owe you."

"Why, you smart selqarth."

"Now, now," the pilot scolded. Some insults were just too far out of bounds.

"Kingsman 3 advises Queen's Squadron patrol gate till resonators are back up. Oh, and don't run into the defensive fire."

The woman's voice: "That's neither here nor there."

Queen's Knight: "Neither are we."

And the small flock veered away and became lost in the sun.

Ashata fled to her residence in the Autumn Quarter. There the shaking overtook her. She opened her mouth to breathe, heard the air catch in a rasp. Her heart hammered in her chest. A thudding vibration drummed in her fingertips; she thought it was her pulse overspeeding to a blur. She feared for her life.

But I am not alive. I exist.

She pictured those dangerous ephemeral beasts snapping at each other in fun. Ilu. Ilu. How could they be laughing?

Here. The invaders had come *here*. There was no such thing as a safe place. Nowhere to hide.

The soldiers could afford to play tag with their lives; they were finite anyway.

But my life. My life.

She was squatting on the floor, hugging her knees. Fingers curled into claws, closed on the silk rug. She tore it from the floor, spilled a delicate sandwood table and sent the crystal chimes crashing to the mosaic-tiled floor. She seized up anything within grasp, all her beautiful decorations. She tore down the gossamer curtains, kicked over the pedestals, hurled the vases against the frescoed wall till there was nothing whole left to throw.

She caught sight of movement, froze, stared. The exquisite, alabaster-skinned, petite creature flushed red, panting over the rubble, stared back with blue eyes. It was herself, her own image in the glass.

She walked up to it.

And smashed her new pretty face into the mirror.

"This was the Garden of Eden. The sin of Adam was that he could not leave anything. All was his and he left nothing untouched. As you see on your mortal world Earth, the apple is consumed. There is nothing there for us."

"Point of clarification: Eve did it."

"She was mortal too and the two have been pointing fingers at each other ever since. You leap upon your own tiny differences and fail to notice how same you are. Sex, what is that? It becomes all when the two of you are not the same. Mortals must rank things. Between any two, the question is immediately: which is better? No matter how irrelevant the question they must do this. Man and woman, which is better? Oak and maple, which is better? Left or right, which is better? Tall or short, which is better? And better is usually that which one has or is. The prime criterion is the possession or composition of the speaker. In the enormity of your ego, you fail to look past your own sphere and see what utter worms you are—destructive worms in our woodwork, and we with a long vision don't give a damn if you are an Adam worm or an Eve worm, a black worm or a white worm, or your worm god is named Allah or Jehovah or Schickelgruber."

"You who are immortal, so immortal is better."

"If you like."

—The Immortal/Mortal Dialogues.
Vol. II ℗ 1784

Fort Ujiji, New Earth (Telegonia)
EtaCas
5 September 5241
XIV. 23. 1788

III.

Major Paul Strand sifted through a pile of assorted misplaced things on the floor with his bare foot, looking for his shoe. He found a recorder, the image-control box for his monitor, a shirt, one of his telephones—crushed—and ten computer bubbles, but no shoe. He sat down, not really wanting to find it.

The air filter had sucked away all the smoke, but the smell still clung to the carpet and the furniture, and Paul was very high. By his consideration, it was the only condition in which to be when talking to Space Fleet admirals. He had no doubt that Admiral Bertrand Krestly braced himself with something before talking to Paul; he either drank, smoked, shot or plugged himself into something nice, Paul was certain.

Paul found his shoe.

His aide came in. "Sir, your ship is waiting."

"For what?" he growled, forcing his foot into the shoe that seemed to have shrunk a size or two. When he sat up, the aide was gone. A moment later Trevor and Bristol were there. Tweedledette and Tweedledum. The Bobbsey Twins in light and dark chocolate.

"He sang on me," said Paul.

"Why don't you ever wear a phone?" Trevor scolded.

Paul activated the phones. From all points in the shambles, including the waste receptacle, sounded a jangling chorus of hailing beeps. He turned them off.

Bristol sniffed the stale air, wrinkled his nose. "What'd you do? Torch your couch? Weird goddam habit, Paul."

"Whaddaya want?"

Trevor circled in on Paul's left, draped herself on the arm of his chair like a piece of silk. "Did we graduate in '30 or '31?"

Paul tried to focus. His thoughts were muddled. Why she would ask such an inane question at this time never crossed his scrambled brain. Whatever time this was. He was distracted by Trevor's smile and her rusty red hair. He did not know how Trevor could be so pretty while looking just like that bum Bristol. He frowned, concentrated. What was the question? " '30—ow!" He jerked in his right hand and glared at Bristol who had moved in on his right and jabbed a soberant into Paul's wrist.

Bristol shrugged apologetically. "Carl said you were flying without a ship."

"That was intentional, dammit," Paul growled, his head clearing. The four intruders in his office merged to two. He pointed a finger at Trevor. "You, I don't love anymore."

"Bon voyage, sir."

"Fuck you both."

"We'll get on that right away, sir."

Paul headed for the door. "Just don't spawn any immortal mutants while you're at it."

"Immortals aren't mutants. They're aliens," said Bristol.

"No, sweetheart," Trevor said seriously. She never joked about immortals. "You think so? If they're alien to Earth that means EtaCas is really their planet."

"Yeah, but mutant means progression up an evolutionary ladder, like they're perfect or something."

"They're not perfect," said Paul. "They have assholes just like everyone else."

"Have or are?" said Bristol.

"Always did have trouble with my verbs." Paul winked.

Trevor wagged a warning finger at him. "You could be arrested for that kind of talk in the Empire."

"We aren't Empire, sweetness."

"Yet," said Trevor. She was genuinely afraid. "They mean to do something about that." Annexation was a word heard too often these days.

"Over my rotting carcass," said Paul cheerfully.

"They can probably arrange that too."

"You have so little faith in our defenses? In your fearless commanders?" He brought his hand dramatically over his chest. And, walking backwards, tripped over a fold in the carpet and fell on his imperfection.

"I have faith in c ships," said Trevor.

Admiral Krestly received Paul with a malevolent stare. Dark eyes glowered from under a great flat shelf of a brow that seemed to be made of stone etched with horizontal lines. The admiral was a big rugged Caucasian, his features battered as if he'd lived his life under fire. All his scars went unrepaired and he looked like a weathered old dog. But the scars were all from training. Admiral Krestly had never been in battle.

"Are you coherent?" said the admiral.

"Yes, sir," said Paul.

"We have reason to believe that the Vikrhalt has just crashed a c ship."

"What!"

"One of the Queen's Squadron. Their elite fighters."

"Yes, I know." He'd seen them once, ten years ago. Had it really been ten years since he'd shoveled bodies out of Aithar's abattoir? Eight. Eight. Count in local time. It sounded better. That made Paul twenty-six instead of thirty years old.

"Don't get uppity with me, Strand. I know where you've been. Don't think it makes you better than me. It doesn't."

"Sir?"

"I didn't choose you for this. This order does not exist. Neither does this mission. Go see if there is anything to find."

"Where's the crash? What system?"

"This one."

"Hello?"

"They're on the far side of the sun. I.I.N. believes they've planted one into Eta Cassiopeia A VII. We need a real close look and souvenirs wouldn't hurt. There's a courier ship at your disposal. Officially you're carrying a message and you will detour out of mercy."

"Why not send one of your own?"

"Too incendiary. I am under a higher mandate to make it look casual."

"Army is casual?"

"From my viewpoint it is. Any more questions?"

"No, sir. I'm gone."

"Strand."

"Sir?"

"I'd go myself. I'm under orders."

"No doubt, sir."

"Is that sarcasm?" The admiral rose, actually reaching for his sidearm.

"No, sir."

"Get out of here."

Paul saluted and hastened for the waiting ship.

Actually he did have a question. For what supposed reason was he to detour out of mercy if there was no SOS? C ships never called for help. They would sooner self-destruct. Paul did not ask the question because it was a moot point anyway. He did not need an alibi. No one was going to ask Paul Strand what he was doing at the crash site. If the Vikhens caught him, they would shoot him.

The idea of sending Paul Strand on a mission requiring discretion was not without its humor value. Paul was as discreet as a brick and always had been. But he had the highest security clearance. He'd won his first medal while still a cadet.

He did not fit Admiral Krestly's image of a hero. Or anyone else's for that matter.

Admiral Krestly looked like the battleworn veteran he wished he were. There had been few enough incidents for seasoning anyone to real war. Krestly missed them all. It was not cowardice. Paul was sure that the man was nuts and would have been in the thick of it given a quarter of a chance. Bad luck, Krestly would call it.

Paul had been involved in two of the incidents. Bad luck, Paul called it.

"If that's the way you feel, why the hell did you enlist?" Krestly would ask him.

"I don't like to pay taxes?" Paul would offer.

Krestly had once taken one of Paul's lit cigarettes and held it to his finger. "That's what they used to do with these back when men were men. Know what I'm saying, bet you do."

"Funny, I always thought they put the unlit end in their mouths and sucked smoke out of them. But what do I know?" Paul had regarded his returned cigarette with distaste, fancied it tasted like seared flesh. He stamped it out.

"You know what I mean," said Krestly. "You have to know if you can take it."

"I'll find that out if the time ever comes."

"You're weak, Strand."

Paul had simply shrugged.

He approached the crash site cautiously.

There was no chance that he would not have company, not when the Empire dropped a jewel of this size, the fabulous technology that was the Empire's ace in the balance of power.

Normal interstellar travel took conventional ships through the stargates, the spacefolds which shortcut journeys of light years. Still the journeys from planet to stargate were limited to some percentage of light speed, no faster.

C ships could take or leave the stargates. No one knew their top speed, but New Earth's Interstellar Intelligence Network had recently confirmed without a doubt that a c ship had made the round trip from EtaCas to Earth in thirty-six hours without making an appearance at the Aithar stargate, giving it an average speed of 8800 times light.

8800 times.

But it was the initial passing of the light barrier that was so difficult to credit and impossible to duplicate.

So you broke one of your supertoys, did you? Paul thought as he swung into low orbit round the seventh planet. *What'd you leave for me?*

There was a brand new crater on the seventh planet all right, red as a fresh wound and huge enough to mark the death of something of immense power.

Paul made a slow low pass over it. His ship's sensors detected nearly nothing of non-native matter. The c ship had managed to annihilate itself very nicely on impact. What anomalous matter there was, was a tiny wafer of no more than five grams. Paul swept it up and climbed clear of the crater.

By sheer luck he spotted a movement. It did not read on his sensors, for it was well cloaked. He just happened to see it through his viewport. A small slow-moving capsule in high-orbit.

Paul moved in, couldn't believe his luck. A Kingsman pod. It must have jettisoned from the c ship before impact. This was a prize.

Paul opened his cargo doors.

Suddenly there was a ship on him.

Shitska!

He hadn't seen it, hadn't detected it. Faster than he could think about, it was here and shooting.

Paul threw his ship sideways, took a scrape on the cargo doors.

The Vikhen ship hurtled past him like an arrow-head. The sleek silhouette of a c ship.

Paul threw his ship into pursuit. Folly, it occurred to him even as he did it. These ships could go faster than light. 8800 times faster than light.

But it had to get to light speed first. And Paul had an idea, because of where the ship was headed, that it needed the sun to do it.

Paul pushed his ship screaming at the limit, ninety percent c. The c ship was not pulling ahead.

You bastard, without the sun, you're no faster than I am!

The c ship began a curving course as it approached the sun.

Yes. It was going to catapult itself around the sun to faster than light.

Paul moved to cut it off. He started around the sun in the opposite direction and computed the c ship's parabola to put himself directly in its path. He would catch it swinging around the other side as it tried to slingshot itself to FTL.

I may swallow you, but you're not getting away from me.

Paul rounded the sun.

To vacant space.

Dammit.

He scanned for kilometers on all sides. Not high, not low, not tight, not wide. Just . . . not.

How had it done it so fast? Paul only had the ship out of his sensors for a millisecond.

Where could he have gone? FTL? Then it hadn't been a slingshot. He'd just *gone.*

Paul wondered how he was going to report this, when suddenly his computer guard was ringing.

Found him. *There he is. BEHIND ME!*

The blast sent him spinning.

Acceleration compensators failed. Crushing whirl. Nose gushed blood. Ears buffeted in by the abrupt sealing of the cockpit. Hull breached. G-pull sank his hands to his seat and plastered them there. Could not reach the controls. Could not move. Could not breathe.

Auto equalizer kicked in. The world stopped spinning. Paul's vision continued round a few more orbits. Ruptured sinuses dripped a sticky pool from his nose onto his chest.

First thing he did when he could lift his hands was transmit an SOS.

His viewport had filled with the image of a long streamlined ship. Paul estimated it at 12 meters in length. It nosed up close as if looking in the window. Like being inspected by a great dolphin. He memorized every detail he could see though he did not expect to live to report this. It was hard to focus on, so stealthy his gaze seemed to slide right off it. The light itself found the swift ship difficult to hold.

Lord, it's pretty.

It was long and lean and slippery-skinned, its wings swept hard back, enormous engines tucked underneath them. It was the most elegant craft anywhere among the stars. But why why, why was it aerodynamic?

Paul's radio still functioned. Someone was hailing him. Paul gingerly switched on his com.

A Vikhinden-accented voice asked if there were survivors on board.

"Yes," said Paul. And he expected the Vikhindens to pick him up. They didn't. They stranded him there with a message, a warning, to pass on to anyone who might pick him up. "Stay away from World Seven until the Empire advises otherwise."

The c ship sped away.

Someone answered Paul's distress signal before his ship fell into the sun.

"Came back empty-handed, did you," said Krestly.

"I came back handed, thank you for your concern."

Paul had come back via a med station. And on second thought his hands were not precisely empty. "Found this." He turned in the small disk he had pulled up from the crash site.

"That's it?" Krestly frowned at the little wafer.

"That's all there was."

It was pale, light-weight, and vaguely glowing. "Is this thing hot?"

"I'm carrying it in my pocket next to my family jewels and you're asking me if it's hot?"

"So maybe you're stupid."

"No, sir. It's not radioactive."

Back at the Army base, Paul's own corps was not delighted with him either. General Conchetta Alejos met him by saying: "You transmitted a rescue vessel SOS."

"Yes."

The general purpled with outrage. "Do you realize if they had shot you, it would have been an act of war!"

"Well, yes, ma'am. I kinda hoped that *they* realized it."

"How dare you hold a planet hostage to save your own skin! The fact is, you *weren't* a rescue vessel. We don't want to go to war over you. If they had shot

you, we would have to admit that you were not a
rescue vessel, that you were a spy, and where would
that have left us?"

"I don't know, ma'am. We're not there."

"We're not where?" said the general, lost on the
curve.

"Wherever that would have left us. It didn't
happen."

"Don't think you get any points for this stunt. I
hope you realize why you were chosen for this
mission."

"I think I can figure it out, yes."

Paul held high enough clearance to be trusted with
whatever he might have picked up of c technology,
yet tarnished with enough reprimands that in case he
were caught, New Earth government could discredit
and disavow him, and the Empire just might believe
it.

"And I want to tell you something, major. The
corps is not happy with your 'excess use of
soberants.' "

"An excess use of *soberants?*"

"You know the implication. An excess use of various substances."

"None of which I use on duty, so you can't charge
me with an excess of anything actionable."

"No. More's the pity. But I can assure you, unless
you make drastic changes in your lifestyle, you will
never see colonel."

"Ma'am, if I never see another colonel again as long
as I live, I'll be real happy."

"Major Strand, you aren't going anywhere."

Paul was stalking away, hunched over, intent on
using something that would require excessive soberants, when he picked up two shadows on his flanks.

"Buck up, Paul," said Bristol. "Conchetta would be
singing a different tune, with a definite blues note, if
you'da picked up that Kingsman pod."

"Hm?" Paul grunted.

"Rumor has it, you almost bagged Rachelson."

Paul stopped. Brown-green eyes regained their customary spark. "Are you shittin' me?"

"Negs."

"Rachelson is commander of the Queen's Squadron."

"Yeah, I know the name. Queen's Knight."

Trevor nodded. "Leader of the snottiest bunch of boys and girls in the Out There. You missed him, but you can't say he got away. He's disappeared from the star map."

"What?"

"I guess the Empire wasn't happy with him."

"He's *gone*, your majorness sir. Commander of the Queen's Squadron *used* to be named Rachelson."

"Oh, hello. You mean I brought down someone's career besides mine? Can I stand you a drink, Freddie and Flossie?"

"We can. You can't. I.I.N. wants you."

"Aw, shitness."

"Don't worry. I.I.N.'s the only branch of the Service that doesn't want you hung from a yardarm. You're due in the Hive."

"When?"

"Now-ness."

The Hive was the subterranean wing of Fort Ujiji, the rock under which the I.I.N. dwelled.

Waiting for Paul in the Hive was the prettiest agent he had ever seen. He flashed a smile. She took one look at him and said, "Are you lucid?"

"Yes. Why?"

"I was warned you might not be."

"It can be arranged. Is this social?"

The I.I.N. agent's flat expression said that she found him tiresome. The Interstellar Intelligence Network was generally a humorless bunch. This one was entirely too pretty to be so dour, thought Paul.

"How is your relativity, Major?" she said.

"Relative."

"Does this look familiar?" She lit up a graph on a vid sheet.

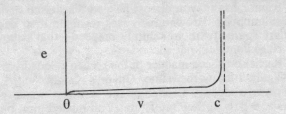

"Incompetence/rank relation. Sure."

The I.I.N. agent covered her eyes.

Paul elaborated. "The dotted line at c—c stands for colonel—is the point at which you have to have your brain surgically removed to advance any further in this man's Army. All that blank space to the right represents the generals and the admiralty."

The intelligence agent pushed back her soft brown hair and forged ahead as if he hadn't spoken. "On the x axis is plotted velocity. The y axis is energy required for acceleration. The 'dotted line' as you so technically put it, is an asymptote. No matter how far you extend this curve it will never reach the asymptote. No matter how much energy you expend, you can never reach c."

"I've been told that," said Paul.

"C is the speed of light. By the laws of physics as we know them, you cannot reach the speed of light because you cannot gather the energy required. Does this look familiar?"

$$M = \frac{M_O}{[1 - (V/c)]^2}$$

"No."

"M is the mass of the object in motion. M_O is the mass of the object at rest. V is of course velocity. At normal speeds V/c is a very negligible quantity, so your mass in motion for all practical purposes equals your mass at rest. Even speeds of thousands of kilometers an hour are insignificant relativistically speaking."

"Please don't use seven-syllable words. It makes my brain hurt."

"At a velocity of one tenth light speed—that's about 30,000 kilometers per second—"

"Thank you."

"The difference in mass becomes significant for spacecraft propulsion. Your mass in motion is 1.23 times your mass at rest. So if $F = Ma$, then—"

"Then it takes 1.23 more F to A your M," said Paul brightly.

"Don't ever join the scientific corps, will you do that for me, Major?"

"For you, anything."

"Stay with the scenario."

She may have been cuter than the average agent, but she talked like every other field ferret Paul had ever known. The two catchwords of the I.I.N. were *scenario* and *ticket*. "At a velocity of 90 percent c, the load you are trying to accelerate is 100 times as massive as the one you started with. Which is why conventional ships stay well below this speed. As you approach light speed itself, your mass increases geometrically until it approaches this—"

$$M = \frac{M_O}{[\,1 - 1\,]^2}$$

"You can't do that," said Paul.

"Correct. You're trying to divide your mass at rest by zero. How many zeros go into any number?"

"Infinite."

"At light speed your mass equals infinity. So does time by the same relation. Put t's in for the m's in the equation, and you have it."

"No, you keep it, please."

"At light speed, a second lasts for an infinite amount of time. You could say time stops. Or becomes eternal."

"Will this be on the test?"

The agent grit her teeth, her lower jaw forward, in

tried patience. She was young and freckled and it made her look cute. "Am I dumbing this down enough for you, Major?"

"It's sufficiently dumb, yes."

"I have to ident you now."

"Go ahead."

"Can you read?"

"Yes."

"Good. We don't like to put this on audio."

And after exhaustive scrutiny, which verified for a red card level that Paul Strand was truly Paul Strand, the I.I.N. agent brought out the reason for this refresher course.

Paul had a feeling she was going to fry his minimal brain.

File.

EYES ONLY

CODE NAME: LOOKING GLASS

The first thing that appeared was a familiar-looking graph, only extended:

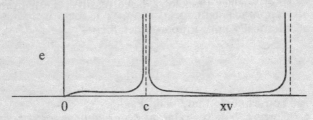

"Eyes only? Why bother? I don't know what I'm looking at."

"Faster than light physics."

"I knew that."

"I will explain. Now look."

"I'd rather look at your eyes. They have little gold lights in them, did you ever notice?"

If the major were not so good-natured he would be obnoxious. Or maybe he was anyway. "Pay attention."

"Why?"

"Because, for some reason known only to the government and probably not to God, you have red card clearance—"

"Couldn't trust a lesser man around those eyes."

"You no doubt think you're charming."

"Oh." He looked a bit astonished. "I'm not?"

"You are annoying me."

"I'm sorry," he said sounding sincere. He folded his hands on the table and became attentive and business-like. There hadn't even been an insulted edge in his apology and she almost wished she could retract what she'd said, or at least rephrase. His boyish—juvenile—humor wasn't all that offensive and it suited him. Without the smile he looked quite ordinary. He was short when any man of means was tall. Height augmentation was a facemaker's most popular operation. If a short, cross-eyed, gap-tooth, bow-legged, balding man walked into a facemaker, you knew what he would say. "Make me tall."

Major Paul Strand was short. He was who he was.

He made her think of a piece of silver fresh from the ground, tarnished black and a bit disgusting but of elemental worth. She wished she hadn't snapped.

The I.I.N. agent inhaled, got on with it. "This is what we've managed to sketch in of how the Empire travels FTL. If you look at the graph you'll notice that c is as impossible to reach from either side of the light barrier."

"So how do we get there from here?"

"Just as the stargates fold normal space, allowing us to go from point x to point z without going through point y, the Empire manages to get from sublight to faster than light without ever going the speed of light. They never reach the singularity. Remember I said time stops here at the asymptote?"

"They pass through light speed because it isn't there."

She paused, hesitant to agree with him. "Yes. I guess you could say that."

"But how?"

"I don't know and the Vikrhalt isn't saying. I doubt the pilots of the c ships are even told. The Empire killed the workers who built the c ships, you know."

"Shitska."

"And you thought your retirement benefits were crummy, Major."

Paul grinned. It had been a kind of apology, the jest.

She continued. "We're not sure at what speed they make the crossing or what precisely is the mechanism for catapulting them through the light barrier. From a sublight observer's point of view they must cease to exist. Only if you're massless can you go the speed of light. But then, general relativity isn't the best yardstick of spacetime and matter under extreme conditions. Near c the universe warps. In normal spacetime, you appear to be approaching light speed and never make it. You cease to exist in the universe as we know it. At some point faster than 96 percent c, they tunnel through the timefold and all the laws reverse for the c ships—they're suddenly on the far side of the looking glass and *de*celeration becomes the difficulty. Faster than light travel is impossible in normal spacetime. Light speed is impossible everywhere and at all times to all observers."

"Timefold?" said Paul. "It's a fold in the goddam reality."

"That is the ticket." She nodded.

"What happens to their sense of time over there? Can they come back before they leave?"

"No. According to the equations, time is flowing backwards for the faster than light traveler. However, the laws of physics don't really care which direction time is flowing, when the c ships reappear in this universe, it's *later* by the quantity of the absolute value of time experienced by the traveler. Whatever happens to you crossing the asymptote, un-happens coming back."

"You're starting to talk like me."

"I know. This is dreadful. Are you still with me?"

"No, but keep going."

"At the point of crossing from sublight to FTL, the traveler disappears from this universe, but there is no energy flash to account for the destruction of the matter. We postulate that the traveler switches places with a doppelgänger, one that does not exist in real space-time, so we don't see it. And the conservation of matter is maintained, because he was never there. It's the uncertainty principle in action at a macroscopic level."

"That does it. That does it. You can't do that."

"Major Strand?"

"You cannot apply rules of subatomic interaction to the macroscopic universe."

She gave a slight pout. He was following her better than she'd thought. "Major Strand, this close to c, all bets are off."

"We're not talking about an uncertainty here," said Paul. "We're talking about sending a very substantial, 7000 kilogram object that shot my ship to pieces into the other side of something that doesn't exist, through which he doesn't exist either."

She paused a moment to absorb this, and nodded. "Yes. You have it."

"I'm having a son of a hard time with this."

"This was not my choice of assignments."

" 'Kay, so what keeps the g forces from squashing a c pilot flat on his way to 96 percent c?"

"Obviously the Empire's compensators are better than ours."

"I've never seen anyone go 96 percent c," said Paul.

"Neither have I."

" 'Kay. Suppose we're FTL. However we got there." He pointed at the second graph. "What's xv there at the bottom of the curve?"

"That is what the c pilots call cruising velocity. It's quantity is unknown. It's the speed at which no energy is required to accelerate a mass. Once a c ship accelerates to faster than light, it can cut engines and it will naturally accelerate up to cruising velocity and stay at that speed quite literally forever. From the graph it looks like cruising velocity ought to be one and a half times c, but we think it's considerably faster than that."

"Since the Queen's Squadron is clocking 8800 times c without breathing hard, I guess that's a safe bet."

"Just so."

"We can't see them at those speeds. Can they see us?"

"Don't know. Don't think so. They don't exist in normal spacetime."

"How do they navigate?"

"Don't know."

"What happens to transmissions between c ships traveling FTL? Can they signal each other?"

"We postulated that they could, since they send out c ships in squadron strength and not solo. Can they see each other? That would require light to travel faster than light. Perhaps it's not FTL at all, but a sidestep into an alternate universe."

"Hello?"

"I don't know if it's possible to differentiate, or even necessary. Either way, they don't exist in real spacetime. FTL is impossible in this universe; they aren't in it. The end result is the same. They leave *here* and turn up *there* faster than the normal laws of physics allow. What we need from you now is anything you might have seen that could fit into this scenario."

Paul shook his head. "It's what I didn't see. He didn't come around the goddam sun. I don't know how he reached his 96 percent c. How he did it between the time I lost him and the time I should've met him again doesn't compute by anybody's bean count."

"I know. I was hoping you would change your story."

"Nope."

"What else can you give us?"

"What about that little round thing I picked up?"

"The disk. Now that's another story."

"Is it as complicated as this one?"

"Stickier," said the agent and secured the room for desensitization.

When the doors were opened a man was waiting.

Vreeland Forgil, the Peacemaker.

How hot was this situation that someone the caliber of Forgil was here? In his hand was the disk Paul had retrieved from the crash site.

"You should not have touched this," said Forgil.

Before Paul could say something caustic, recognition crossed the ambassador's handsome face. "Captain Paul Strand, isn't it?"

Paul could not help but warm up to a famous man who remembered his name ten years later. "Major," Paul corrected.

"Yes, of course you would be by now. Major Strand, do you know what this is?"

"I'm wishing someone would tell me."

"It's an immortal disk. It seems there was an immortal accidently taken out by that c crash."

"The pilot was an immortal?"

"No. Immortals never risk themselves in combat ships. Possibly a passenger who wanted to get somewhere very fast, more likely just someone in the wrong place at the wrong time. Anyway, you picked up the body—all that was left of it—and by the grace of God the Empire hasn't cried murder."

"Oh, fuck them!" Paul said irritably.

The I.I.N. agent said, "We need to tread more delicately than that. War with Vikhinde is out of the question so long as they have a monopoly on c technology. That comes from the top. *We can't afford it.*"

Forgil murmured, "Perhaps so."

Paul said, "What do we need to go FTL for? What do we even need space ships for? In case anybody misplaced it, can I remind you that Vikhinde is right across the pond?"

The I.I.N. agent explained, "Fighting, if there is to be any, won't be on EtaCas. It'll be in space. Nobody wants to swing Sebastionique into this. Sebastionique has lots of friends. They're all that stands between us.

Draw Sebastionique into the fray and we'll see who gets across the pond to take a shot at whom."

"You don't think Sebastionique would side with us, if it came to it? They're free mortals too."

Forgil answered, "They have great admiration and sympathy for the Empire. It's not a gamble anyone can afford to lose."

Paul returned the immortal disk to Forgil. "The Empire can't blame this one on me. They crashed the c ship and they took out that immortal."

"For one thing, they are not admitting that they crashed one of their superships. And for another, the Empire has a standing threat to kill one thousand mortals for any immortal who dies by human agency. I must convince them not to enforce it this time."

"It was their ship. It wasn't a free mortal who did it. It was their own ace, Rachelson. And it was an accident."

"Immaterial. When an immortal dies there is nowhere to hide. The idea is to make everyone take extraordinary measures to insure the comfort and safety of the immortals. I must convince them it would be counterproductive in this case."

"Have they threatened to? I mean this time?"

"We're getting the impression that they don't even know yet that one of their own has died. I must break this to the Vikrhalt. Gently."

In ancient times they killed the bearer of bad news. So that was what Vreeland Forgil was doing with this affair. A political firefighter, it was said Vreeland Forgil could put out a type O sun.

Paul pointed at the immortal disk. "So who was that? Who got nailed?"

"This disk idents to the one called Ashata."

The c ship had crashed into the seventh planet with a terrific blaze of light. Ashata took her viper and went to see. The viper was the type of ship the Empire used as a spyship. Immortals used them as personal hacks. Immortals liked to move without notice.

She stepped outside in her environmental suit. Instruments muttered out the extreme readings. The radiation counter clicked a solid blur. Her suit advised her not to spend more than five degrees out here.

The vast flat burning landscape before her was glassy smooth. She stared at the enormity of the crater, smooth sided and flowing red hot. The rocks themselves were slick underfoot, on fire. The cavity was as huge as some continents, and so deep that as she looked up the cliff it appeared to extend to the stars.

Before she thought about it her hand moved. Her immortal disk jettisoned from her suit and went into the inferno.

Suddenly she felt wonderfully light and free and dead.

She smiled.

She was tired of being a smoldering ember shrouded in ash, clinging so tight to life that she wondered if she were alive at all. She would turn up the flame.

I will be mortal. Not just pass as one for an afternoon. To be one. Live as one. Spend her one small coin instead of passing eternal days guarding her hoard. One must risk death to become alive.

She climbed back into her viper, leaving all that was Ashata behind her.

*If you accept the immortality of the soul, then
nothing is more important than the individual. Not
temporal institutions, not governments. I matter.*
                    —Against Annexation
                      Archbishop Andrea deMontagne
                      c. 5240

Beltava, Vikhinde
EtaCas
3 December 5241
XX. 17. 1788

IV.

In the capital city Beltava there was a crooked maze
of narrow streets and stepped alleys called, if you
knew where to find it, the Artists' Quarter. Crouched
within its tight maze were clubs without signs, un-
marked doors to marvellous secret places, dens of ar-
tistry and decadence, culture and counter-culture. Its
denizens lived a private game, part of which was to
discover the rules, and the casual tourist could not
play.

The great shining private vehicle pulled in as far as
its size would allow and came to a stop. Splendid beings disembarked.

Its arrival sent a scurrying of things into the woodwork, petty criminals and service dodgers. At first
came the cry, "Press gang!" And the inhabitants ran
for cover; the streets emptied. In a moment the cry
was amended, "Rhalt!" And the Artists' Quarter
pulled itself in tight and bolted everything it had. Then
the cry escalated yet again, "It's the *Vik*rhalt!" And
the bohemians crept back out to see. This was too big
a gun to be here for the likes of them. Curiosity over-

came dread. An immortal had come among them in the flesh.

The immortal was not interested in them. Some lower member of the Rhalt could weed this crop later. The Empire's rulers kept a loose hand on the Artists' Quarter. The Vikrhalt valued its artists and did not want to pull up the jewelflowers along with the weeds.

The immortal was tall, his hair jet black. The gray at the temples was a facemaker's artifice. His hair was pulled off his square face and cinched in a ponytail that hung dead straight to his mid-back. The face was red-bronze, with strong square jaw and high heavy cheekbones framing coal eyes. His appearance never varied, and the watchers knew at once this was Marchale.

The shadow of a woman waited in the car. That would have to be Kveta. The two were never found far apart.

Marchale navigated the twisty stepped alleys like a native. He came to a house of five and let himself in. He walked the cluttered hallways of the student grade quarters and mounted the stairs. He found whom he sought without asking names. The door opened to a startled youth holding a lyranope at his side. Marchale had never seen him before but knew him at once.

Marchale was shocked into a moment of deja vu. He had expected the boy to run true to strain, being vondesi on both sides, but Ilu, Ilu, he had recreated the prototype. Down to the quiet, startled look.

In the Earth year 3912, the immortal Marchale accidentally imported the first truthsayer into the Vikrhalt.

The planet was in a zone off limits to both Vikhinde and Telegonia by international treaty. The inhabitants were human, so one hesitated to call them natives, though no one knew how else they came to be spawned here.

"Here" was not on any map. The planet lay through the far gate, on one of the destinations called the Far

Worlds. No one knew quite how far they were—no one had precisely found them yet. The jump took seven days one way, assuming a symmetrical jump, which was unverifiable. The turnaround time through the stargate was fourteen days. But observers could not find the star pattern surrounding the Far Worlds from here—here being the Milky Way galaxy. The only thing for certain was that those stars were not in the Milky Way or in any galaxy within 100 million light years of it. It was a very dense part of the universe, in one of the great walls, which was doubtlessly why space bent through the gate this way.

And here on a far world were humans, not just homonids, not even merely humanoid, but pure homo sapiens. It lent strong support for the theory of resonant evolution.

The inhabitants' level of technology was primitive. Their most advanced nations had just invented gunpowder and had made a messy job of each other with it.

Fortunately it was cold. Red blotted the snow and ice in paling patches under many bodies.

Marchale and his companion came upon one still breathing. A faint tendril of frost steamed from his nostrils. It was a truly artistic face, and so very young. He had fine features, high cheekbones, a narrow nose. The lips though blue were well formed. His hair and the lashes of his closed eyes were startling in their darkness on his nearly white face. He bore all his wound in front, and he had fallen near the flag, the very picture of a valiant young soldier.

"Will he die?" said Marchale.

"Undoubtedly."

"Would you swear to it?"

"You're not thinking of taking him with us."

"And why not? If he is dead, what law would it break?"

"It would stress one rather severely. What if someone takes a body count? Look at him. He *is* someone."

"Yes, I can see that. And he's no more good to them. I want him. Call a transport."

"The Queen won't be happy."

"She'll live," said Marchale wryly. "You would begrudge me a pet?"

"We're trespassing. This counts as interference."

"I'll say he died and I revived him. You can certify a mortal dead, can't you?"

"He's dead."

"Thank you."

Marchale bent down on one knee as his companion went to see about a transport. The immortal took his gloves off, brushed the dark forelock from the white face with his gloves. The black lashes fluttered, lids lifted. Dark eyes fixed Marchale with a fuzzy glazed stare of numb bloodless shock.

"I know you cannot understand what I say, and it doesn't matter. You will. You're mine now."

Aboard ship, the young soldier was repaired. He came to consciousness alone. When Marchale entered the cabin he saw the mortal's thoughts logjam in his open mouth.

A translator had been set up, and Marchale said, "My dear child. Maybe it's better if I tell you what you ought to know. You did not die on the battlefield, but you may as well have. You have passed into another world. Forget what you know to be true. The bulk of it isn't."

"Are you a man?" the soldier asked in quivering voice, his nerves betraying his best efforts at a brave front.

"Yes and no. More like a demigod. You needn't worship me, I didn't create anything. You must however obey me. I am your liege. I saved your life and you owe the rest of it to me."

The mortal took well to obedience. Marchale gave him a new name for his new life. To disguise his illegal origin, Marchale gave him a foreign name. He closed his eyes and pointed at a map of Old Earth and named him after whatever city, lake, or mountain he happened upon. He named him Rainier.

It was a new game for Marchale, who was very

old and bored with most pursuits. Watching his pet's bewildered reaction to everything made it new again.

The tables turned and Marchale received a shock the first time he lied to Rainier. His pet stared at him uncomprehendingly and asked him why he was saying something that he knew to be untrue. Marchale insisted upon his lie, and the mortal said perplexedly, "No."

It happened several times before Marchale caught on. The youth never used the word "lie." He didn't know it. It did not exist in the vocabulary the Empire had for his people. Evidently one could not get away with one back on his world.

A weapon, thought Marchale. *I have imported an exotic weapon.*

The Queen was, as Marchale's companion predicted, not happy. But she agreed that the potential was too great to throw away now that they had it. "Just never let on to the Telegonians where this being came from."

Marchale was given leave to breed his new pet. To his delight the mortal was breedable with ordinary mortals, and the truthsense turned out to be a dominant trait. Marchale tended his little crop like a fussy gardener with prize blooms.

The vondesi were as loyal as they were unnerving. They kept him honest.

They flourished at first, but then withered outside of his protection. When he set them loose on the Empire, the reaction was virulent. The truthsayers were the object of loathing, fear, and too often of murder.

It seemed humanity could not survive without its deceptions. Humanity attacked these truthsayers as if they were deadly organisms in its host.

There had been an outright purge 500 years ago that nearly got all of them. But there had been an immortal behind that one. Selqarth, the Deceiver.

Selqarth had been caught in too many lies and decided to be quit of these creatures. These creatures could say that he plotted to overthrow the Queen, that he had killed another immortal. And people believed them.

Taking the life of an immortal was an unthinkable crime. And sentencing one to death took the unanimous vote of all immortals. Selqarth, of all immortals who had ever lived, gained a unanimous vote. The Vikrhalt put a price on his head—as he was by then a fugitive. A mortal did the deed and was rewarded. Selqarth's name lived on as byword of villainy. The Deceiver himself was gone.

Too late for Marchale's pets which were reduced to a precious few. And now, after the uprising on Aithar eight Eta Cassiopeian years ago, they were almost gone. Marchale should never have let them clot together like that. All of them in one basket. It was not as if Aithar was a safe fortress like Valhalla.

Near extinction, Marchale's pets were down to one. Maybe two if this one could See. His name was Penetanguishene.

Marchale said without preface, "Do you have the Sight?"

The question sounded unnecessary even as he spoke it. Did he have the Sight. How could he not and look like that? He looked exactly like Rainier.

Penetanguishene shifted his hold on his lyranope. Mother had told him never to answer that question. Unless an immortal asked it. "Yes."

Stifled gasps and whispers burst out from down the hall where Penetanguishene's housemates were spying from a guarded distance. They shuffled in retreat, conferring in a buzz of whispers. They hadn't known. You could almost hear them taking account of the lies they'd told in his presence.

Downstairs a door slammed open, shut. A thudding of heavy footsteps stamped up the stairs, and a girl bumbled by with a precariously held musical instrument under her arm. She squeezed between Marchale and the wall, unaware whom she jostled. She was a sloppy young woman with kicked-down socks, shirt

tails hanging out, jacket falling off her shoulders, and
her face directed firmly on the floor in front of her.
One could not say she walked; she charged at a sham-
bling march.

Eventually she looked back to see who was clogging
the hallway. "Damn a ram is that an immortal? I
mean—hi, ehre . . . mat."

Penetanguishene pulled her jacket up onto her
shoulders, smoothed down the wildest of her cowlicks,
straightened her com which stuck out skewed on her
ear like the broken antenna of a half-squashed ant.

The attention alarmed Marchale. He was not about
to break up a pair. Humans lived so much longer and
took better care of themselves in mated pairs, and
they pined so when one broke them up. He might
have to take the girl too—or else leave the boy, because Marchale had a bad feeling that she was Natalya
Nakaji, one of those talents who come along once in
a millennium. She had a genius that even a tin Telegonian ear could hear. Her social instincts were lacking entirely. She stood at an awkward stance and
made funny faces when she played. Penetanguishene
was decorous always. Marchale had heard him audi-
tion for the conservatory. Emotion showed only as a
slight pinch in his brow. And you thought he was brilliant until Natalya tore in and found things in the
music you never knew were there, inventing colors
and making you see them as she went.

Marchale watched the nuances between the two for
a moment, and he relaxed. No. Not a pair. He saw
not love but a brotherly concern, or the concern one
would show to a big sloppy dog.

She was clutching his shirtsleeve, realizing that
someone was about to be taken away. Penetanguishene murmured to her, "It's all right, Tally. Go to
your room. I think I'm the one they want." He gave
her a firm gentle push.

He guessed he was being conscripted into the Service. It happened to most young men, but he had not
been expecting it. He was older than the usual con-

script. He was fifteen years old, seventeen Earth standard. Perhaps he'd thought it had passed him by.

Marchale informed him officially, "You are being summoned."

"Yes, ehremat," said Penetanguishene. No question, no protest. No reaction at all really.

"Question first," said Marchale. "Do you have a calling to music?"

The Vikrhalt esteemed its artists the way Telegonians could never fathom, so wrapped up were the free mortals in the utile, the commercial, the immediately accessible. Pure art was beyond their grasp.

Marchale said, "Your duty to the Vikrhalt is best served where your talents lie. Are you one of those touched by divine gift?"

Penetanguishene withdrew into a serious introspective look. He was about to speak, it looked like a question, when from the room across the hall where the bumbling figure of Natalya Nakaji had retreated, poured forth a spate of sound, pure, beautiful and gifted.

Expression flickered on the normally impassive face, desolation almost to bitterness, then returned to blank resignation. "No, ehremat," said Penetanguishene. "I am not."

Marchale sent him to pack his things. Penetanguishene reappeared a brief time later. He owned terribly little. Like those windblown weeds with shallow roots, he uprooted easily and put down wherever he might alight next.

He followed the overlord to a new life, his past every bit as alien and dead to him as Rainier's.

Marchale would think back later and wonder if it would not have been kinder to let Rainier die in the snow.

Dark room. Alone. Scared. Limbs hurt. Joints would not move. Saw dark circles under her eyes when she clawed to the basin and dared look in the mirror. She would only dare in deep shadow. She shivered in the heat, sweated in the cold. She could not close her enormous hulking hands. Something had gone wrong. Growing out, but did she really look like this? She could not even change her mind and run to a facemaker. She did not have her disk. She could not show herself like this.

What unholy thing have I become? Would that nose never stop? Swollen breasts felt like cow's udders. She had shaved her head of its two-tone hair. The last light, pretty, fine white-blond was gone. Now there was only this coarse black-brown stuff. She was hideous. It had been so long since she had seen her real self, was it possible that her body did not remember?

That was what was happening, she convinced herself. Her body was trying to grow back and got lost. She saw herself in nightmares. Fears loomed large and concrete. Images so vivid they could only be real. *What have I done?*

She existed in hiding. No day, no night. Boarded up windows kept the world out. Sometimes brightness limned the cracks. She had become something the sun should not see.

It had to stop some time, finish. She could not be doomed to this sick grotesque hybrid state forever. *What do I look like?* Would she ever revert or not? This misshapen thing was not who she was.

She kept out the lights, and suffered in darkness. Hugged her misery close to her. Abide in this limbo in shades of hell. No time. No light. Only dark. And wonder if she would ever come out again.

Fort Ujiji, New Earth (Telegonia)
EtaCas
29 December 5244
VIII. 2. 1791

"Paul?"

"Go away."

"Paul." Bristol reached for the bottle, but Paul yanked it back with some force.

Paul lifted his head from the couch, his face as rumpled as his clothes. "Look. I am thirty-three today. Earth years. The age when one has to face the fact that he hasn't conquered the world, composed the Magic Flute, or walked on water. I can, however, kill this soldier." He swilled the bottle. "Know your limits, Admiral Krestly always says. This is something I can do. Now leave me alone unless you brought a cake. Didn't think so." He rolled over.

"Get up. We're on the brink of war."

Paul's voice sounded muffled, directed into the couch. "Again? Still?"

"Looks like the big one."

"What'd they do now?"

"We did."

"Who fucked up?"

"Admiral Krestly."

Paul pulled a knee rug over his head. A tuft of light brown hair bristled over the hem. "Come back when you can tell me something new."

Trevor dragged the knee rug away from him. "Banzai Krestly led a commando raid on a Vikhen factory."

"Krestly ain't a commando."

"Rat right," said Bristol.

Trevor said, "Krestly made a raid on the Vikhindens' c ship factory. They blew it up."

Paul turned to look up with pink eyes. "Who did? They who?"

"The Vikhindens. Suicide save. They obliterated the site entirely—raiders and all. They killed their own workers."

"Sure they did."

"They did. You find that beyond their ruthlessness?"

"No. I'm finding that below their level of stupidity. You're telling me that the Empire is not building and maintaining c ships anymore."

Trevor and Bristol paused. They had assumed that once the factory was gone, that was it. It had seemed obvious. They were not sure now. Following Paul's line of thought Bristol said, "They moved the factory."

"Of course they did. The Vikhindens had to be ready and waiting for that one. Praying for it, probably. And those workers may very well have disappeared from the face of the world, but you can bet my next pay chit they ain't dead."

"Interesting possibility," said Trevor.

"Possibility? Bank it." He sat up. "Now you've ruined my binge. Get me some coffee."

Bristol searched for a clean cup in Paul's office. He picked up one cup after another, and replaced them gingerly. Some he would not touch at all. "Paul, you growing a cure for something in these?"

Paul was buzzing his aide's office. "Carl, where are the files that were on my desk?"

"There were no files on your desk, sir. The ones that were on the floor are in the file library."

"What a novel place for them."

"You were shooting marbles with them."

"Where's my other shirt?"

"In the cleaner."

"It was clean, Carl."

"Not after you stepped on it, sir. By the way my name is Daryl, sir."

There were five of these efficient and vacuous young men out of the same tube. All aides in this complex. Paul swore they switched places just to confuse him. "What'd they do to you guys. What kind of names are those? Daryl, Carl, Earl, Merl. Those aren't names. Those are noises I make when I'm trying to throw up. I want my fucking shirt."

Trevor retrieved the shirt from the cleaner in the wall. "You don't think we're on the brink of war?"

"Oh. No brinker than we were yesterday. Admiral Krestly just gave this hand to the Vikhindens, in spades. They get to up stix and move their factory to a safer place and blame us for the demolition of the old one, which they wanted demolished anyway. And they get a grievance against us in the interstellar court, for whatever that counts for. This round is all theirs. Unless of course the raiders managed to get something out of that factory before . . . ?"

"No."

"Didn't think so."

"They were quite blown up."

"You don't think the Vikhindens will declare war over this?" said Trevor.

"Hell no. Relax." He rubbed his hands up and down her arms. She was shivering. "When it comes, *we* will do the declaring."

"They've called in Vreeland Forgil to negotiate."

"Oh, brills. I could settle this one."

"Yes, you have a future in diplomacy. Carl, Earl and Daryl can be your references."

"The Empire's technology is way over ours. They could crush us at any moment, if they were of the crushing mind. So why don't they? The intercession of Forgil? Well, bullshitness. No. The Empire doesn't crush us 'cause the Empire don't wanna. Vikhinde doesn't want war. They want to peacefully take over everything.

"Ever talk to tourists who've been to Vikhinde? They're a little afraid to go; that's why they go. And they come back with glazed eyes and glowing smiles and they gush over it. It's Sebastionique without the underside. It's all sophistication and courtesy, and local color and charm. Guests are sacred. The cities are appallingly beautiful. You can see happy healthy children with their mothers on the street after dark watching a snowflake festival. You never see the cruelty that underlies it. They have no creeps in the all-night coffee shops, no one sleeping on the subway or panhandling on the concourse to the bullet. No strange men wander into martial arts classes and tell you they can teach you how to kill with a drinking straw. No one spoils the picture-pretty main streets. Because they've killed them all. That's the beauty and terror of Vikhinde. Illness if not easily cured is excised. I have to believe our homeless are treated more humanely for our neglect than being put down like stray cats. Vikhinde will never declare war. Too messy. That's our job. We'll do it to keep them from annexing us to the immortals' spotless doll house. Never ever fear a declaration from Vikhinde."

"Even after we attacked their strategic weapons factory?"

"Nah. We needed this. A nice little earthquake to blow off pressure and stave off the big one. A good self-inflicted black eye. Now if Vikhinde can keep from rubbing our noses in this incident too much—doubtful they can do that—but if they do, we're okay. Trouble is that someday Vikhinde will be so overbearing, totalitarian and unbearable that we'll have to declare. That's how it will happen when it does."

" 'When'? Not 'if'?"

"When," said Paul. "But not today."

Life is short. Honor is long.
Dishonor is even longer.
       —Race Rachelson

Alpha Base
15 September 5245
VI. 5. 1792

V.

The soldier woke with the gentle thud of her craft's landing. The top of her prison slid open to bright light, a vapid sky, and dust-scented heat.

She sat up and climbed out slowly. The thing that had brought her looked like a casket and she had not been convinced that it was not one when her commanders had sealed her into it. It did not appear suited to a journey of any length, but she was a long way from home now.

Where she was she did not recognize. Surface pressure was between Earth's and EtaCas', so it was not uncomfortable. The air was breathable, if hazy. The land was adamantly flat and grudgingly bore vegetation, a brown-green tattered scrub.

She had come down on a wide landing flat of a military installation. The outpost appeared crude, without sentries or obvious security measures. Great solar collectors stretching over low buildings were of a size to suggest heavy underground industry. The horizons were featureless.

Overhead burned a sun she had never seen, and she thought she had seen them all. Near it hovered a diffuse red smudge of a companion star.

She accessed all the maps in her implant. This place was not even mapped. It was inaccessible. There was not a stargate within light years. It could mean only one thing.

You have just been on board a c ship.

She regarded the flying casket which had brought her. *So that is a Kingsman pod.* A c ship could carry three of them.

The pod closed itself as she watched. She stepped wide of it as it lifted itself heavenward to return to its orbiting carrier.

Stranded on the dirt field she turned toward the low buildings. Her arrival provoked no alarm, no interest even.

She shouldered her small pack and walked toward where she heard voices drifting over the open ground.

There were no fences, no guards. And she supposed there could be no sneaking up on this base even if anyone knew it existed.

I didn't know this was here!

As she walked into the compound area she crossed paths with a knot of burly young men. Kingsmen. They parted for her.

They knew on sight that this was a new c pup, as sure as they were Kingsmen. They all had that look, arrogant even in confusion. She'd come walking out of the dusty landing track like a leopardess, sultry and aloof in her drab fatigues. She gave a predatory survey of the scene. She was lost. One of the Kingsmen jerked his thumb in the direction she wanted to go.

They closed ranks behind her. She heard their murmurs in her wake. She went looking for the person in charge.

She found him with the others, half out of uniform like everyone else, apparent as the commander only because he was the one who owned the attention of everyone around him. Though he was seated she could tell he was tall. His shoulders were wide, but he was greyhound slender so he hadn't the formidable presence of the Kingsmen. He was light-skinned, his hair dark blond with a sun-scorched blaze. He wore it very short on the sides, longer on top. Though young, he was the oldest of the youthful faces ringing him.

He was bent over a vid sheet which he had balanced on his knees. Energy bristled even in his smallest movements, springing, alert. She imagined he was surrounded in light. Something drew the eyes to focus there.

She approached the circle, waited for a moment. When no one took notice, she said politely, "*Parakaloh?*"

He looked up. She was struck senseless. This for two reasons. The eyes themselves were lovely to behold even when they had been downcast. For clarity and brilliance they could have been gemstones, and had she been a Dr. Frankenstein she would have murdered the man just to have those eyes, not to give to any creation but to give to herself. Then they had looked up and passed through her, painlessly as a sharp knife or a shaft of light. His focus and intensity were an invasion, as if he could see straight through her, was in her and wandering around her core and already knew what she was thinking—which would have been convenient because she was suddenly incapable of uttering a word.

Still the gaze persisted in the benign questioning face.

Finally she remembered why she was here. "Are you the I.C.?"

"Rachelson," the Instructional Commander affirmed, introducing himself.

"Bastard," she said. It flew out before she could consider. She was not used to screening her comments.

"Yes," he said.

She was trying to decide on the best course of retreat, but the guard was already up; she could see it, a mask over the clear eyes. The vertical line above the bridge of the nose.

No retreat was possible. She pushed ahead with her own introduction. "Maya of the Timberlines."

"Rhalt," he said like a counter accusation, as if she were not a cadet but an agent sent by the ruling class to keep an eye on him. Her accent was pure aristocratic.

"No," she said.

"Bull*shit*."

"You are calling me a liar," said Maya.

"Yes. No. Why bother?" he turned his head. This was settled easily enough. "Penetanguishene."

To Rachelson's summons came a cadet, who must have been a truthsayer because Rachelson challenged her to repeat her denial. "Are you Rhalt?"

Maya looked to the cadet whom Race had called to witness. He was short, dark eyed, neat and quiet as a cat. He looked like a child of the Rhalt himself. He was the only one who did not look dusty. A vague sadness haunted him like a perpetual shadow.

A vondesi. The last sort of creature she wanted to meet here.

Luckily this was a question she could answer. Rachelson had only asked if she were a ruling *mortal*. "No," she said. "I am not Rhalt."

"Penetanguishene?" said Race to the vondesi, but his clear gray eyes never left Maya.

"Truth," said the cadet, but he regarded her with reservation as if he saw something else.

Race stared in surprise. He thought he'd had her. On a less attractive face the look would have been stupid.

Maya kept a bland expression of patient superiority. *Don't think you can outflank me, you ridiculous child. I am older than the rotted bones of your great great grandmother!*

"Who sent you?" Someone else backed up Race's challenge.

"I swear," said Maya. "And hear this." She grabbed the vondesi who looked weary and pained, a trick dog tired of performing its one trick. "No one sent me. I came of no agency but my own. I just want to be a c pilot."

The vondesi nodded ever so slowly as if it were painful and his head would split if he moved faster.

"Actually," said Maya, "I wanted to be a Kingsman, but they wouldn't take me. I had to settle to be one of you."

An explosion of hoots and laughter broke from the techies, and incredulous gurgled outrage from the c pilot cadets who had never heard of becoming part of their elite cadre in terms of *settling*.

A small group of Kingsmen within earshot cheered. One gave Maya a wink. "You're all right for a c pup." He looked her up and down. She was too small to be a Kingsman. "What happened? Flunk the physical?"

"No," Race snapped. "She *passed* the IQ test. That did it. Out on her ass. Don't you baboons have something to do?"

The Kingsmen moved on, chortling.

Race returned his gaze to Maya, dumbfounded. She who would settle to be a c pilot. "I'll be damned," he said at last.

"Undoubtedly," said Maya, thinking she could hardly have got off to a worse start.

Days were blazing hot, nights abruptly cold in the thin air. Dust dulled Maya's black shirt, which was patched darker in front and back from sweat. She peeled it off and stripped down to her matador pants.

She had never liked her real looks. She had spent a fortune keeping her skin fair, her hair white-blond and short, her eyes ice blue, her stature petite and thinner than her build was ever meant to be. Her natural muscles tended to slight bulk. She had kept them daintily sleek and her form flat and neat as a porcelain doll. She had not seen herself since she was of an age to say anything about it. She had not been a cute child. She remembered a caretaker saying, "You would think someone meant to last forever would be prettier."

One virtue of the centuries of deception was that in her natural guise no one would know her. In order to hide, she need only stand in plain sight.

Her hair was black and coarse, her dark deep eyes a warm brown. Heavy brows looked woeful to her. Full lips kept a perpetual pout, and her long nose added to her look of arrogance. Her jaw was firm and rounded. She was tall for a woman, sturdy-boned; she felt like a hulk. She had wide hips, a narrow enough waist, and heavy breasts that obeyed the laws of gravity, not the stand up high globes of actresses. She wore no support. Whether envious or trying to be helpful, a woman on base commented to Maya that she would need a facemaker by the time she was twenty-three.

"Don't bet the Rhaltbank," said Maya.

She felt secure that no one would know her looking like this, and that no one she had known in her past could happen upon her out here. Then, while Rachelson was explaining something to the new cadets on the simulators, Maya closed her eyes and listened to the voice, Race's light middle baritone.

She had heard it before. Seven Eta Cassiopeian years ago.

Hello hello. Anyone at Valhalla. This is Queen's Knight. Queen's Squadron victorious. For the Queen. For honor. Come in, Valhalla.

Maya felt suddenly dizzy and naked. As if the clear gray eyes could see through to the porcelain doll beneath the hulk. In quiet panic, she reminded herself that he had not seen or heard her then. Or ever. She had heard him, a disconnected voice from space.

Race was looking at her inquiringly. "What?"

The hunter's eye spied something.

Waiting for the world to stop spinning, Maya continued to stare at him, at his long, thin-fingered hands so she would not meet his eyes. Maya said, "You used to be the Queen's Knight."

He stiffened as if she'd stepped on a nerve. "Yes," he said, like a prompt, a dare, for her to explain. *And so what of it?*

"Why are you here teaching cadets?"

A look like anger crossed his face. Then for an instant like tears. He got up from the simulator and walked away as if he were carrying an arrow in his back.

"Good shot, Maya," someone said dryly.

The others had been here longer and knew things that she did not. "Well?" she said. It was a demand for someone to explain.

"You don't know, do you?"

"Why would I be asking if I knew?"

"Because you're a bitch?" someone offered.

She had landed a telling blow somehow. She watched the retreating figure. Ever since she had arrived she'd been catching herself watching him, memorizing the form. His poetic thinness gave him a look of fragility now, his wide shoulders held straight across, his back too straight as if fighting to stay upright. It was the walk that was remarkable. They all had it. He patented it. Even wounded, he moved at a rolling strut.

"Race Rachelson was the best there ever was," a techie answered, a great flat-faced slab of a man named Sun. "Any of you will be lucky to be a quarter as good." Sun went on at length to say that Race Rachelson had shot down more enemies of the Empire than anyone in any sort of ship. Race was overage for a c pilot and his reactions were down from his peak, but he was still faster than the best of his c pups. "Better, there isn't."

"So why is he not active?" said Maya.

"About four years ago he crashed a c ship."

Maya felt herself pale. Ashata knew many things that Maya could not have access to. Afraid to look around, she tried to determine where was the vondesi. *Careful what you say here.* She said nothing.

"He didn't ride it down," Sun continued.

"Obviously," Maya said strangledly.

"It wasn't Race's ship. His Echo was in trouble. The pilots switched places FTL. Rhaltcommand got hysterical about that stunt. They don't understand what it's like FTL."

"You've been?"

"No," said Sun. "But if Race did it, it must be all right."

She would hear that statement over and over. She

was learning already that if Race said it, it came from a burning bush. And hard as she kept up her guard, something of his charm got through to her, too. A clarity of soul was all she could call it.

"Race brought his Echo's ship in. Pointed it at an uninhabited planet and baled out in a Kingsman pod. The ship's crash took out an immortal who just happened by some cosmic coincidence to be there, and that was the end of Rachelson's career."

Words came to Maya's lips but she did not speak them. They were unfamiliar to her and she'd never said them in her life: *I am sorry.*

Race may have been young for a mortal, but he was ancient for a c pilot. He was 24 Eta Cassiopeian. 27 Earth years. By the time the Empire got around to forgiving him, if it ever did, it would be too late for Rachelson. His career was over.

I didn't step on a wound. I am the wound.

She had an impulse to tell him. *You didn't kill me. The coincidence was too cosmic; I wasn't really there. I am alive. Reclaim your place while you still have a few heartbeats left.* Her eyes were burning.

His voice behind her made her jump, the familiar baritone. "It wasn't that. It was the engine loss." Race had circled back, composed now. He picked up a chair, planted it back down backwards and sat astride. "Nobody cried when that bitch died. I don't think I was canned on account of Ashata. It was the security risk. They say I almost handed c tech to the free mortals."

Maya tried to keep her breath even and natural as she choked down wrath. *No one cried.* She looked up casually as if studying the sky, bored. *I did!*

She fought to keep it in perspective. No one hated Ashata more than she had. So why so angry and hurt when he said that no one cried? Because she'd almost told him her closest secret, and he turned on her like that.

Take the fall, bastard!

Quivering inside, she wondered why had she almost

torpedoed everything she wanted. What had she been thinking? Her thoughts had latched onto him. She would not let it lead her into stupidity. She had been to the mouth of hell and spent four years clawing and plotting and now that she was getting where she wanted to be, she almost gave it away for an ephemeral too old mortal with an appealing way.

No one cried!

A hundred years from now, you'll all be dead and who will give a damn? What was I thinking?

The conversation continued without her.

"There is a c engine missing to this day," someone commented.

Race said, "I'm not worried about that. It's safe."

"Where is it?"

"I don't know. Out There. The Elsewhere." So he referred to faster than light. "It's not a security risk. We're the only ones who can chase it."

"Why don't we?" said a c pup.

"Actually I'm not sure even we can bring it back. C ships are designed to haul their own carefully distributed mass back and forth. The only cargo is the pilot, the fuel, and up to three Kingsman pods occupied by a maximum of 350 kilos. I don't know if we could tow an engine back. Why try and maybe lose another c ship? The engine is safe. It won't slow down with inertia, that's not how things happen Out There. In the Elsewhere, things speed up. Nothing ever falls out of the Elsewhere. So we leave it."

"Then how do you know it's still in the Elsewhere?"

"Kit up. I'll show you pups something."

The Presence waited out on the flat, its stillness that of something ready to spring. Dust devils kicked up round it like spitting smoke.

Like all legendary ships it had its own personality. The Presence spoke with the most powerful voice she had ever encountered. For arrogant belligerence it out-did even Maya, and she approached with due respect.

The ship stood delicately on tricycle gear, twelve meters long and of variable span with a flexible nose, aggressive lines, sleek as an arrow head. It was very light, all its mass in those huge engines. Its skin was tissue thin, tough as an elastic diamond, and frictionless. Its armament was all of the beam variety. It carried no physical missiles to add mass. A c ship weighed in at 7000 kilos fully loaded.

There was a way to climb up to the cockpit directly if one knew where to hold on. Maya did not feel like entertaining the ground crew by trying to climb up the frictionless skin, so she entered through the side hatch, crawled up the catwalk, and swung herself feet first into the access tube and into the cockpit. She raised and locked the firewall behind her.

Half of the instruments on the panel were masked off, with only one unfamiliar gauge allowed to peek through. The rest of the uncovered instruments were very familiar sublight standard fighter craft equipment, logically arranged.

Race mounted the wing, swung himself up as if onto a familiar steed, and leaned on the edge of the cockpit. There was a trick to it. She watched Race do it. There was an intimate familiarity in his touch. He hooked an elbow into the cockpit to hold himself up while he briefed her. "She takes off just like a K 14 Black Adder. If you want, you can put her on auto and she'll take herself off."

"Not a chance."

Race gave a half shrug. All c cadets said that. If they didn't, something was wrong with them. "You escape atmosphere just like a Hawk 92 and she handles in space like a Razor only more so. Don't panic slam unless you really mean it. You'll be downtown yesterday. There's nothing else here that should be strange to you."

"Except those," Maya pointed at the masked bank of instruments.

"Not today. Those are for FTL. Don't go playing with nine quadrillion Rhaltmus worth of gadgets."

"That the price tag on this?"

"Try not to break it."

She checked over the sublight instruments. "Nothing here that lesser beings haven't handled before me."

"Coming back she lands like an Adder. With the wings spread she does know how to glide and she has a very low stall speed. There's a target circle on the field for the hot shots. Not feeling cocky today, there's 20,000 klicks of flat here. Just get her down on the same continent, this side up. Questions?"

"What's that?"

She pointed at the only unfamiliar gauge left uncovered.

"That's your sun reader. You're going to use that."

She watched his dismount from the slick machine. It was a balanced glide off the wing to land springingly on his feet.

He walked over to another machine to brief another cadet. The pups were going up two at a time. Only three c ships were available for the training unit, and Race would be going up in the third.

The best ever.

Maya could see it now, the open wound. He carried a pained wistfulness as he trained his charges to go to a magic place forever locked to him.

The canopy slid shut over Maya's head, locked, and sealed.

Analytical calm balanced against exhilaration. An intrusive pang lingered:

I almost gave this up for you.

Her stature that was too small to allow her to become a Kingsman became a virtue now inside the snug cockpit. It was the kind of fit that made a pilot feel one with the ship. She turned on the electrics, listened to the different voices of the different gauges. Normal green glowed on all the readouts. Brakes gleamed red. Seals secured, she pressurized and ran through an instrument check.

At the signal, she started her take-off sequence. The engines quickened with her heart. The Presence moved with the prowl of a menacing predator, rolled, and then streaked off the earth and up.

For a thousand years Maya had feared, loathed, spaceflight. Every bump signaled something wrong. It was a different thing entirely being the pilot. Her fate lay in her own hands and she could face the fear. She was glad now that she'd failed to make Kingsman. She had not been able to press the requisite 250 kilos in an Eta Cassiopeian gravity. But she hated to be a passenger for space travel; and to reach their battlegrounds, Kingsmen were stuck back in those little pods while someone else held the c ship's controls. Maya wanted to meet her terrors head on, to stop her endless running and go to the front and look the monster in the teeth. She wanted to be in front of the front, where even fear does not go. The quivering inside her now was a different brand of fear, one she could become addicted to, an exhilarated rush instead of a clawing sickness.

The powerful ship achieved escape velocity in no time.

The voices murmured normally, the readouts stayed green.

Maya met up with Race and the other c pup.

Race gave them a heading toward the sun.

Even at conventional sublight speeds this ship was exciting for its power and responsiveness. Maya felt an immediate bond with the machine, a sense that for once in her life she belonged somewhere.

Race's heading took them into a wide orbit around the sun, in and out of the tenuous outer corona. The inner corona was one million degrees.

She was careful going through the widest of its fans which spread from the most active regions. Her ship skirted the puffs where the chromosphere was about to shoot out tons of matter at hundreds of kilometers per second.

A dazzling loop prominence rained fire back to the surface along magnetized lines in a molten storm.

The roiling mass of the surface filled her view from horizon to horizon, granulated with titanic rising columns of gas which mushroomed and fell away.

Race's voice sounded on the com to bid the cadets

turn their magnetographs on and tell the sun reader to search for a sunspot having no polarity.

Maya did as she was told. Flying over a sunspot she could not see that it was a spot. It was too close, too huge, and only its relative temperature had ever made it look dark in the first place. They came in varying sizes of enormity. The tiny ones were thousands of kilometers across. They were all dangerous. The ship veered of its own accord with flashing red on the screen, taking her wide of a sudden violent spray.

"Careful here, pups. Alpha's shooting at us."

Maya looked back at the molten fire geysering up. She heard another voice on the com, the other cadet. "Wow."

"Sightseeing, are we?" said Race.

"Uh, Race? I didn't get a read of those spots back there."

"They were magnetized. Trust me. Get these."

At the end of a few orbits, Maya's magnetograph had isolated nine sunspots lacking any polarity.

She sent, "Ehre, I have nine spots so far."

"That's all of them. Go back and ask your sun reader for a mass."

"Mass of what?"

"It knows."

"Mass!" she demanded, and the sun reader's measured vaguely male voice intoned: "6988 kilos, 6924 kilos, 6980 kilos . . ." in a series of nine, all close to 7000 kilos except one.

"All right, bring her home," said Race.

Returning to base, Maya tried to put down on the target circle, missed. The other pups in their turns, overexcited and awed by the Presence, came down even wider. Race touched it precisely, every time.

When they had all gone up and taken the reading, Race told them what they had been looking at.

"C ships leave holes in the spacetime where they pass from this universe into the Elsewhere. The hole looks like a small sunspot, but real sunspots are magnetic. This is just a cooler spot and it doesn't go away in a few days like real sunspots. Your magnetograph can recognize the holes and the sun reader can tell you how big a mass made it. The hole only heals when the mass that made it returns to real spacetime. Doesn't matter where you return. The wound heals. You saw eight 7000 kilo readings. That means the Queen's Squadron is somewhere Out There. They went in here and they're not out yet."

"There are nine holes."

"I know. One only measures 2900 kilos. That's the engine I lost. And that, children, is how I know it's still Out There."

Maya frowned. *It leaves a wound where it leaves spacetime.*

The wound was below the photosphere.

In fact it was below the convection zone and more toward the core where temperatures approached 15 million degrees with pressures to crush worlds and even the light created therein could not get out to the surface.

She said aloud, "That hole is inside the sun."

Race looked his pups straight in the eyes, each one, in a kind of challenge and said, "Uh huh."

They all squinted at the sun where they would be headed at full speed. If they ever wondered why the designers had bothered to make a spaceship aerodynamic, the answer was here: They hadn't. Its aerodynamics were a side effect of a design made to plunge into the densest, hottest matter in the solar system.

"For the next vants, you will be doing this on simulators. Not that it gives you any real idea what it's like, but you will know exactly what you have to do. When it comes to the real thing, you get one shot. Get it perfect the first time. This is where we separate the very quick from the dead." Then he added wistfully, "Life begins at 293,796 klicks per tick."

A small wave of impressed muttering and grim chuckles rose and fell.

A c pup murmured to any of his companions. "Think you can do it?"

Maya said, "I know I can."

In a sense she already had.

The trouble with annihilation is that you never quite know where all the bodies are buried.
—Eta Cassiopeian saying

VI.

Into the sun.

The inferno loomed. The viewports photo-adjusted, the full fury allowed to show only on the instruments. The seething slow churning of its cells took on true dimensions as the c ship neared.

Closer the granulation went. The relative darkness of the cracks became a single huge blaze, the sun reader clicking a quiet storm. Suns were ever in flux. Maya needed to plot a course and execute it immediately or the terrain would change on her within minutes—or in degrees as Eta Cassiopeians kept time.

Analyze. Plot. Commit. Execute.

She chose a low point in the corona, avoiding the sunspots and other BMRs. None of the sun's surges, puffs, and mass ejections would kill her; what they would do to her trajectory would.

Time the rotation. Plot the depth. Account for the oscillation.

She would need all the momentum she could muster. Go into the doppler blue and meet the advancing side.

Drive into a solid wall of fire.

And come out where?

Depends on if you get it right. You dive into the sun and one way or the other you are no longer of this universe. You are either destroyed or you go Elsewhere. As far as the universe is concerned, you cease to exist.

Only if you are fast enough will you live to see the other side.

A tick from now, it will all be over.

Maya took a quick final read.

Decided. Point of no return. Execute. Slam the accelerator. Dive speed!

Thousands of kilometers of atmosphere in a flash, the corona a millionth as dense as air. She was through before she was ever rightly there.

Through the photosphere. Intakes filled with hydrogen. A c ship could not possibly carry the fuel it needed. She collected it on the way, in the only place to find it in the quantity and density needed.

Into the sun at near the speed of light, a dive that would either force her through or squash her to a size to dance on the head of a pin with the rest of the angels.

Crash into the wall.

Before she could register a single thought, connect a single synapse, before she knew anything at all, she felt a pull as if she had been grabbed from the other side. No transition, just instantly past center. Spacetime had flexed and she was through the looking glass, speeding into darkness. Silence. The sun was gone and the engines had shut down. Still she accelerated as if sucked through a venturi tube. She blinked in the sudden empty blackness, so vacant that even vacuum was too substantial a word to define it.

The Elsewhere.

No past, no future, no here and now. The only landmarks showed on the instruments, the warping in the nothingness which corresponded to black holes in real spacetime.

A few muffled thumps sounded behind her within the ship. That would be Race crawling out of the Kingsman pod where he'd been secured. She heard him moving forward through the hold.

A tapping came directly behind her head.

She lowered the headrest and opened the hatch behind her. Race elbowed up the narrow passage to look over her shoulder. "I take it we're still alive."

Maya said nothing.

Race reached in over her shoulder and cocked a mirror so he could see her face. He gave a small sound of approval. Maya supposed he was checking to see whether she was in the grip of frozen fear or this glow of wonderment which she wore now.

Life begins at 293,796 klicks per tick.

Finally Race spoke, for every moment she spent dreaming was taking them a million kilometers away from the base. Not that she could run into anything Out Here. There was no mass except what she had brought.

The Elsewhere was cartoon flat like a bad movie. Without depth or infinitely deep, like an optical illusion it shifted back and forth with no in between.

"Remember when they first explained the positively curved universe to you and you pictured a ball expanding from the Big Bang, and you wondered what was *outside* the positively curved universe? This is it," he presented proudly as if it were his. She supposed if anyone could make a claim on the Elsewhere, it was Race Rachelson. He was like a kid showing off his most exclusive of secret hiding places. "Any problems?"

"No," she said, then asked, "Why am I not going backwards when I pass through the light barrier?"

"You are. We think. But the universe around you is inside out too. So you sense forward motion. Your senses lie like hell Out Here. Doesn't matter too much because most of the lies are consistent.

"Trust your instruments. You have nothing else." Even the arti-grav had gone. She was weightless. "Your bearings go. Spend time Out Here, you get real confused. There's no such thing as dead reckoning Out Here. Well, there is, but it's well named," he amended. "Feel like another hit, or you want to go home?"

"Let's fly," said Maya.

A c ship had the ability to decelerate anywhere its pilot chose, but the problem was where do you go from there? Never, Maya was told, decelerate any great distance from a star or a stargate. To do so was to maroon oneself. And never try to dive into a black hole or neutron star. But where there was a black hole there was a stargate—though it was usually one leading farther than you wanted. If you ended up in another galaxy with a one-way gate, even your c ship won't get you home again. At ten thousand times the speed of light, a journey of trillions of light years was still a long hike.

The other thing to avoid was a singly formed red giant. Red death, the c pilots called it. A red giant star hadn't the density to send a ship FTL. You may as well be nowhere.

Maya's destination was a blue star. It had no planets, making it an easy destination for a training flight.

Getting back to real spacetime was easy, requiring nothing so spectacular as colliding with a star. She need only achieve the speed at which she made the crossing, and spacetime would drag her back through.

Maya punched it. Speeding down hard as if into a wall. She missed the transition again. Instantly her engines had cut power, their work done, and there were stars! On her starboard side blazed a field of intense violet fire. The blue giant.

If anything could daunt a new c pilot it would be the alien violence of a gargantuan blue star. Maya was eager to have at it.

Race retreated to his secure berth back in the Kingsman pod for the plunge. All he said to Maya was, "She's a fast one. Make it shallow."

The only problem he could see with Maya was going to be getting her back to base.

Disembarking at last at Alpha Base, Maya slid off the wing and landed on her feet.

"Ilu, Maya has teeth!"

What did that mean? she wondered, then realized that they had never seen her smile.

Race crawled out of the side hatch. "I'm gonna take a piss and we're off again. Somebody get in the cockpit and run a pre-flight. *Next!*"

The pups watched each other go up and return.

Maya listened to them talk. She was not sure what the proper reaction was in many situations. When in doubt, keep your mouth shut. That was always a safe approach. Mortals would fill in the blank with something, if not proper, then at least human.

At day's end Race gathered his pups around him for a few words before he released them.

"Don't break a leading edge. If your ship is injured in combat, we have to shoot the horse. A broken ship will not go FTL.

"If you are in danger of capture, take whatever means necessary to annihilate the engines. If there is an empty Kingsman pod on board, you may choose to save yourself or go down with your ship."

The pilots, all of whom were very much enamored of their own lives, were startled by the suggestion of a choice. "If the engines are secure and you can save yourself, what's to decide?"

Race, who could hold anyone's gaze, turned his eyes from all of them. "Had I to do it again, I wouldn't."

As they continued training, the cadets watched each other and wondered who was going to make it to the top, to the elite Queen's Squadron. Most of them were destined to the reserve squadron, or worse still, to be reserve pilots to the reserve squadron.

Maya walked on a fine edge. She could not afford to be as belligerent as she was and not be the best. The others were waiting to eat her alive. They never got the chance. There grew a grudging admission among them that Maya was as good as her attitude. Everyone picked her as second best of the group. They picked themselves first.

What Maya was so good at was taking in the barrage of information, analyzing, coming to the proper response and executing in proper order without confusion, panic, overload or miscalculation. The ship was a joy and a challenge. The cockpit her cocoon. Outside of it she had a sense she was being stalked.

Passing as a mortal was harder than piloting a c ship. Everyone knew the rules but her. And there were so many of them. Her reactions were often inappropriate.

The c base was a tight community of c pilots, Kingsmen, techies and support personnel. The canteen, christened Nebuchadnezzer's, was lively every night, especially when there were Kingsmen on planet. Maya dreaded the off hours.

Casual conversation was dangerous. She almost hung herself when she missed a reference to "three and a half decks," within a group of women. What was so important about thirty-five Eta Cassiopeian days? It was a menstrual period. She didn't have them. Immortals didn't.

She had heard, though she would sooner jump off a bridge than verify first hand, that if an immortal had sex and did not become immediately pregnant, she would menstruate two decks later. A scarlet letter for bestial behavior, Maya thought.

The topic was a popular one among the women. Days were different here, and all the women were off rhythm. And they all it seemed had cause for worry when they missed.

Maya watched their mating games in embarrassment. Not that the drive was wholly absent in immortals, but someone who did not die was not driven to replace herself. Pride and shame were the stronger forces. Among mortals, desire threw shame out the window. There was no threat, no taboo, no sanction legal or moral that could keep them from rutting. Well, mortals must reproduce. The drive insured it. Maya suspected that nature had overdone it.

She felt as if she were being dissected as she walked past the males. She would catch herself thinking: *I can make you go away. I can feed you your eyes.*

Then quickly, *No, Maya. You are not Vikrhalt. You are not even pretending to be Rhalt. You can't just kill people when you want to. You're one of them now. How do they stand each other?*

They said Race was promiscuous. Strange, because he looked like a clean scrubbed boy soldier. She never saw him making an ass of himself—not in that way at least.

She was becoming aware that Race was out of step so that even she could see it. He was not well spoken, sometimes clumsy of expression then abruptly poetic. He could read. Slowly. They would see him in his off hours trudging through a book, for himself, the way no one else would read except under threat of an advanced test.

Difficult to categorize, he refused to rest easy in any pigeonhole in which she tried to perch him. Contradictory. Singular.

He was supremely coordinated, yet clumsy in gestures of expression. Aggressive, gregarious, shy, reserved. Emotions sputtered out in a gush as if breaking a dam. He kept his mouth shut when he smiled, but the merriment leaked out his eyes. He always blushed when he laughed, and when he broke a full smile he hid crooked teeth behind a long-fingered hand.

He could be a picture of quiet dignified leadership, then it would all dissolve into childish enthusiasm.

He observed the coming of the survival trials with a fiendish glee. It was not true malice, more the devious joy of a boyish prank, as if it were great sport to dump these star children into the wilds of an unspecified planet and watch them try to find the nearest friendly base.

Maya thought Race would be out of his element in a survival situation. He was so perfectly the pilot. He wore his uniform like a lion wore its mane, all his strength in the machine, power to level cities at the tips of those long fragile-looking fingers.

Out of his element he never looked more in it. He was lean but tough as a Kingsman. He could move silently in a forest and he set some very rugged trials for his pups.

However this outing was marred by the unexpected

appearance of ferals who carved up one of the cadets. Ferals were not to have been part of the test.

"Bogus ferals," said Race back at Alpha Base.

"The land around Alquon is full of ferals," someone argued.

"I'm from Alquon," Race snapped. "It's not *full* of ferals."

"They looked like ferals," said Maya watching the recording.

Race turned on her. "And you'd know a feral if you saw one, would you, Maya?"

"It looks obvious."

"This is obvious." Race uprooted a flower and pushed it at her.

Perplexed Maya took it. "What am I to make of this? This is a plant."

"That's good. So were the ferals," Race declared and walked away in a pout.

She had always thought he must be a colonial for his awkward ways and polite schoolboy manners in the presence of superiors. The record said he was Eta Cassiopeian. Alquon province, was it? Alquon was the most unsettled region on the world. Race Rachelson was a back woods bastard made good.

He was intelligent, but sometimes the man was stone stupid. All mortals were to a degree, but this one acted like he just got into town. And she had to wonder where he'd been all his life. Alquon province?

Maya became aware there was a secret here, besides the bastardy which was as obvious as his name. She had been so wrapped up in protecting her own secret, that she hadn't noticed someone else playing close to the vest.

Race was much more direct in his prying; he would ask bluntly what he wanted to know. He was fishing into Maya's past when finally Maya said, "Let sleeping dogs lie. As a matter of fact, they're not even sleeping dogs. They're dead dogs. I killed them. They rotted away to skeletons and I hung them up in my closet and locked the door and annihilated the key."

"This is a hell of an outfit to get into with any kind of baggage," said Race.

"You're a fine one to talk," said Maya.

Race flinched, stared at her in horror, something like a cornered beast. He said nothing for a long time then finally choked out, "What do you mean?"

"I haven't the vaguest. It was a random shot. You shouldn't have bled. I wouldn't have known I hit anything."

Race retreated looking rattled.

It became a game of chess, each maneuvering for a glimpse behind the other's line. And watching all the time to see where was the vondesi.

Maya feared, loathed, the quiet truthsayer. She avoided him, and no one thought it odd because they all did. It had been the worst luck to find him here. A vondesi was an incognito immortal's worst enemy save death.

Immortals had a few extra powers—or maybe they were human qualities which immortals simply had time to practice and develop.

An immortal could mesmerize a person in the way that vampires were fabled to. An immortal could not become invisible, but they could convince a weaker mind that they had not been here.

A truthsayer's mind could not be clouded. Furthermore, a truthsayer could detect falsehood within a mind that had been altered. A mortal could swear that he did not see anyone, and truly believe that he hadn't seen. The vondesi would hear two signals, the clouded answer as well as an echo of part of the mortal mind that had seen and resonated a lie.

It made the vondesi a natural predator of a being who lived by deception. A vondesi could see through the artifice which immortals used to survive.

This one, Penetanguishene, was talented and patient as a pack animal. He hadn't the temperament of the other pilots, no soaring enthusiasm. He was a correct, decorous, educated child of the Rhalt though not Rhalt himself, not yet. And Maya suspected that even he suspected he was only here to keep an eye on the c base.

Maya hadn't long to endure him. He was gone sooner than anyone thought.

Maya woke to a sonic boom. It thrummed at her ears and vibrated the cot in the underground barracks. The tremor passed through like an earthquake. Maya thought it was an earthquake until another thundercrack roared from above. Definitely from above though it shook the ground.

War?

Maya climbed out of the barracks.

In the planet's quick twilight before its imminent sudden dawn Maya could see flashes of light on wings high in the atmosphere.

They came plunging down, two ships, one on the other.

Dogfight.

Maya walked to where a knot of techies stood watching in fascination and horror, Sun holding his head and bemoaning what atmosphere does to an engine.

The two were c ships, locked in combat. The fighting looked real. C ships never dogfight each other. It was not taught because it was never needed—all c ships were on the same side.

So what was this?

Maya hugged herself, the night air cold on her sleep-swollen face. She could see her breath. She sniffled, still waking up. "What's going on?"

"Penetanguishene jumped Race."

"What?"

No one could say more. Penetanguishene had always been so quiet. No one knew him. Or what was happening here.

There was a third c ship available to the training unit. The senior cadet asked the senior tech, "Should I go up and help him?"

"No. Race has it under control. He's just trying not to kill the son of a bitch. Not that he doesn't deserve it, but that's an expensive little bird he's got up there."

The battling eagles roared, feinted, deathly beautiful.

They locked and plunged. Voices yelled from the ground, "Pull up! Pull up!"

The two ships disappeared over the dark horizon. The ground crew was silent, waiting for the sound of explosion to arrive.

Sudden roaring split the sky from behind. They all turned as the two c ships blazed chasing overhead.

At last Race forced the errant ship down.

Sunlight lanced over the horizon. Mist rose in tendrils from the landing field, rolled in steam clouds off the heated sides of the c ships.

Race stalked in past Penetanguishene, who waited under his ship's wing with his helmet under his arm. The vondesi's cheeks were blazoned red whether from cold or crying or exertion. His thick black hair fluttered in the wind like a dog's ruff. Race spoke softly in supreme fury, "You are grounded for the rest of your life." He stalked in, roiling the mist behind him like smoke, leaving Penetanguishene standing by his steaming ship.

The others followed Race inside.

"What will happen to him?"

"They'll just reorganize him till he doesn't know his own name."

The other cadets were just waking up. From the buzzing they knew that something big had happened and they'd missed it. "Crasher?"

"Crasher? He detonated."

"Gotta watch them quiet ones."

"Hell of an exit."

"Nice job bringing him down, Race."

Race grunted. He was furious at himself, at Penetanguishene, at everything that had brought them here. How had this happened? "And what the hell got into him?"

"Just nuts."

Race exploded, "They don't send me nuts! They send me best!"

After breakfast, which Race did not eat, he stalked back out. "Where's Penetanguishene?"

"Gone."

"Gone? How can he be *gone*?"

A Kingsman pod had lifted earlier. The reserve squadron had come and picked up a passenger. "I assumed you knew."

Race was about to shout for the orders when they were placed into his hand. The wand was red. Priority. Race replayed the message.

The wand said that Penetanguishene was being recalled by the Vikrhalt. "Cease training at once. We are sending a c ship for pickup." The Rhaltcommander signed off. The wand flashed to indicate that the message not complete. There was a brief addendum. "Agamemnon is dead. Ninthvant first, 1792."

The wand went inert, its message done.

"Is he to be killed?" someone asked.

"I don't know." Race replayed the message for a clue. The thought hadn't occurred to him. "He may have thought so . . . Or . . ."

Agamemnon is dead. Agamemnon was the vondesi at the Empire's intelligence gathering center as Kobandrid Rog was euphemistically known. It was a torture chamber. *Now there's a post worse than death*. Race's mood changed abruptly. He become concerned, upset. "Why didn't he come to me?"

Penetanguishene doesn't come to anyone, thought Maya, then suddenly realized as she said it, "He did, ehre."

He wanted you to shoot him.

Since when is freedom of choice axiomatic? You have no right to choose to rape the future.
                                   —On the Rain Forest
                                    ℗ 1791

VII.

Penetanguishene did not know where he was exactly, only that it was a place most people never saw. The trouble with those kinds of places was that a mortal was likely to die before he was allowed to leave.

He was about to be promoted or executed, one of the two.

There were seven immortals arranged in the chamber, two he recognized as Marchale and Kveta. A mortal, a high ranking member of the Rhalt, was asking the questions for them.

"Are you loyal?" said the Rhaltcommander.

"Yes," said Penetanguishene.

"Do you pledge your life to the Vikrhalt?"

"Yes."

"Then give it."

One of the towering beefy Kingsmen flanking the door stepped in to hand Penetanguishene a revolver. It was an old weapon, projectile style, the sort of weapon used in rituals, antiquated and symbolic as a sword. All of its chambers were loaded.

Dull inner vacancy collided with panic, and left Penetanguishene sinkingly numb. *So it goes.*

He looked around him to gauge where the projectile, should it go all the way through his head, would do the least damage.

"You know how to work it?" someone said, misinterpreting the delay.

"Yes," said Penetanguishene.

He aimed the gun at his temple, its line of fire

pointed toward a blank wall. He closed his eyes and pulled the trigger.

The explosion slammed at his eardrum. Fire stung his temple.

He blinked.

Blood trickled down the side of his face. His head ached, concussed. He stared in bewilderment at the row of judges who lifted their chins in Vikhen approval.

The gun was taken from his slack hand. He stood stunned.

The blood was wiped from the side of his head. Someone was congratulating him.

It must have been a small charge. It had sounded like thunder when he thought it was the end of the world. Even a normal blank would have killed at this range. They had measured it just so.

A mirror was put in his hand. He looked at his face. The bleeding burn at his temple would scar. They told him never to tell how he got it, never to have it removed. Look at it and remember this.

They asked him to swear loyalty, to serve immortals and to protect civilian mortals with his life. Great power, great burden, and great trust were in his hands. Still dazed, as he recited the words he realized what he was saying.

I am in the Rhalt.

Penetanguishene knew where his new posting would be before they told him. Kobandrid Rog.

The Vikrhalt wanted no sadists in the decision-making position. "That kind loses track of what they're about. We need someone who loathes it," Marchale explained. "Unfortunately, that is you."

"Must it be so extreme?" said Penetanguishene.

"Man created the idea of hell," said Marchale. "I assume he had a need for it."

Fort Ujiji, New Earth
EtaCas
17 January 5246
IX. 21. 1792

Trevor saw Paul head for his vid and warned him, "Whatever you do, don't turn on channel 1238."

Channel 1238. Vikhen Broadcasting.

"Why? What's up?"

"The Vikrhalt's broadcasting an execution from Kobandrid Rog." Trevor gave a shudder that rattled her ankle bracelets.

Paul turned it on. "Grotesqueness. Looks like they're airing the autopsy now." Then the corpse screamed. "Shit." Paul slapped it off.

"Told you so," Trevor sang.

Bristol nodded at the now-blank vid sheet. "It's Rhaltcontroller Zebred."

"Couldn'ta happened to a nicer guy," said Paul, feeling only slightly better about this. "What's he in for?"

"Abuse of power."

"Well shit, does that pass for a news flash from the Empire? What took 'em so long?"

"Empire's house cleaning to polish its image."

"You call that image polishing? Granted the man should die, but Jesus."

"The idea as the Vikhens explain it, is the betrayal of supreme trust wins you the ultimate penalty. With a war in the wind, they're trying to get their citizens to believe in their justice and everyone is equal before the law."

"Ha!"

"Zebred was Satan himself."

"Yeah, and what about the guy doing this execution?"

"Donts know. But speaking of mad dogs, Krestly wants you."

"I know. I've been dodging that message all day."

When Paul finally answered the admiral's summons, he found the vid in Krestly's office tuned to Vikhen Broadcasting. "That still on? Can't be the same guy. Oh shit, he can't still be alive."

"Zebred," Krestly said casually. "He's died five times already. They keep bringing him back. They're damnably good at this."

Paul was getting the idea that Krestly had been watching this from the beginning.

"Is that Agamemnon's pleasure palace?"

"No," said the admiral. "It's Kobandrid Rog all right, but Agamemnon died. This here's a mean little fuck, Rhaltcaptain with a name five klicks long. Pentateuch. Penultimate. Pendulum. Pentameter. Pen on and on and on."

"What do you need from me, sir?"

Krestly swivelled his chair around, a kind of sitting-down swagger. "I don't *need* you. Never think I *need* you," the admiral prefaced. "The Empire claims we planted bogus ferals in a globular cluster."

Paul laughed humorlessly. "They think we're stupid?"

"Also in Alquon."

"They're sure those ones weren't real?"

"Empire says they're ours."

"The Empire—" Paul began, squirmed as a scream rose from the vid. He was losing the thread of what he was saying. "Ah . . . can we turn that off?"

"I find it informative," said Krestly lazily, relishing Paul's discomfort.

"Know these men?" Krestly rolled some picture globes his way. Paul illuminated each, dropped them in turn. "Mercs. Generic."

"Are they red cards?"

"Hell no, sir."

"Who are they?"

"Fucking idiots, sir."

"Army?"

"No. Fleet maybe."

"Your friends in I.I.N.?"

"I don't have any friends in the I.I.N."

"Oh yeah? They seem to like you just rat fine. Listen, Strand. I don't like operations going down without my knowledge. Especially ones that make my Fleet look bad."

"It's a stupid stunt. It's not our guys." He glanced at the vid, felt his gorge rise, swallowed it.

Krestly intoned like a tour guide, or a lecturer, "The machine monitors his brain waves. When he turns veg and can't appreciate the pain and horror any more, they'll let him die. The idea is to put it off as long as—"

"Excuse me, sir." Paul edged for the exit.

"You're weak, Strand."

A scream and Krestly's laughter followed him out the door. He drowned them out with his own gagging.

Fort Ujiji, New Earth
EtaCas
9 April 5246
XII. 3. 1792

"Sebastionique has just issued rules of war."

"Why, those assholes," said Paul in a reasonable tone. He snatched the sheet from Bristol. "Well, that's not good, *is* it? Makes the whole thing bloody possible, doesn't it? *Ass*holes!" He took an unlit cigarette from his lips and repeated with a jerk of his head, "*Ass*holes."

He replaced his cigarette and played the list. A cultured female voice recited, "Violation of any one of the following mandates shall cause the sovereign nation of Sebastionique to ally on any warring side against the perpetrator.

"There shall be no biological weaponry in the Eta Cassiopeian atmosphere, either contained in a laboratory above or below ground, or free, affecting either animal or vegetable hosts.

"There shall be no alien life forms introduced to EtaCas not previously admitted by the Quant Act.

"There shall be no nuclear radiation released into the Eta Cassiopeian atmosphere.

"There shall be no interference with Sebastionique's shipping or trade.

"There shall be no . . .

"There shall be no . . .

"There shall be no . . ."

Paul threw the list away. It muttered from the corner of the floor. Paul searched for his lighter in the shambles of his office. "Where the fuck was Ambassador Vreeland fucking Forgil when they were drawing up this?" Paul snarled.

"I think he negotiated it."

Paul found his lighter. He lit his cigarette and smoked like a dragon, brandishing the lighter flame as he spoke. "Well, thank you, Sebastionique ever so much. And you too, Forgil." Paul stepped on the list to silence it. He looked to Trevor. "*Now*, Ms. Ambletonian, we're on the brink of war."

Bristol offered a tentative argument. "But these rules restrict everything. How can either side make a move without drawing Sebastionique in to join the other side?"

"They restrict all warfare on EtaCas," said Paul. "*Space* is a wide open battlefield."

An alert stirred the c ships' hidden base before dawn.

The reserve squadron, en route to patrol EtaCas, detoured a ship to Alpha to collect Race as a passenger with orders to report to Rhaltcommand at Beltava.

Race answered the summons with a lump in his throat. It was difficult enough being grounded in peacetime. Launching his fledglings to fight a war barred to him was too much to bear.

The c ship took him to Beltava where a grim military board informed Race Rachelson that he was being reactivated as Queen's Knight to resume command of the Queen's Squadron.

Race did not dare blink, his gray eyes gone watery. "But I . . . am in disgrace."

"You were never in disgrace. We just wanted to see how you would handle the charge. This was only a test of character. Do you really think we would let someone convicted of negligence train c pilots?"

Thunderstruck, Race opened his mouth and shut it again.

"You brought this trial on yourself. There were certain things you chose to withhold from your background. We needed to be sure. Your loyalty never wavered and we have seen fit to restore you in your country's time of need. Here are your wings. Your squadron will meet you at the Aithar Gate. Choose an Echo, anyone from the Queen's Squadron or the reserves or the trainees. Whoever you want on your wing."

Never good at containing emotion, Race saluted with a vibrating fist across his heart as two giant tears spilled over his lower lids. He exited the room, ran down the corridor, gave a screech like a wild animal, and ran to the shuttle that would take him to his ship.

The Queen's Squadron was on patrol at the Aithar stargate.

The Telegonians (who persisted in calling themselves New Terrans) had decided to clear vast areas of their rain forest and send the material to Earth. Vikhinde forbade any such thing. The destruction of an irreplaceable habitat affected the world atmosphere, and Vikhinde considered it an act of aggression with forethought. The rain forest was the reason that Vikhinde never incorporated the land into their own nation. They had intended for it to remain undeveloped.

Telegonia ignored the mandate and went ahead with their destructive harvest. Vikhinde sent a party of warships to blockade the Aithar Gate which connected EtaCas with Earth's solar system. By treaty the Aithar Gate was exclusive to neither side, but Telegonia did not understand treaty, so neither would Vikhinde.

New Earth, as Telegonia called itself, sent its own contingent of warships in answer. All of them swarmed in waiting when two more c ships appeared out of nowhere.

"Hello hello. Queen's Knight to Queen's Squadron. For honor."

A detonation of space flares lit the vacuum in welcome, alarming the edgy combat vessels in the area. The Queen's Squadron's laughter filled the coms, drowning out the cursing from the nervous sublight warships.

"It's Race!"

A hooting and howling like a pack of wolves greeted the returning hero.

Queen's Castle yowled like a dog in concert with Race as Queen's Pawn gave a high-pitched series of yips. Queen's Bishop spoke a bored and rather disgusted, "*Must* you?"

Queen's Castle Echo sent, "Hey Race, who is Queen's Knight Echo?"

Who is Queen's Knight Echo? There was not a simple answer. Her name was not enough to contain her.

Race had seen her coming a long way off. He had not looked up lest he stare, and at first he was not sure he hadn't made her up. She came walking out of the dust like a mirage, with an easy arrogant stroll, unconsciously sexual as an animal. Closer he saw deep dark eyes, a wild brown-black mane, and beautiful pouting face. She walked up to him and in a sweet rich mezzo soprano with her ever-so-better-than-you accent, called him a bastard.

"This is Maya of the Timberlines."

"Reservee?"

"Just out of training."

"Yo ho ho."

"Maiden?"

"Aye aye."

"My, my, Maya."

"Hello hello, hate to disturb this chat. On the nines, hostile, approaching the gate. Does anyone care?"

The ship making the move was a Telegonian cargo vessel, putting the Vikhinden blockade to the test.

"Hello, mousie, this cat will not be belled. Why don't you go back where you came from?"

The ship plodded onward at a non-threatening but determined pace. The Empire was protective of civilians, its own and others. Would they hit a civilian ship? New Earth was gambling that they wouldn't.

As the Empire vessels moved in to intercept, the ship sent emphatically, "We are unarmed."

"Jolly *good.*"

"Turkey shoot. Who wants him?"

"We could let the Rook gum on him."

"I want him! I want him!"

The sublight Vikhinden flagship broke up the chatter, "Commander Rachelson, will you silence your wardogs? Telegonian vessel, this is Rhaltadmiral Nizer. These are not idle threats or bluffs. Continuation on your present course is an act of war. Lack of weapons will not protect you."

The ship continued toward the gate, protesting that it was carrying food.

"Your cargo is destructive to EtaCas and you have been classified as a warship accordingly."

The cargo ship kept repeating, "We are an unarmed, peaceful civilian vessel." Right up to the moment Rhaltadmiral Nizer ordered a sublight sentry ship to open fire.

The remaining combat ships immediately altered and realtered defensive/offensive formations round each other, squaring for a shootout.

After a brief tense ballet, the Telegonians withdrew to a wide orbit of the fifth planet of the Aithar system to await orders.

The Queen's Squadron took up a close orbit of the sun. "Circle the wagons, boys and girls. This may be awhile."

New Earth issued a statement of outrage. They demanded restitution for their destroyed vessel, its cargo, and its butchered crew. They demanded the indignation of Sebastionique.

Vikhinde demanded the indignation of Sebastionique against Telegonia's harming of their mutual atmosphere.

Sebastionique issued a statement, coolly announcing that either side was asking for whatever it got. "Do what you will to each other. Leave us out of it."

New Earth then gave Vikhinde twenty-four standard hours in which to lift the Aithar blockade.

The news reached the forces at Aithar five hours into the ultimatum. No orders arrived for the Vikhinden warships to leave the area.

"Queen's Castle to Queen's Knight. We're not going to, are we?"

"Don't think so, children."

Maya in her ship swallowed, dry. She turned off her transmitter, heard her own breath shudder against the mike.

This is it. This is war.

PART TWO

THE EMPIRE AT WAR

*Mortals are so enamored of your own death that
you must make your gods die. Osirus, Dionysos,
Jesus. You kill them all. You hate life. You
rehearse your death through your own gods.
And now you have come for us.*
> —from the Vikhinden declaration of war.

Fort Ujiji, New Earth
EtaCas
28 April 5246
XIII. 1. 1792

I.

"Admiral Krestly called while you were out."

"When was I out?" said Paul.

"Out cold. Out of it. Out of touch."

"Yeah, I'll get to it."

"He wants a reply now."

"And I want a Sterling Taylor Space Yacht. You
know when I told Monica to get over here and help
with the GC, something a little more nowish is what
I had in mind," said Paul, turning on a landing field
monitor. "But they're identing everyone, and she
probably can't get in the gate, and screw whoever
started this really."

"Hey Paul, do I need an ident too?" Bristol came
breezing in the door, swinging Trevor in with him.

"No, you two I'm *sure* are traitors. Get outta here."

The panel under the ground control monitor lit up
solid. "Almighty. Hey Paul, this is real," Bristol said
in amazement.

"Yes dammit, this is real." Phones clamored from
the floor. Paul pointed at one with his cigarette. "If
that's my brother, tell him to shoot himself— Why is

that Voyager moving?'' He pointed at the monitor. "Carl! Get him on the horn.''

"He says he's just getting out of the way.''

"Out of the way of what? We're fucking blockaded!''

Before the ultimatum even ran out, both nations moved to close each other's ports. Except at Sebastionique, there was no incoming traffic.

Paul slung his arm over the back of his chair in a slouch. "I had plans. I had a holiday coming.''

Trevor, who was on the verge of tears, said, "It's hard to tell when you're kidding. Is that just a front or do you really not care?''

"It's a front, of course. I'm scared out of my fuckin' mind.''

"I wish your mind wouldn't fuck so much. One gets weary of the word.''

"You're right, dear. Actions speak louder than words. Wanna act?''

"O Paul!'' She ran from the room in tears.

"Everyone's scared,'' said Bristol.

"Have to be a complete idiot not to be scared.''

"STRAND!'' Admiral Krestly's voice sounded, a muffled shout—Carl was holding a phone inside the office.

"*He*'s not scared,'' Bristol muttered with a sideways nod toward the phone.

"I rest my case. I'M COMING, SIR!'' Paul yelled back at the phone and motioned Carl to hang it up.

On the monitor came a persistent hailing from an Army ship, which wanted to land but all of New Earth's bases were shut down and, as it carried bombs, the ship was not allowed to land at Sebastionique either.

Paul grabbed the com. "Did the controller give you an orbit?''

"Yes, but—''

"Stay in it!'' He shut off. Finally he threw all the phones and radios into his aide's adjoining office. He dragged on a jacket to go out.

Bristol moved out of his way. "Some idjot already tried to land," Bristol said. "Fleet shot him before he hit the breathable stuff. Don't know who it was. Trouble with annihilation is you don't know who you nailed."

Paul pointed at the monitor. "I want to know why that Voyager is still moving."

"He tries to take off, the Vikhens will shoot him," said Bristol.

"He tries to take off, hell, I'll shoot him." Paul leaned over the console, beat a com open. "Park it!"

He straightened up, turned to Bristol. "Out of here Anyone asks, I've run away to an island in the Antoine chain and I'm living in a grass hut with three feral girls who have never seen a man before and they keep asking me to show them how it works."

"Life is hard, Paul."

"Life ain't fucking fair. I'm going to see what Krestly wants."

Admiral Krestly did not want him. The I.I.N. was using Krestly to get Paul out of his office. Paul dialed in the spaceport, but his public car shanghaied him, turned around and brought him back to Fort Ujiji and down into the Hive.

"Goddammed cloak and dagger shit. What do you people want?"

The agent was not even the cute one. This was a more typical, tall sapient stone block, of a middle shade of black with short shaven silvering moss for hair.

"We know where Valhalla is," said the mossy stone.

"Where, and how do we know this?" Paul always checked his sources. It was Strand's law: Don't check your source, you end up with compound shit.

"Eight standard years ago a terrorist organization sent mercenaries through the Cerberus Gate, a.k.a. Empire stargate 49. They did not come back."

"A terrorist organization. Sure that wasn't us?"

"It may have been." That was I.I.N.-ese for yes.

"Rat strange that the Vikrhalt didn't try to pin the attack on us," said Paul.

"It's the Vikrhalt's lack of finger-pointing that drew our interest. They've been rat good and quiet about this one."

"Where does the Cerberus Gate go?" He'd never heard of it. No one ever used it. One had to assume it led to hell.

"Twenty-nine light hours from Mu Cassiopeia."

"I think your mercs deserted."

"This was a little over eight years ago."

"And Mu Cassiopeia is if I remember . . . ?"

"A little over eight light years away."

"Ah ha. What did our junior star gazers see in the heavens last night?"

"On the night of 26 April, our observatories recorded a disturbance in the Mu Cassiopeia system."

"26 April. And the next day we forced the Aithar Gate. You guys aren't subtle, are you?"

"A brief flare of fireworks appeared, energy flares not solar. Now all's quiet again. The only scenario which fits indicates there was a shootout at Mu Cassiopeia eight years ago."

"And that makes it Valhalla? MuCas? 'Snot likely."

"There *is* a planet between the two suns."

"Hell, so what? Well done or burnt to a crisp?"

"Neither, we think. We ran all available information through the computer and the planet could be habitable."

"How? The two stars are what, ten astronomical units apart?"

"Seven."

"Seven. Shit. How do you fit a habitable world between two stars that are as far apart as Jupiter is from Sol?"

"Mu Cassiopeia A is a G5V yellow subdwarf about 75 percent as massive as Sol, its luminosity a mere 40 percent. The planet is approximately six astronomical units from Mu Cassiopeia A—a little closer than Venus is to Sol."

"What about the companion star?"

"Mu Cassiopeia B is a red dwarf only 209 times the mass of Jupiter, and as you said, about as far away. It's almost a brown hole. It has more in common with Jupiter than it has with Sol. Its luminosity is .03 that of the sun and it might perturb the planet's orbit a bit, but that is all. We suspect the planet is more cold than burnt. Its ideal distance from the stargate—"

"Which is?"

"Twenty-nine light hours. Get with the scenario. That distance makes it unassailable to a conventional invasion force."

"Sure, since they call their c ships instantly on the resonator and the Queen's Squadron has twenty-nine hours to come and shoot you down. Yeah, that works."

"Valhalla is probably an artificial fortress oasis. They probably haven't settled the whole planet. Valhalla is somewhere on it, a compact target if we could locate it. Now I need to ident you again."

"Why?"

"Because I'm about to tell you something very few people know because it's going to win us the war."

Paul was cleared for red card level, and the I.I.N. agent told him a plan codenamed Götterdämmerung.

Maya felt like she was going to die, and for the first time in her very long life she really didn't think she would mind. It wasn't the war. It was her new squadron that was going to finish her.

The beating on the door felt and sounded as if it were coming from inside her skull. "Maya, how are we this morning?" Eric entered with a cheerful singing and bouncing on the bed. "Get up. You're only a third of the way through."

Maya retched.

No one had warned her about the ritual drinking of the bar.

The Queen's Squadron had left Aithar when the declaration of war moved the hotspots elsewhere. They had been on duty for ten straight days, picking up Kingsmen and sending them into enemy territory, or diving themselves into battles which would break up at their mere approach. It left an itch to know how strong they really were. Maya hadn't fired a shot. She had grown into the cockpit and swore she'd taken root.

When finally they touched down on a friendly planet, Maya got to see who she had been flying with, who belonged to those voices.

They were, all of them, beautiful, each in their own unique way, all uncorrected with nothing to correct. Maya felt like a blot in their presence and she wanted to run back to a facemaker.

They had come out of their cockpits, sliding down the wings and straightaway they jumped on Race like a litter of puppies all bunched together and bouncing off each other except for Maya and the Queen's Bishop, known as QB.

QB had assigned himself the role of insouciant intellectual snob. QB was Beltavan born and let no one forget it. His accent to a trained ear was strictly bourgeoise, but Maya kept her mouth shut about it. She was already familiar with his flat dry comments over the com, laconic and cynical. In trouble he would be at your side faster than anyone. He sounded in battle as excitable as a tree. Maya already liked him sight unseen. He was squarely built, wore his wavy brown hair in a Roman cut, and he looked down his Roman nose at the others. Indulgent beautifully curved lips didn't need much to effect a sneer. He was someone you could easily imagine being called Centurion in a past life. He was Race's right hand, highest in rank after Race and oldest after Race. He was the first one to introduce himself to Maya. While the rest were piling on top of Race, QB turned to her with offered hand. "I'm the only other adult in this outfit. QB. You must be Maya."

The only other woman in the squadron was the Queen's Pawn. Her name was Ionnina. Everyone called her Nina, except QB who called her Ion. She was biting Race on the ear.

Ionnina was next in age to QB, very tall, a hipless breastless willow who danced when she moved, fluid as a river. She never sat; she coiled like a silken serpent. Her features were sharp and thin. Almond eyes slanted above high sharp cheekbones. Her hair was very long, black, and poker straight, pulled back into a high pony tail that swayed when she walked. She extended a hand to Maya in greeting. "May? Nina."

Ionnina's Echo was the only one of the squadron who was truly big. He was a strapping, light-skinned brown-haired Olympian. Ionnina claimed she had bought him at a slave auction on the Far Worlds for eighteen goats. His name was Yuri but he was called

Jav, short for Javelin, as everyone in this squadron had a penchant for monosyllables. Quiet, Jav did not say much on the com, and Maya sometimes forgot he was there.

QB's Echo was an affable blond brat whom QB threatened three times a day with murder. Eric was youngest of a young group, raffish, energetic as a puppy. Eric had been in the Queen's Squadron since he was fourteen, drafted straight into pilot training. Together QB and Eric were the best and longest established team, and QB loved him dearly but would die before he said so.

Queen's Castle was a dramatic rugged man with a seething sexuality which made Maya look away as if he would burn the eyes if she looked at him too long. He was sizzling in motion, precise as a dancer, with the raw edge of an athlete. She didn't know his name. Everyone called him Whip. Even through his drawling trash accent, he sounded good-hearted, sweet and polite when he wasn't fighting. Whip loved a good fight. Low born, he was the kind they called a city feral. He had come up through the boy troops trained as a hand-to-hand fighter before he was picked out to be a pilot.

His thick mass of brown hair curled into loose rings like a decadent god. He had blue eyes, and a crooked sensual mouth. He gave Maya a kiss. Or he took one. She had nothing to say about it.

Whip was known as a reckless player. He was Race's old Echo. It was Whip's injured ship which Race had crashed.

Queen's Castle Echo was a small golden man named Tak Yoshizawa, newest of the squadron before Maya. His eyes were opaque black. He kept his black hair cut very close to his head, "So I don't look stupid at zero g."

"Who cares what you look like at zero g?" Maya asked.

Tak grinned.

These pilots were all old hands, either members of

the Queen's Squadron when Race had commanded it four years ago, or else, as Tak and Jav, they were students whom Race had trained. They were ecstatic to see Race back in command.

After Race told them the story of his demotion and restoration, Whip became very angry. His upper arms bulged with the clenching of his fists. "Don't you hate them for what they did to you?"

"It was a test," said Race. "I passed."

"Speaking of tests," said Tak. "Initiations are overdue here." He flicked Maya's shiny new brass wings on her black flight suit.

Eric's eyes lit up. "Yo ho ho, where's a bottle of rum?"

"From the top, darlin'," said Whip.

It was then that Maya learned she had to drink the bar, starting with anisette and going down the list. It was something they had all done, so there was no way around it. She'd left off last night somewhere around the jackhammer.

Fortunately someone had taken her into the bushes before that point and stuck his fingers down her throat so she'd lost the first twenty shots. QB, she remembered now, his flat voice saying, "Let's not murder the girl before she's fledged, shall we." And he matter-of-factly stuck his fingers down her throat.

"What are you doing?" she'd asked.

"Saving your life. You hold your liquor too well. Something you really don't want to do right now."

In the fuzziness of the morning Maya wondered if Race had seen that. She pulled the coverlet over her head to make the intruders go away. Jav dragged her from the bed.

"This is barbaric," Maya screeched, clinging to the sheets.

"Up you go."

"It's sophomoric."

"I don't believe our Maya is happy with our customs."

"Can't I just kill something?"

"That's next."

"You for starters." She sounded hopeful.

"My, my, Maya."

"They always want to run before they crawl."

"I'm crawling, thank you. I don't want to run. I don't want to drink. I want to kill you."

"Dieu, dieu, she sounds like she means it."

Suddenly an alert sounded with the Queen's Squadron's signature three note summons, A G C.

"Queen's Squadron. Queen's Squadron. Patrol Citadel. Patrol Citadel. Bring cargo."

Citadel was the Empire's code word for EtaCas. Cargo meant Kingsmen.

"Ilu!"

"Party time, All Good Children."

Whip's deep urgent shout banged in Maya's ears as he propped her up. "Get a soberant here!"

QB had one standing by and blandly passed it over with a look of long-suffering.

The Queen's Squadron traced a weaving path through the Elsewhere, constantly changing relative positions, lining up mock attacks on each other. There were no enemies Out Here, which was not a situation a fighter ought to become accustomed to. So they played their own attack games as they sped toward their destination.

They kept up a constant chattering, talking over the raucous music which they had blaring on the com. Maya kept hearing, "Queen's Castle Echo to Queen's Rook." And she wondered, *Who is Queen's Rook?* Maya had been hearing that name, but there was no Queen's Rook. She thought they were calling Whip, the Queen's Castle, until she heard Whip's low drawl, "Queen's Castle to Queen's Rook."

"Who is Queen's Rook?" said Maya at last.

Race answered, "I'm afraid that's you, Maya, until your first kill."

Queen's Rook. Queen's Rookie.

No. Oh no. I refuse. I refuse to go through one more

*imbecilic right of passage. Enough. Enough. I have
dutifully played all your baboon games. When do I get
to belong? Every time I think I've made it, they build
another step.*

"No," said Maya.

"What do you mean, 'No'?"

"I believe it's Empirese. No. I don't recognize that
call sign."

Tak, the Queen's Castle Echo, sounded like a nasty
little boy. "Oh yes, you will."

Maya took her ship wide of the formation, high off
Race's port side.

"Hey, Rook," Tak called.

The only sound on the com was blaring music.

"Hey, Rook. Rook. Come in and that's an order."

Maya hummed to the music.

Tak appealed to a higher authority, "Race—?"

Race sent: "Com check. Com check. I've picked up
a whine from somewhere."

Chuckles reechoed on the com. Tak fell into cha-
grined silence. A misstep, that had been. First point
went to the rookie.

Maya was aware of what was happening. *Ah. So
this isn't official. I don't have to play.*

They continued the game, calling her Rook and
excluding her when she did not answer. But one
thing an immortal learned better than any mortal
was how to wait. *Until you are dust, I will not answer
to Rook.*

They all called her Queen's Rook, though Race
only used it in the third person. Tak had it in for her.
He used the name all the time. New to power was
always eager to sling it around. And Tak would have
been the last Rook. He was eager to turn the tables
on someone else. *Too eager and not with me.* He was
lowest member of this baboon troop, and Maya did
not need to listen to him.

Race must have sensed when she was feeling partic-
ularly put upon because he came to her defense.
"Maya was the most extraordinary cadet ever to come
through the wringer—except for me of course."

"Of course," said QB.

"I'd like to run you through a scanner someday, Maya, and see what makes you tick."

"No," said Maya. A scanner would reveal that she was not mortal.

"Too fast," said Tak. "Hiding some reconstruction there, Rook?"

Maya barked a laugh. "You think I would look like this if I had been reconstructed?"

"Why?" said Race sounding genuinely bewildered.

"This?" she said and thought bitterly, *You haven't really looked at me, have you?* He would have seen her heavy breasts, her long nose, those doleful eyes and big bones.

A directional signal, ship to ship, entered her com. Race: "You are the most strong, sultry, beautiful woman I have ever seen in my life."

Panic burned behind her face. She was struck dumb, all her thoughts stampeded away.

The com dialog continued non-stop, gone off in another direction. Race had rejoined them.

Maya turned her cockpit mirror inward and looked at her unreconstructed self. *I am what?*

When she tuned into the com conversation again, QB was saying, "This war has now lasted twelve days longer than I thought it would."

"It's twelve days old."

"Astute of you, Eric."

"The free mortals began this war with some idea that they could win it," said Jav. "They must have something."

"They do," said Ionnina. "They have a secret plan. Götterdämmerung. It's supposed to win the war for them."

"But they can't," said Eric. "Can they?"

"Technological superiority by itself never decided a conflict," said QB. "Overconfidence has however lost many a war."

"I don't believe there is a Götterdämmerung," said

Maya. "Not one that will work. The naming is the all of it. They want us to worry, and I shan't."

Race summed it up for all of them: "There can be no Götterdämmerung as long as we *are*."

When Paul Strand requisitioned a Fleet spyship, Admiral Krestly asked who he was sending.

"You mean who am I taking," said Paul.

"Exactly what are you implying."

"I'm not implying nothing. I'm going and taking a crew."

"Yeah, and—?"

"And what?"

"Just so, you miserable son of a bitch. I know what you're saying."

"Wish I did."

"Let me make this clear, mister. I'm not going because I didn't get the orders or clearance."

"No one was questioning—"

"Oh no? Is that right? 'You mean who am I taking.' I know what you're implying."

"I thought I was saying I was going instead of delegating."

"You were saying that you're going and I'm not. Don't bullshit me. I know what you say behind my back, but God help me you can't get away with it to my face!"

His face was purple.

"The ship, sir?" Paul prompted.

"Where are you *taking* it?"

"I can't tell you."

"Then I can't give you the ship."

"Fine, sir. Give it to the I.I.N."

Krestly put through the authorization for Paul.

"Götterdämmerung? They're sending you on Götterdämmerung?"

"What's a Götterdämmerung?" Paul said ingenuously.

"Don't bullshit me!"

"Does everyone know about this fucking secret plan?"

"I am not everyone," said Krestly. "And the name is well known. The plan is locked up tight."

"Well, that's something."

"Are you assigned to Götterdämmerung?" There was an awful desperation, almost to pleading in his voice. Krestly sounded like he would do anything, even try to be Paul's friend to get on this mission.

"Hell no," said Paul. "Just a little non-essential recce to pretend I'm useful." He took the authorization and went outside.

A public car had pulled up to the door and the robot control switched over to manual. It was a square and boxy vehicle. No money had been wasted on styling which would be indicative of private ownership. It was dulled standard white, much used, kicked a few times, ever on call to whoever summoned. Paul climbed in and joined the crowded grid.

At Fort Ujiji he found Bristol and Trevor in his office. Bristol looked up. "Hiya Paul. I'm into my book for a few. Got any state secrets I can sell?"

"Admiral Krestly was a rabid mastiff in his past life."

"That would explain a lot."

"Don't it though? I liked that one myself. Look, I got a ship leaving orbit tomorrow. Seeings how I command the tin can, I better be on it," Paul said, getting organized, something not easily done. "Trevor, sweetness, can you give me a hand?"

"I have to process these sightings for the general."

"Then piss on you. Bristol, are you busy?"

"Nothing worth being pissed on for. What do you need?"

"Find me a fifth on a shadow class crew. Picture taker. At least blue clearance for a field trip."

"I'll go."

"One. Only one."

"I'll go."

Paul glanced toward Trevor and back to Bristol. "What? And break up a set?"

Bristol sidled in confidentially. "I need it to boost my clearance. I can't marry Trevor while I'm not the same clearance level. She's gots more secrets than me."

"That's 'cause she's discreet."

"Yeah? You're discreet as a toilet seat and they gave you a red card."

"I'm cuter than you are. Get that woman's eyes checked. Does *she* want to marry *you*?"

"Yeah, and it'll be two years if I wait through channels. I don't want to wait two fucking procedural years. I need to kick start this show. She's going to drop a bundle in five vants and I want my name on it."

"How Vikhen," said Paul.

Vikhinden society was concerned with questions of legitimacy and cute nuclear families.

"That was a low shot, Paul."

"I have a better idea," Paul said. "I'll marry her."

"Get fucked."

"We'll name it after you."

"Like hell."

"You're right. Who wants to make a kid go through life named Dumb Shit."

"Paul Strand, if you are not the biggest jack off in the galaxy, you are surely a contender."

"Love you, too."

"Hugs and kisses." Bristol slobbered a big wet one all over Paul's cheek. "Am I on the crew?"

"This is dangerous," Paul said seriously, too low for Trevor to hear.

"*You* intend on coming back, don't you?"

"In time for the game. I got money on the Wilddogs."

"You disloyal swine."

"Pack your kit. Don't pack clothes. They'll be issued on board. Report to the starbase at 0300."

Trevor looked over like a woodland creature that had sensed something different in the sounds of the forest. "Going somewhere?"

Bristol looked to Paul.

Paul cracked his knuckles, told a breezy lie, the last one he ever got away with: "Earth."

Vikhinden airspace
EtaCas
13 May 5246
XIII. 13. 1792

As the spyship took off, the crew was surprised
when Paul gave them the trajectory.

"Uh, Major, that takes us two meters off the
ground."

Paul knew that.

Current speed was that of a flying boat. Military
ships were often dressed as innocuous civil craft then
parked in plain sight for the spy satellites to see. The
disguises burned off in ascent. This one, however, was
playing the part for which it was dressed.

"It's an almighty long trip to Earth at this rate,"
said Bristol. He had already figured out that they were
not going to Earth.

Paul gave heading to the navigator. "Beltava."

The spyship flew up the river under the Empire's
nose, directly into Vikhinde's capital city. The crew
parked the spyship with the pleasure boats and walked
up the pier.

The riveredge was dotted with ale houses and shops
and waterfront cafes in a melange of styles, domi-
nated from the heights by Beltava's landmark, the
soaring turrets of the retro-romantic fairy-tale Castle
Vikhinde.

Paul walked up the parquet promenade reserved for
pedestrians and *portans*, the Vikhinden rickshaws. He
marched into a government record center as if he belonged there, entered a security area unchallenged,

and tried out the access codes with which the I.I.N. had supplied him.

The message he received was not the one which the I.I.N. told him to anticipate. It was benign enough but it told him to wait.

Paul returned to the ship at a jaunty walk, spoke through a clench-tooth grin in a cheerful voice: "We tripped something. Abort. Abort. Scrub mission. Get us the fuck out of here."

They boarded the ship. Paul did not breathe until the hatch shut. He put on his uniform jacket over his civilian disguise, suddenly feeling cold. The spyship wended its way down the river. When they reached the ocean the pilot, Danyella March, put on some speed.

"Slow down," said Paul. "You'll trip another flag."

"We'll be in Sebastionique airspace in two minutes, Major. I don't think we tripped any flags."

"Bristol, what's in the rear?"

"Nothin."

"What's the bird?"

"It's configured like a Sebastionique liner and it's not acting interested."

But something was speaking louder from inside, a sixth sense Paul never knew he had. "They're after us."

The satellite monitor beeped a warning. The Vik-hinden controller rang up the offending sighting on her screen. She plotted it moving over the Western ocean. It was too hot to be a flying boat, its initial output too fast though it was proceeding at normal speed now.

She called a supervisor over. As he looked over her shoulder, she reported, "Shell looks like a flying boat. Too much muscle in it though."

"Magnify. Extrapolate infrastructure."

The image of a flying boat appeared on the screen, then a skeleton sketch of its framework.

"What is that?"

"Telegonian spyship."

The controller got on the security com. "Hello. Hello. Skywriters, are you up there?"

Three notes chimed, A G C. "Aye aye. Hi. Hi. This is Queen's Knight."

"Ah, the big leagues. Queen's Knight, we have an intruder at North 01 095 035 and shrinking, by 280 001 002, Vector 17 on the compass rose. Estimated time until Sebastionique airspace 30 ticks."

Eric: "There. Low on the water."

Race: "I have him."

Ground Control: "Alive, if you please."

Race: "Best shot."

Ground Control: "Thank you."

Eric: "I want him."

Ionnina: "Mine."

Ground Control: "Decide fast up there. We're losing him. We will settle for him dead. He hits the equator, he's gone."

QB had begun and continued a quiet countdown: "Fifteen ticks to Sebastionique airspace. Fourteen."

Race: "Mine."

Ground Control: "Clean, if you can."

QB: "Ten ticks. Nine. Eight."

Race focused on the rear engines where they connected to the fuselage.

QB: "Seven. Six."

Ground Control: "Hello, Queen's Knight?"

QB: "Five."

A beam cut into the atmosphere, excising the engines from the craft neatly as a surgeon's cut. The fuselage torpedoed into the water of its own inertia.

"For honor. For the Queen."

Howls and yips filled the com.

Eric: "Nice shot!"

Tak: "Perfect!"

"Actually two microns to the north would have been perfect," said QB blandly. "All in all, a spectacular shot, Race."

"Queen's Knight to Squadron. Wake up some babies and give 'em a bath."

Maya revived from suspended animation the three Kingsmen she carried in their pods in her hold. She briefed them of their situation and shot them down into the ocean to retrieve the intruders.

Paul bobbed up, gasped, floundered in the Eta Cassiopeian fresh water sea. He swam toward his ship's orange life raft.

Suddenly a hand closed on his ankle. He tried to kick. A masked face rose up before him. Frogman. Men. They were popping up all over like something in a horror vid.

Paul grabbed the breathing apparatus away from the nearest face, tried to get an arm above the water long enough to get in a swing with his fist.

His own face felt to explode as the Kingsman rabbit punched him and he went under to oblivion.

Fort Ujiji, New Earth
EtaCas
13 May 5246

"Carl! Carl!"

Trevor stormed into Paul's office. "Carl!"

"Merl," the aide said as Trevor grabbed him by the lapels and shouted into his face, "*I don't give a shit!*" She released him only to shove a report under his nose. "What the fuck is this?"

He fumbled to replay the bubble, flustered to hear gentle, soft-spoken Trevor using all Paul's words. The bubble listed Bristol Derrah as Missing In Action.

"What is this?" Trevor shouted so he could barely hear the bubble.

"Oh," said Merl. "This isn't accurate."

Trevor slumped. Her knees buckled inward like a colt's and she sank, groped for the nearest chair and sat, all her strength gone in the relief following terror. "God." Her knees wobbled. She held her heart and abdomen.

"He's not precisely missing," said Merl. "They'll update that upon confirmation to P.O.W."

Trevor bolted to her feet. "What?" She grabbed the back of the chair and shook it, as if about to pick it up and throw it. "What!"

"Lieutenant Derrah ought to be all right, ma'am. He doesn't know anything."

Trevor's brown eyes roamed without seeing, full of water, wide and lost. "How could Paul do this to me? Why did he take Bristol? Why did he take Bristol?" She pounced on something of Paul's, a pack of cigarettes on Paul's desk, tore it and threw it. "Paul Strand, I hope you're dead!"

Merl nodded. "I do hope he has sense enough to kill himself before he gets where they're taking him."

Vikhinde
EtaCas
13 May 5246
XIII. 13. 1792

I know where this is. I've heard of this place.

Wet and waiting. Waiting so long they were no longer wet. Five crewmembers standing in a line. Paul shifted uncomfortably, the last dampness clinging to his stiffening clothes. His bruises had cooled and started to ache. He wanted to squat and take the kink out of his lower back. Big apes with weapons would not let him move. Waiting. Clock tick.

I know where I am and I don't want in this or any lifetime to be here.

This is Kobandrid Rog.

Space
XIII. 13. 1792

II.

Queen's Squadron, proceed to Starstation Gamma. Yesterday.

"Hide fox and all after."

Race's ship swung round the sun and in, his squadron behind him answering the summons to battle. "Yesterday" was the Empire's code word for as fast as possible.

The c ships raced, weaving through the Elsewhere.

"Yo!" said Tak on Maya's back.

"Ho," she said, evading.

"Ho ho," said Race, from an attack position on Tak's tail. "Very careless." Then he wove out from under the guns of Whip who had come to his Echo's aid.

The mock attacks kept them keen. According to the unwritten rules of the game, a pilot could call a rest; then his Echo became responsible for guarding him. Such time-outs did not exist in the real world. A secure place to sleep was a luxury and they used the privilege seldom.

A c ship never flew straight and level unless he had called a rest, and he never attacked his own Echo. One's Echo was one's friend and responsibility always, anywhere.

Maya assumed that was the only reason that Race did not join in tormenting her with the name Rook like everyone else.

The Queen's Squadron arrived at its destination within hours. They had been told to expect a battle.

"Let's into it."

The squadron sublighted.

An uproar crackled onto the coms as suddenly back in realtime the Queen's Squadron was not alone.

Maya had never seen so many ships in or out of a shipyard. They were tangled in a melee around Starstation Gamma.

A New Earth emblem directly in front of Maya was instantly gone just as she realized she ought to be shooting at it. Race had nailed it over her wing.

Maya took aim at another enemy ship, fired. Too far. Her intended victim had a tachyon warning and tipped in the split second lag to deflect the shot.

Shortly into the fray, Tak called that he was out of fuel. "Rook, cover me while I recharge." He started toward the sun.

Maya stayed in the melee with Race.

Tak's calls on the com escalated to shouts as enemy ships converged on him. Whip was not in a position to help his Echo, in trouble himself. Whip liked to dive into the middle and shoot his way out. Without his Echo he was having trouble.

QB sent, "Eric, cover Queen's Castle."

Queen's Castle Echo was dodging the enemy ships which escorted him sunward, when suddenly his engines shut down entirely and Tak was sailing on inertia, with no power in his beam guns.

A steady target, he saw a New Earth fighter take its time lining up a shot. The fighter exploded and a voice on the com said, "That was badly done, you know."

"QB! Thank God."

"No, thank *me*. Get on with it."

QB kept the fighters off him as Tak glided toward the sun. Nearer, his engines showed glimmers of life and he was able to accelerate. The two c ships dipped into the photosphere, swung round the sun and sped back into battle recharged, guns blazing.

Maya saw none of it. Didn't care. She was busy keeping up with Race and shooting anything that tried to lock on him. She had already killed a few.

She had not been counting. She thought only moment to moment.

It wasn't the killing that was new. She was acquainted with erasing mortals from her existence. But these were shooting back! *I could die here.*

But she had put herself here and she had something to say about her own living and dying. She had been trained. Her weapons were the best.

This was what it meant to be mortal, to live in the shadow of death, and each close brush confirmed that she was not dead yet.

She shot them down, her bad dreams, the phantoms, her helplessness. She raked through the enemy with the vehemence of killing a nightmare.

She remained peripherally aware of the others. QB's voice never varied. "Empire fighter, that was 60 gigawatts you just put into my wing."

"Sorry," said the sublighter.

"Is that an apology or a self-description?"

Periodically she would hear Eric's excited, "Did you see that? Did you see that?"

And QB would pick someone off his bragging back and ask him if he had seen that.

Maya took out two at once, with her port and starboard beam cannon at two different ranges.

"Some pretty shootin' there, darlin'," Whip sent.

Tak sent: "Sure those were flying green and white flags?"

He was questioning her ident. They *had* been hostiles. Her cannon would not have fired had they been friendlies. For her first battle, she'd kept the firing fail-safe on.

Space was laced thickly with missed crossfire. Tachyon echoes enabled the c ships to evade the beams—unless they decided to intercept. Into a long streaming shot toward the starstation, Race angled out a slippery wing to deflect it into a hostile compatriot.

Whip howled, Eric laughed, and Maya was not sure she had even seen it. Even the inexcitable QB managed a toneless, "My God."

Maya had thought she doing quite well. The man simply dazzled.

They would replay their recordings later and find that for shots expended to kill ratio there was no one close to Race.

As the melee was breaking up, the Queen's Squadron withdrew. They pulled back to Alpha Base where the techs could inspect the ships for battle damage.

Tak came down fuming. He wanted Maya drummed out of the service for endangering the squadron.

Maya took off her helmet. The squadron was staring at her, with what she fancied were accusing eyes. She met their gazes. Tak's. Race's. QB had settled back like a spectator at the fights.

Maya said, "If you have a problem, you take me to military court." She headed for the crew quarters. She wanted a bath.

"Hey, Rook!"

"I am not Queen's Rook! And furthermore, I am not Queen's Castle Echo Echo!"

"Whip was engaged! The order to assist was not unusual!"

Maya circled back to him. "No, the order was nonexistent. You wanted me to cover you, yet you screamed nonexistent names into the void. I didn't ignore a direct order, ehre. I never got one!"

Maya tossed back her sweat drenched hair and left the group again.

Tak turned to Race, "She knew—"

"So did you."

QB added like a footnote, "She has you. Queen's Rook is not a legal call sign."

"But—"

"You broke all the rules of hardball," said Race. "You didn't have anything she wanted and you couldn't afford to lose and you underestimated Maya's willingness to let you die."

"That's the point!" Tak threw down his helmet. "How can a team member let someone else die just to prove a point?"

"Same team that can afford a member willing to die for the ritual hazing of a new member. You were the one who needed help and you'da had to die to prove it and it wasn't worth it, was it? Anyway game's over. There is no more Queen's Rook."

"Race, she—"

"Excuse me, I can't seem to get rid of that whine."

Race walked away. He passed Maya, looked at her in silence and walked on.

His disapproval hung inside, a dull vague unsettled canker, shrouding what should have been a victory. *Why do I care?* thought Maya.

I do.

She ran after him and fell in step alongside. "What would you have done?"

"Not what you did."

"I am being held liable for a debt I did not contract."

He said coolly, "You are legally free."

"I mean the court of the Queen's Squadron. Everybody disapproves."

"This isn't a Telegonian junior scout troop. My boys and girls play for keeps. You won. What's your problem?"

"You tell me."

"Now everyone knows you're a hard player. But they don't know if they can trust you."

"Do you?"

"Who, me? With my life. Come on."

"What."

"You're out of uniform."

Maya went with him, quizzically. She had to pick up her step to keep up with his long stride.

The uniforms of the c pilots were black, and, at rest, baggy, cinched at the ankles, wrists, waist, and collar. They tightened in response to g forces. There was also a short boxy jacket they often wore on the ground. Maya did not have hers on, and she thought that's what he meant.

Race said no.

"Squadron badge?" she guessed next.

Her sleeve was blank where other squadron's wore a unit badge.

"We don't have one," said Race. "If it isn't there, it means you're Queen's Squadron."

"It could also mean you are no one."

"Like my old Echo says, 'If you ain't Queen's Squadron, you *ain't* no one.' "

"Why do we not have a badge?"

"Because you can't see things that are FTL," said Race. "It's neither here nor there."

"So how am I out of uniform?"

Race gave her an earring of feathers sprouting from a small white spike. Maya inspected the spike. "What is this?"

"A catwolf fang."

Grotesque. "Why would I want this?"

"That one's your first kill. We wear our feathers and fangs when we go among the grounders. So they know who we are."

Oh. My tribe. How quaint.

And he tied a leather thong around her head, a cluster of feathered fangs hanging from behind her ear, numbering the kills recorded by her ship in the battle.

I look like a savage.

That evening the whole squadron wore feathers and fangs. Lots of fangs. The Queen's Squadron's pre-war skirmishes added up when one saw the tally on their headdresses.

In the glow of celebration, the squadron's mood was thawing and they were forgetting that they had been angry with Maya.

Tak had cooled down and realized that if he tried to divide the squad, he could easily end up on the outside looking in. He'd been called a whiner twice; he decided to accept the new tough guy in their midst before that tag stuck for good.

He poured a bottle of xylan over Maya's head. She ducked. Burning liquid trickled round her face and made wet strings of her feathers and hair. The others barked and howled at her baptism.

As long as I don't have to drink it.

When the bottle was empty, she sat up and shook her hair dog style, sending the squadron ducking and diving for cover. The catwolf teeth of her headdress smacked her in the side of the head as she swung it. She caught them and looked over her trophies as her companions laughingly restored themselves to their seats and retrieved their drinks. She was soaring.

I am Maya. I am alive.

Kobandrid Rog, Vikhinde
EtaCas
May 5246
XIII. 1792

"What is Götterdämmerung?" Penetanguishene asked, not really expecting an answer.

"I don't know," said Paul Strand.

Lie! Penetanguishene barely contained his inner tumult. *I have in my den the key to Götterdämmerung.*

The prisoner lied again, under oath. Major Paul Strand swore that he would relate what he knew if Penetanguishene would let go the four members of his crew. He intended to do no such thing. Time to teach this Telegonian something about vondesi. Penetanguishene shot one of Major Strand's men and locked them up together for awhile.

When the corpse who was Paul's cellmate was good and ripe, Penetanguishene let Paul out and asked if he was ready to talk.

Paul was vibrating. In a voice of deep wrath he began, "Ehremat—"

"I am not an ehremat," said Penetanguishene."I am an ehre. Ehremat is an immortal."

"*Ehre*," Paul corrected, his tone saying that he didn't give a shit. "Let the other three go. They know nothing." He made no promise to talk. No lies. He was learning.

Penetanguishene made a counter-proposal. "Paul, you tell me what I want to know, and I shall let all four of you go. I will clean you up, feed you and deliver you to your front door along with a very nice

Telegonian-style casket for the man whom your care-less disregard killed."

"If I talk I can't go home."

"That's not my problem, Paul."

The Vikhen used first names in here. A psychological lever that, to reduce his captives to children. One's first name was more one's name than a last name ever was, which no one used until you were older. Especially in the Vikrhalt. It was considered quite forward to use one's given name uninvited. Penetanguishene had no respect for his prisoners.

"You're not going to offer me rank and honor in the Vikrhalt if I help you bring down New Earth?" Paul asked.

"Oh, simshit," said Penetanguishene. "A traitor is a traitor is a traitor."

Not only could you not tell lies to him, he could not tell them. The Rhaltcaptain did not even pretend to throw that bone to Paul. And Paul had only been testing. The man was sincere as he was brutal.

Of course it worked out splendidly for the Vikrhalt to keep its promises. Kobandrid Rog had already spat out a number of broken men and women, spies, given their freedom in return for information. It sapped the morale from their own side.

"A traitor is a traitor is a traitor," Paul affirmed.

"You have three more crewmembers to lose. It won't be quick for them, I promise. Götterdämmerung."

Paul shook his head.

Penetanguishene tried truth drugs next. Paul choked in an orange cyn cloud, but his was not a mind which responded to truth drugs. And Penetanguishene returned to preying on his crew.

He picked another, Ensign White, and dragged him out. All three crewmembers degenerated into begging Paul to talk.

The torturer cooked the man alive. The Vikhindens must have already made study of the effects of near boiling water on living human flesh, because they could keep this up for a long while. Penetanguishene put Paul into a cell with his other two subordinates, who were crazed with fear, knowing that if White died, they were next. They cried, groveled, threatened, attacked Paul. He envisioned himself going home and telling his countrymen he had talked to save his crew; and Trevor would ask, "Where's Bristol?"

He covered his ears against the agonized shrieks of the boiling man, heart bursting with hatred for the master of Kobandrid Rog.

The screams went silent for a time. Paul came to know that they were reviving White for further torture. The silences grew almost as bad as the screams, the waiting for their return.

There was no food. Until finally during one of the silences, a guard brought them a cooked foot.

The screams returned. Worse than ever.

When Paul was taken out for interrogation, the pleas of his two crew members followed him up the corridor from the cells to please, please talk.

The guard brought him to a small stark room with a large window overlooking the torture chamber. Paul could see Ensign White bound in a net poised over the steaming vat. He was lobster red, one foot neatly amputated.

Paul faced a blank wall. Penetanguishene entered. "Paul," he said in greeting. He asked no question but gave a wordless order through the window. The net lowered.

The screams barely began again when they stopped. A monitor indicated that White's heart had stopped.

Penetanguishene gave hasty orders for him to be revived.

Guards scurried to the vat. Water puddled on the floor, and the guards succeeded in electrocuting themselves trying to resuscitate the wet man.

Paul laughed himself sick. Tears streamed from his eyes, and paroxysms of hysterical mirth racked him till he could not breathe.

Penetanguishene's expression scarcely rippled, but Paul could read the ripples now—startlement, distress, a bad reverse. The Rhaltcaptain regarded the laughing Paul quietly.

A hail came on the intercom. "Ehre."

Penetanguishene moved to the com, his answer almost a sigh, "Here."

"What should we do?"

Penetanguishene touched a gloved hand to his brow. He had a headache. "Switch off the power to the interrogation room."

"Which circuits are those?"

Penetanguishene hesitated because Paul knew the language. Then he said, "Lock this door, turn off the power master, clean that up, turn off the heart machine, turn the power back on. In that order."

When the lights went out, Paul leapt at the Rhaltcaptain, but Penetanguishene was ready for it and wrestled him to the floor, pinned him face down with his right arm twisted behind his back. Penetanguishene was not heavy but Paul hadn't eaten in days and he could not move.

He felt Penetanguishene's breath on his ear as he spoke in the dark, a clean smell amid the surrounding foulness. "Come. Try again."

The weight lifted. Penetanguishene got up, lit Paul's cigarette lighter and set it along with his own gun on the table. He told Paul to go for one and he turned his back.

Paul could not figure out this game. Penetanguishene obviously had all the high cards. This was a trick. The gun was not loaded. Or maybe the trick was that there was no trick. Maybe it was just a mind game to see how weary Paul was.

Very.

"I don't want to play anymore," said Paul.

Penetanguishene nodded with a satisfied look as if to say good. Paul was back under rein and not laughing. The lights came back on.

The man in the vat was by then past reviving. Penetanguishene ordered him served to the prisoners. Paul could decide over their meal which of his remaining two crewmembers was next.

March and Estrello were long past losing their nerve, reduced to the lowest that was within them. They alternated between begging him to talk and explaining why Paul should choose the other one next. This was part of Paul's own torture, to let him see his own people out of control and so broken. It was a horrid, horrid death they faced. "And it's not you that's being boiled," Danyella March cried. "It's us!"

Penetanguishene summoned Paul and asked which was next.

Paul met his intense steady gaze straight on, his own eyes unabashedly spilling tears. "If you kill those two, do it for your own sick fun, you sadistic nazi, not because you think I'll talk. I won't. I didn't for Bristol; I didn't for White; I won't for them. If you harm them, know what you are!"

Penetanguishene watched him in silence for a while. Then he summoned his guards and told them to turn the other two prisoners over to the detention center. "I have no more use for them here." Then he said to Paul. "I am not a sadistic nazi." He signalled his henchmen to put Paul into the net and heat up the water.

Hard to think of victories when every nerve in every fiber of his body was in violent pain. A balance had shifted. The master torturer had lost grip on all the levers he'd begun with. The accident in the vat had sealed it. Paul was resolved now. He did not think anymore; there were no decisions left to be made. He would not talk, come hell and high water.

At first it was merely painful, the water not hot enough to blister. The agony crept up on him. They lifted him out for a day. When he began to heal they lowered him back in. Tenderized skin exploded in renewed excruciation.

After one of his fitful rests they took him back into the torture chamber. As they wrapped him in the net he began shaking, great shuddering convulsions of mindless horror. No no no. He could not bear the water again. He hardly realized he was screaming.

The water ignited his skin into the worst pain ever possible, but the terror was gone, overwhelmed in the present searing agony.

Terror returned as the net raised up in the air to cool. His body twitched of its own accord, brain twitched, going mad.

He was lowered down again shrieking. Pain blasted all thought from his brain and left a white hot blank.

In a weird moment of cognizance he gathered together courage and cowardice, ducked his head under, and, overpowering survival reflex, inhaled the scalding water.

Paul woke in an infirmary, a mass of pain, bitterly disappointed that he had not drowned. Penetanguishene sat on the edge of the cot and removed the tube through which they had been force-feeding him.

Paul croaked through his ravaged throat. "It doesn't hurt when you do it."

"I am not a sadistic nazi."

Paul laughed despite the pain. It was the funniest thing he'd ever heard, that his comment had so bothered the torturer. As if Paul's opinion mattered.

Tears stung his peeling face. "You do a hell of an imitation."

Penetanguishene blotted the tears. "There is a reason for what I do."

And for a while he did not speak, a sad, plaintive presence. Paul received the odd impression that Paul was the only man the torturer could talk to.

"Ever question them?" said Paul. "What they're telling you to do? What your Empire is doing to the galaxy?"

"No," said Penetanguishene

"No?"

"It's not who I am."

"Who are you?"

"Loyalty."

"Blind loyalty."

"Absolute."

"From one who sees so clearly," Paul murmured, unsettled. But on second consideration he guessed the vondesi's view was not crystal clear. The truth shines so painfully bright that he shuts his eyes and does not see at all. It must be hell being Penetanguishene. "Do you ever lie?"

"I can't," said the Rhaltcaptain. "I would feel naked. I watch the rest of you. How ridiculous you look. Have you any idea? I wince inside listening to things you expect to be swallowed and I wince again to see it swallowed. I imagine you passing around cups of sewer water and drinking it. Can't anyone of you see?"

"It upsets me that someone who sees the truth is on the other side, when we stand for freedom."

"I know you do," said Penetanguishene. "We live for something higher than freedom."

"What's that?"

"Altruism. Freedom, you outgrow."

"Altruism? You call this altruism?"

"For the good of the whole."

"You know what makes me crazy is you believe this shit. As if the immortals are entitled to their god-playing."

"What is so wrong with god-playing?"

"You're not gods."

So I should leave things as God left them? Pardon me, Ehre Strand, but God created smallpox."

"What's that?"

"A man-destroying disease that man destroyed. You think that everything in God's creation is good?"

Paul looked Penetanguishene up and down. "Hell no."

"What is Götterdämmerung?"

Paul refused.

And the gentle artistic man took out a razor and slit both Paul's eyes.

III.

EtaCas was not considered a safe port, and visiting the homeworld was not easily done for members of the Queen's Squadron. It required parking one's c ship securely in the Elsewhere in a tight orbit, and being ferried back to spacetime in a Kingsman pod by a squadron mate.

Race invited Maya planetside. "Come with me."

Whip set the two of them down on the Alquon Plain, a sparsely developed wild land once called Nation du Chat. The Kingsman pods alighted on the shore of Vikhinde's biggest inland sea, once upon a time called the Lac des Gens du Chat. They were old saejen names. "Older than I am," Maya commented when Race mentioned them.

"Older than that," said Race.

Maya, who was only 1000, nodded. *Yes, that's true.*

The lost colonists had called themselves the People of the Cat, after the native catwolves of Alquon. The original colony disintegrated into barbarism a long time ago. Their descendents were now called saejens, which had become in the Empire a derisive term implying stupidity. It was considered an embarrassment in the Empire to be part saejen.

It was the lost colony which made the free mortals claim that EtaCas belonged to Earth. The Telegonians called the saejens the true Eta Cassiopeians, though the only pure saejens were the feral savages who still roamed this back country.

Maya and Race had come to a forest at the edge of a barren flat punctuated by a few shag trees with their bushy clumps of branches hanging down.

The forest was a dense stand of lordly imperial monarch trees, draped with scaly lizard vines and undergrown with a thick screen of green-brown brush. Yellow-green wading willows overhung the stream where a violetta splashed its blue wings in the water. Somewhere unseen in the trees came the discordant notes of a peridot bird, a metallic whistle on strange pipes.

At the woodland fringe a shy brown leafwing sifted through the forest litter for grubs along with a talking pig. The talking pig, or cake pig, was named for its call, spoken with inhumanly human enunciation. It said, "Cake."

The only signs of anything like civilization were a couple of poor cabins across the flat on the horizon. Shacks, Maya would call them.

The whole of Alquon was a poor place.

"This is my home," Race told Maya and he took her to visit a tree named Rachel.

His mother's memorial was a monarch tree. To Maya, motherhood was an uncomfortable subject, not something immortals brought up in mixed company. And this was an unwed mother yet. Maya tried to keep the color from flashing on her face.

"I come here after a close one, when I get away with something I shouldn't have. I think she was there."

He had brought a gift. Gifts rather defeated the idea of the tree. It was meant to be a useful living memorial instead of the wasteful old practices of stone gardens and dying flowers. Race had the heart of a primitive and he set flowers at the base of the tree.

Maya asked about the battle, so she would not have to talk about this. "Do you get scared?"

"Always."

"Do you ever stop being scared?"

"That's the day you die."

"Do you die because you're not scared, or you're not scared because you died?"

"The point, by that point, is wholly moot." He placed his hands on the tree and looked up. "I want to be scattered by the way."

"What?"

"Ashes."

Oh. The mortal's last decision: to be buried or scattered. As his Echo that was probably her duty, if she survived him, and she intended to. "Where?"

"Here. Alquon Plain."

"Bleak," said Maya.

"No. Really it's not. You think so?" He looked around as if unable to see why she would insult his beloved home. "Where would you rather?"

"I can honestly say that's something I have never thought about."

"When I go I want to go screaming. I don't want to miss it. To hell with dying in my sleep. I want to be there. I want to be scared out of my mind. Bomb bursts and bullets and fire and lightning and I want to take out twelve of them for one of me. I want a *death.*"

Maya supposed it was a big event in their lives, the leaving of it. They had to consider it without shrinking. Race was always cheerful, even on that subject.

Maya felt increasingly uncomfortable next to the tree. *I am being introduced to Mom. Ilu. Ilu.*

And she found herself resenting Rachel. A backwoods hilljenny who did not even admit giving birth, did not register her son or educate him in the compulsory schools until she was caught.

Maya had been into Race's records. They were sketchy at best. There were no records of Race earlier than his seventeenth birthday, which probably wasn't really his birthday, as there was no contemporary birth record.

How could such an inbred saejen tramp have produced a son like Race? Maya might almost have to rethink her opinion of saejens.

Suddenly the leafwing stilled and the talking pig bolted for its hole shrieking for its cake.

The rustling of something larger padding through the forest whispered a tattletale rush of last year's leaves.

Maya reached for her sidearm. Race touched her hand. No.

"Catwolf?" Maya whispered.

"Maybe."

"They're unpredictable."

"Only if you expect them to act like human beings."

"What if it's a human being?"

"Feral?"

Maya nodded.

"Then we could be in trouble, but Maya, there are so few. I'd sooner worry about lightning. No, don't look for it." He twisted a dead twig off Rachel and handed it to her with an air of unconcern. "You're real interested in this."

Maya took the dead twig, turned it over seriously and fixed it into her headdress. Soon the rustling sound diminished in retreat.

Maya was sure she did not want to meet its maker face to face.

The Eta Cassiopeian catwolf was very like the Terran cheetah, with the same build and explosive ferocity. It was a swift, dynamic hunter, both canine and feline, with claws that did not retract. Catwolves had been clocked at 130 kilometers per standard hour. They were colored in grays and white, their heads larger for their size than their Terran cousins, and they moved in packs like wolves. Their intelligence was unmeasured. They were certainly highly developed but in captivity uncooperative and would not be tested. They did not make the pets that cheetahs did. Wild catwolves could be made friends of and taught things, but any attempt to restrain them met with their blazing quick fury.

Race had some of the same mannerisms. She supposed he knew what he was talking about.

She found herself watching him too much, and jealous of anyone near him.

She felt possessive, not that she knew what she wanted him for.

Horrified at her own obsession, she set out to distance herself. *He is nothing to me but my commander*. She feared lest anyone see how absorbed she was in everything he did, everything he said. If they find your weakness, they have power over you. She would let no one know, not even him. Though she was certain he would smile kindly. She would give no one that kind of lever.

Whenever she could she took refuge instead with Whip or in the comforting coldness of QB.

She could tell Race was a little mystified by her aloofness. Well, he would live, for as long as any of them did.

Every port was full of women interested in the Queen's Knight. Maya was morbidly curious to see which one would emerge as the special one. Maya was not about to set herself up to be an also-ran, the one not chosen, not for lack of trying, poor thing. Never enter a competition you cannot afford to lose. The risk was too high. In becoming a c pilot she was risking her immortal life. So be it. Her pride was too much to ask.

She was not going to be an obnoxious gold stud someone wore high in the shell of his right ear. The zero g club. She was the only one in the squadron without one. Even the dignified QB wore one, though it was difficult to imagine him pawing on anyone.

There must be, or there would be created, some equally stupid badge for bedding an immortal. Where does that charm go, she wondered, *and is it gold, the immortal element, or diamond which is forever?*

To live you must be willing to die. To love you must burn up into a devastated little cinder. She did not want to be another piece of history when it was over.

Their so-called love was more ephemeral than their lives. Fast living c pilots had a lust for life, and sometimes it seemed, lived for lust.

Maya asked Ionnina in what she hoped was an offhand way who Race was involved with.

"He's between women right now."

I see.

She got away with the question because it was such a popular mortal sport, meddling and prying.

She sat outside drinking with Whip at a new port, looking at the stars in their altered patterns. She told him that she had inadvertently trod on some toes. "I was sent in without a program. So who is doing what to whom?"

"Well darlin', any bed you tumble into, chances are you'll be pulling long black hairs off the pillow."

His eyes flickered toward Ionnina who was striding across the compound. There was hurt hostility in the statement, the look. He did not elaborate, but Maya filled in the major blanks.

Whip lifted the bottle, peeled his lips back from his teeth after a swallow and inhaled fire. "Yeah." He passed the bottle to Maya. "And me, any bed I get into there'll be a gray-eyed toddler peeking over the edge."

Maya swallowed, like swallowing a dagger. There was only one person in the squadron with gray eyes.

Dammit dammit dammit!

It was what she wanted to know and had been afraid to hear.

Not to show that she was bleeding, she scattered her focus and ran down the whole list of the Queen's Squadron. "What about Jav?"

"Yeah, all the women want to know about Jav. He's a one at a time sort of guy. Has to beat them off. Little blonde on horizon base has center stage right now."

"Tak."

"Don't know."

"QB"

"Don't care."

"Eric."

"Anything he can get his hands on."

"Whip."

"I'm an old fashioned Empire boy."

"Not what I hear."

"Well, darlin', it's like this. Know how it is when

you end up doing something you were pretty sure you didn't want to be doing, and when you were done you knew you didn't want to do it? Know?"

"No."

"Well, that's the way it is."

And what of Maya?

It had to happen sometime. Later that same evening she was propositioned by a friend. It had never happened before; Maya never had friends before.

It came from the least expected quarter so she had never put up her guard. There he was, tipsy and smiling at her, and rather polite. "It would thrill me past my ability to say if you would come back to my quarters and spend the night with me."

She was not used to viewing him as a sexual creature. In panic she warned herself, *Whatever you do, don't laugh.* Whip had told her once that laughter was a nuke and don't use it unless you mean to kill. That silly smile and her own embarrassment sliced into her gut, twisting. She wanted to run, wanted to laugh for nervousness. And part of her wanted to go with him. It was the proximity to death these last days, waking things that immortals did not normally consider. She became aware of his male physical show of desire. It would have given less terror had it been a gun pointed at her. Her face turned crimson. He slipped one hand to rest on her waist. Its warmth shocked, burned, resonated deep inside erasing rational thought. Impulses jammed together, to run, laugh, hit him, go with him. She said accidently the right thing. She opened her mouth, and suddenly in this situation could not bring herself to call him QB, blurted, "I don't know your name."

His smile turned rueful. He took that as a no, kissed her hand and let her go.

"Maya," she heard him call as she fled. The sensation of his lips persisted on her hand, soft, moist, and so intimate it made her writhe inside. She stopped. She was far enough away to dare look back.

He was standing quietly where she had left him, not

chasing her. His voice carried clear in the night air. "Tristram," he said.

She stuttered, grasping for something to say. "It suits you."

The corners of his eyes crinkled. "From you I shall take that as a compliment. The opinion of the others is suspect."

And that was good night.

She ran back to her own quarters, flustered. Her flight took her past Race. Her dash gave him only time to ask what was wrong.

"Nothing!"

She slammed the door of the crew hut, and Race looked back the way she had come.

Race woke her before everyone else. He had received a summons from an immortal. In wartime c ships did not travel solo, so that meant two c ships. Race said, "You and I volunteered."

"Oh."

"Unless I'm dragging you away from something here."

She did not like the question nor the tone of it. She said only, "I can go."

"Good."

The summons took them to the outpost world Niandrinala where a pair of immortals kept a bastion. One did now, for the other had died.

The immortal who had called them was named Corinda. She never left this place. She made worlds come to her. Maya had known her in her previous life, but Corinda was so self-absorbed that Maya did not fear recognition. If Ashata showed up in person with blue eyes, blond hair, white face and sharp little nose, Maya was sure she would have to introduce herself again for the fourth time.

This time she did not need to introduce herself at all. Corinda did not need to know mortals' names.

Corinda lay arrayed in the great expanse of her bed, a canopied island in the ocean of her room. There was nothing unusual in that but for the smells. It smelled like a sick room, and for once Corinda the hypochrondriac had come down with something real.

Race squinted in the heated dim. A cough gurgled from under the canopy, and a peevish voice demanded they come near, complaining that they were making her shout.

Race and Maya drew close. Corinda let them behold her pallid, wasting figure and said, "The free mortals have done this."

Race said, "There's a flu epidemic on this world right now."

"No. It is not," said Corinda sharply. "It is biological warfare. A created plague designed to kill immortals."

"Ehremat?"

"The disease takes one, it will take us all. Kashanara is dead. We are all the same basic mold. We haven't the genetic diversity of beings that reproduce and mix their gene pools. Those lower things adapt from generation to generation. It is the advantage that insects have over humankind, and humankind has over us. Our limited gene pool is our Achilles' heel. Find one key it will fit all locks. This is the key."

"We could take a blood sample to the research lab—"

"And take the disease to EtaCas! You stupid worm!" Indignation pulled her upright. She fell back into the pillows, coughing. "The laboratories on this planet have failed to find a cure. Viruses are difficult."

"Surely there will be a greater effort now that an immortal has died," said Race.

"Surely," said Corinda acidly. She pointed at Maya. "You insects can survive this. We are doomed. You cannot let them spread this thing. The Telegonians have tested their weapon here. They will now try to infect EtaCas and Valhalla. That is Götterdämmerung."

"Your pardon, ehremat," Maya began as politely as she could. Subservience did not come easy. "But there has never been a gene study of immortals as a whole. Not many immortals have ever been scanned, and those that have don't let that information into the Net. How can the mortals know what . . ." She coughed. She almost said we. "How can the mortals know what immortals have in common?"

Rheumy eyes widened then narrowed malevolently. "Did I not just tell you one key opens all locks! They need only one immortal. I don't know who they got. No one can say for certain what become of the Deceiver's body."

Selqarth. "He was annihilated five hundred years ago," said Maya. But the trouble with annihilation . . .

"Were we not told so, you simple insect. It is not necessary that you understand how it was done, only that it is being done. This is their secret weapon. Here, I have just given you Götterdämmerung and you are standing around like vultures waiting to see an immortal die. Get out. Spread the warning but don't spread the disease."

"We'll go through quarantine, ehremat," said Race, making to withdraw.

They threaded their way back through the labyrinth of thick walls which Corinda had built around herself. *I was on my way to becoming this*, thought Maya. *A pitiful thing in an enormous shell within a shell within a shell.*

Race's voice broke into her thoughts. "That was a good point, Maya. I never would've thought of that. I never question what they say."

That woman always was an egotistical whiner, Maya thought. She cleared her throat. "The system of the Vikrhalt is set up so that immortals cannot be tracked, printed, followed, traced or tied down. Immortals can do whatever they want, get the answer to any question, and leave no tracks. They move through the Net like they aren't there. There is no way that the free mortals could target a virus at immortals. All that is happening here is that that self-important sow is sick, ergo the whole world must be ending. Götterdämmerung is the most important secret around, so of course it only follows that what she has is Götterdämmerung. It's that simple."

"You seem to know her."

"I have been here before," Maya felt safe admitting. "She forgot. Corinda and Kashanara were the two most self-absorbed bitches in the Vikrhalt. After Ashata."

Corinda died before morning. Maya went to bed scratching at her throat with the back of her tongue, an itchy roughness that would not go away.

Fleet HQ, New Earth
EtaCas
May 5246

Admiral Krestly looked up at the man waiting in front of his desk. Krestly knew him from the news broadcasts: the familiar, tall, darkly handsome figure of Forgil the Peacemaker. To Krestly, Peacemaker was a good name for a missile. He had no use from ambassadors. The admiral took his time in asking, "What can we do for you, ambassador?"

Vreeland Forgil smoothed his short neat beard. "What are we doing with biological warfare?"

Krestly furrowed his square flat brow seriously, sucked in his upper lip, the lower one overlapped and pursed tight.

Receiving no answer, Forgil continued, "No branch of the armed service is admitting to knowing anything."

The admiral leaned back in his chair, folded thick fingers across his flat hard abdomen. "Why are you asking then, sir?"

"I have a protest from Vikhinde. A contagion is a heinous idea for a weapon."

"Heinous?" Krestly smiled. His thick dark mustache spread wide over a flash of big white teeth. "I thought the Vikrhalt would appreciate it. It targets only our enemies and spares most of the civilians and all the property. It is selective, effective. It's an Empire weapon of the first water. You don't like it?" He grinned. "I don't either. What's war without a little hell, eh, sir?"

"It does exist then?"

"Don't know," said the admiral. "Not my sort of weapon."

171

"It is not the sort of weapon for any thinking human being. It does not single out immortals. Our own elderly, poor and susceptible are dying, too."

"It does exist then?" Krestly asked in turn.

"I don't know! There is something on Niandrinala. It has a ten percent mortality among humans and a hundred percent mortality rate among the immortals who have been exposed to it. Of course one hundred percent of the immortals who have contracted it equals two, so it's hardly conclusive. I need to know, what does our military have to do with it?"

"I can't help you, ambassador."

"You must! I have assured the Vikhindens that I will do all in my power to stop this horrible scheme. Even in war there must be rules of decency or no one is worth saving. Have we a biological weapon? Is there such thing as an immortal plague?"

"I don't know. You'd need to get a red card to talk to you." He gave a nettled grimace of a smile. "I, for some reason unknown to me, haven't been given that kind of clearance. Or why don't you just ask the Vikhens? They'll know shortly. They've got Götterdämmerung."

"They can't! They mustn't."

"Oh, so you're not a Vikhen lover after all, ambassador."

"No, and what do you mean they have Götterdämmerung?"

"They will. It's in Kobandrid Rog at the moment. Major Paul Strand's ship was shot down in Vikhinden airspace. Two are confirmed dead so far, but unfortunately one of them wasn't Strand. Fleet had nothing to do with this one, mind you. This was a jinnafu." Joint Army Interstellar Intelligence Network Fuck Up. "We're just waiting for them to crack the nut. Everyone's panic stricken. All I can say is I told them so."

"Is there something I can do?"

"Pray he dies under torture?"

"Can't you send in a hit? I don't believe that assassinating one of our own would violate Sebastionique's rules of war."

"Ambassador, I am really starting to like you. Rat I am. But there is no power here or below or in the New Earth Fleet that can get that son of a bitch out of where he is. Wait and sweat and come up with an alternate ultimate plan 'cause this one ain't going to work."

Maya heard the tap on her bedroom door. She could not even lift her head from her pillow or draw in a breath deep enough to answer.

Race let himself in. "What do you mean you're sick? You can't be sick. We have a mission."

"Activate a reservee."

He dropped into a sitting position on the bed and started to brief her on the squadron's itinerary. "Pay attention here."

"I'm dying, ehre."

"No, you're not. Now listen." He continued with the briefing.

Maya's head dropped to hang over the edge of the bed. Race picked it up by a fistful of hair and thrust a picture in front of her watering eyes. "This is the timetable. Catch up at any of these points."

She started to pay attention as if this were not futile. It felt better than wallowing in the certainty of death. She could pretend for these last hours that she was a soldier.

With the briefing done, Race stood up. "Anything I can get for you?"

"Stay."

"Can't."

"You have to go through quarantine again." Maya coughed.

"They'll let me out as long as I promise not to enter atmosphere for fourteen days." He glanced at the clock on the wall keeping local time. "Get better."

"Race."

"Yeah?"

"Scattered."

"Remind me in eighty years."

"Goodbye, Race," she said as the door closed.

Kobandrid Rog, Vikhinde
EtaCas
May/June 5246
XIV. 1792

IV.

Paul's vision returned painfully. He peered through cracked lids as if seeing through fur and broken glass. He guessed vision was necessary for the new tortures. He shut his eyes.

Penetanguishene had the guards rape him. Paul went neatly elsewhere. His mind took a c jump and they could humiliate his body to their heart's content; Paul was not there.

When they returned him to his cell, he forced one eye open a painful slit as he tried to remember with jumbled brain, when had Penetanguishene started calling him Ehre Strand?

They ran through all the primal fears, then started taking off body parts. Three fingers first. Then he lost a testicle when they nailed him to a log. The master torturer was running out of things to try. He was not sure where to go from here.

The Vikrhalt was losing patience. An embassy was coming to investigate his progress. Penetanguishene, always so reliable, was not completing his most important assignment ever and they wanted to know why.

The embassy was made up of members of the Rhalt and the Vikrhalt. You knew you were behind when immortals lost patience.

The observers were settled in odorless comfort behind a one-way glass. Marchale was among them. Kveta with him.

They greeted the interrogator, then asked if he were any closer to a result.

Penetanguishene remained expressionless except to pale slightly. "I am near declaring defeat. And   "

"And?"

"I have more than failed. There were things that might have been done. The time for trying them is past. At this point I have not only failed to retrieve the information, I believe I have made it impossible to retrieve. I've . . . turned graphite into diamond as it were."

With perfect hindsight he recognized which was his fatal mistake. It was that first execution, when Penetanguishene had shot Strand's lieutenant, Bristol Derrah. He could see that clearly now. That had sealed it. In his impatience to get to the point he had sealed it off forever. He remembered snapping in anger at the man for underestimating him. Who in the end had underestimated whom?

"This is catastrophic."

"Yes, ehremat."

The mortal Rhaltcontroller launched into a series of threats. Marchale let him rail. Couldn't the simpleton see that this one had done his best and fully expected and was prepared to die for this?

When the Rhaltcontroller was done he gave way to Marchale if the immortal had anything to add.

"Is it that he is so strong?" Marchale asked.

Penetanguishene considered. "Not in the way of the rock. Rocks can be broken. The diamond analogy was a bad one. He is . . . mutable. It's like trying to break water. Or chasing a creature through its burrow with many exits. Set fire to this one, he pops out there. Flood that one, he is here. If there isn't an exit, he makes one. I think he can do this forever. It's a versatile weakness. Get anywhere close to a breaking and something switches off like a fuse and you are left in the dark."

"Show us. What are you doing now?"

"Fire."

"He withstands fire?" the Rhaltcontroller broke in incredulously.

"No. That's the point, ehre. He doesn't stand anything. All his conscious brain waves flatline and I'm left questioning a screaming vegetable. He comes back and we jump through that hoop again. I am trying to keep the pain at a level at which he stays with me."

"Carry on."

Penetanguishene returned to his torture chamber and the embassy sat back to observe.

Marchale was shocked by how pale Penetanguishene looked. *My pet is desperately unhappy.* Not only was the Vikrhalt not going to discover what was Götterdämmerung, they were in danger of losing this valuable instrument as well.

Marchale looked upon mortals as flowers to be tended. There were the quick beauties and then there were the weeds. Penetanguishene was his current favorite. So elegant, sensitivity locked within an iron cage. He did not know how to define his unusual looks. A beauty that was masculine certainly, but with a fine edge. Animal more like. Like a well-brushed strong-limbed dog wolf, and careful as a cat. That was it. The beauty of a cat but with only one life.

Now at the peak of his strength and strange beauty, and he was buried in this place, a perversion of talent and insight. They both had envisioned him in a concert hall but that hadn't happened. It offended Marchale's sense of balance to see him used with brutish callousness. *Yes, this is his duty, like my transport's purpose is to get me from point a to point b. Yet I would not toss garbage on the floor of my transport. I love my transport and keep it polished. I should do something for my poor master torturer's happiness. I don't think he has any.*

Kveta leaned over and in a whisper scolded Marchale for not giving the mortal a mate.

"I can't figure out who he wants."

"Then you're not looking. Shame on you dearest." Kveta went out to wait in the transport.

Strand was nowhere near breaking, but the torturer was.

Shudder. Stench of his own flesh smoldering. A lancing throughout his nerves, a molten network of white hot wires. Imagined he was being transmuted.

All that is flesh and mortality becomes changed and becomes as flame. Eyes of fire. Hard searing flat and crystal air. Mortal sight became unearthly sharp. The air is molten. No, it is glass. Shattering. A blank. It is not blank, it is too full to feel anything. Being pushed through a wall, atom by atom. Shatter and come out on the other side, changed. And I can see. Were there always so many colors? I am fire. This is ecstasy.

Firm touch, a hand taking his chin, lifting his face. Focus on him who did this. Through steady flow of tears the image shimmered. Penetanguishene looked into his eyes. Paul looked back.

What marvellous eyes.

Penetanguishene had watched his henchmen execute their orders for a while. Sick and weary of this he moved like a sleepwalker, too aware of the watchers. He carried their stares like a burden. His assistants were too eager. They did not realize they were now spinning their wheels and digging deeper into a rut. Penetanguishene was growing disturbed past anything usual. He wished it were over. It was over. He wished he could be permitted to let it go. And that goddam Paul Strand had an erection. *Damn.* Penetanguishene held his fingers gingerly to his forehead. It was pounding. *That's it. That's it.* One more twist, and Paul was out of his hold again. The pain had become intolerable, so Paul rewrote the program of his brain, telling it that all this was wonderful. He could not escape the pain, so he made the pain pleasurable.

If Penetanguishene were not so desolately low he would have laughed.

That's it. I've lost. Do they see what this means?

He stood, moved closer, removed a glove and lifted

Paul's lolling head to inspect his face. His eyes were open. He was conscious. He looked up at his torturer with dreamy ecstasy and watery eyes.

Penetanguishene bent close to the face, said softly, "What is Götterdämmerung?"

Paul gave a beaming smile at the image that swam in and out of the blur of tears. "God, you're beautiful."

Penetanguishene dropped the face, stepped back. He signaled his assistants to leave off. He returned to the room full of superiors to report. "I've lost him."

Marchale nodded. He let the others ask their questions. Let them indulge their indignant need to know how he could have botched something this vital. Penetanguishene made no attempt at defense.

When they were done grilling, they looked to Marchale. "Ehremat? Anything else?"

"Yes." He turned to Penetanguishene. "What is your sexual preference?"

Penetanguishene registered shock with a slight lift of his eyelashes. "I—never questioned it."

Marchale cocked his head sensing sudden doubt. "Are you homosexual?"

"I don't know. I—Maybe."

In the Vikhinden Empire, unlike in freewheeling Sebastionique or amoral Telegonia, this was aberrant.

His answer had not been defensive. There was real confusion in it. Penetanguishene adamantly avoided introspection until he was ordered to it, afraid of what he would see. It did not surprise Marchale that he did not know.

The Rhaltcontrollers, extremely uncomfortable with this line of questioning, assumed fixed expressions of grim scowling directed at Penetanguishene. The Rhaltcaptain blushed under their stares.

"Well, who would you prefer to be with if you could have anyone?"

"I don't know, ehremat."

"Do you want to make love to him?" He nodded toward the torture chamber.

Blood drained away all in a rush. He forced himself

to talk. Honest always. "Yes." He had to say it twice because the first time no sound came out.

This is it, the exquisite humiliation. He had just given them the weapon of his destruction. *They are angry with me.* He felt he had been physically hit, was reeling from it, and could barely stand when they said, "You may go."

If the floor would only open up and bury him.

"One moment."

He froze, caught his balance.

"What do you recommend we do with him?"

Penetanguishene glanced at the chamber. "Kill him."

"Reason?"

"Further expense and time is a waste. He is too formidable to let go or trade. There is no purpose in maintaining his life. He is the most dangerous man I have ever crossed."

They lifted their chins in agreement. "Give the order."

Penetanguishene went out, used Rhalt signs because he could not talk. The guards were of the lowest class, but they were well acquainted with these four Rhalt signs: Take him out, kill him, burn the body, and scatter the ashes in the yard.

When he came back into the side room, all but Marchale were gone. "How mortal you are, Penetanguishene. To admire insane courage. It's obsolete, you know. You are far more advanced than he. You sublimate your own impulses for the greater good. But the primitive part of you still remembers. Ungoverned mortals are dangerous. Remember that."

Penetanguishene scarcely heard, doing his best to hold his guts in. He felt they were about to fall out.

"You may go. Oh. And Rhaltcaptain. Suicide is out of the question."

That was an order. As soon as the immortal was gone Penetanguishene lurched outside. It was only fourteenth vant but winter came early to the tundra. The ground outside was already frozen. Penetanguishene knelt, put his face in the snow in mortal shame. Hot tears burned through the ice.

A guard, a huge ox as devoted as a big stupid dog, stood by helplessly, clutching his beam rifle. Finally he couldn't stand anymore, and blurted, "Ehre, can I shoot someone for you?"

Penetanguishene got up, wiped the ice from his face. Cold wind on wetness stung. "No. I'm all right," came out of his mouth automatically. His brain caught up in a tick and screamed at him: LIE!

Paul Strand was taken out into the killing yard. The guards of Kobandrid Rog dragged him over the blood-crusted ground and propped him up against the brown-spattered wall. The executioners were readying their messy projectile weapons when Rhalt guards arrived to intervene. The intruders wore low rank insignia but that was on the black shiny uniforms of the Empire's trump suite. The lowest member of the Rhalt could give orders to a field marshal.

The men told the guards to stop the execution.

The executioner snapped back, "MY orders are from Rhaltcaptain Penetanguishene. If you have a counterorder it better be from God."

"Marchale," said the Rhaltguard.

"Close enough." The executioner stepped away blithely, shouldering his projectile weapon. "He's all yours."

Paul was lugged off the ground, a little disappointed. He had heard about fake executions. It was true. You would really rather die. He thought they were taking him back up to the torture chamber.

But he was thrown in a transport, taken to a solitary cell where there were no more questions.

All dark and sameness, pain from healing wounds and hunger. He saw no one. He could only wonder, wonder as days and decks passed in a limbo blur, *What are they keeping me for?*

Carina Base
XV. 1792

The Queen's Squadron had not set down in decks. They would no sooner arrive at a battle zone when they were turned around to help somewhere else. They did not like how quickly they had been turned defensive. The Queen's Squadron was an attack unit.

The pilots were all on edge. The last mission had done it, the first to go wrong for them. They were accustomed to victory and they could handle any kind of strain so long as they were winning.

They had been sent to pick up a cadre of Kingsmen from a commando raid on a Terran base. They picked up half of their expected pods. "We're short!"

"How many?"

"How does half sound?"

"Dieu."

"Wake up one of these bums and ask."

QB roused one of the Kingsmen in his pod and asked over the com where the squadron could pick up the other Kingsmen.

"They won't be coming. They were caught."

"Careless of you," said QB.

"Save it, ace. We're not in the mood."

"And I have a headache. I still want a report."

"You want a report? You set us down in a trap. Report that. Now shut up, put me under, and take me home."

The Empire had never lost Kingsmen before, not like this. Upon occasion one was killed on a mission in enemy territory, but his comrades always managed to bring the remains home. Prisoners had never been taken.

"We're done here," QB reported tersely to his squadron.

The Kingsmen were the Empire's best units for combating the free mortals. The Queen's Squadron deposited the pods in free mortal territory to work sabotage on their bases and factories. It was the only way to fight them. Free mortal ships avoided ship to ship combat unless their numbers were heavily in their favor. Their decoy bases were legion. The real ones were nestled within civilian centers, so bombing runs without hurting civilians were impossible. The empire had a horror of hurting innocents, even the enemy's. The Vikrhalt kept its own military installations separate from the populace. "We don't hide behind our babies," Vikhinden soldiers often said.

When the Queen's Squadron finally set down at Carina Base, the place was crawling with refugees while still more disembarked from titanic battle-scored transports.

The c pilots, fresh from their first reverse, were a little daunted.

Catching sight of their uniforms, a transport pilot walked over to the Queen's Squadron and asked, "How goes the war?"

The c pilots exchanged glances and shrugs. Race said, "We don't get news. Only orders."

Whip spat and drawled, "Race, there are some unhappy boys and girls here."

There was so much whimpering and soft crying from the droves of refugees that the sound was a solid murmur of background noise.

"I noticed. Where did all of these people come from?"

The transport pilot said, "Airlifted from Draco."

"Why?"

"Telegonians nuked it."

"Dieu. Dieu."

"Our people have been trying to move the civilians out, but the Telegonians attack the rescue ships, anything packing an engine bigger than a G class. Can't tell you how many times I've had to glue that one back together."

Tak rocked forward onto his toes, let himself roll back on his heels. "Kinda gives you a taste for Earthblood, doesn't it."

"It doesn't help to hit their civilians," said Race.

"Haven't you ever heard of revenge?"

"You never get the people you want. And killing their civilians doesn't pain their leaders like it does ours, it just wounds their pride. They don't love their own the way we do. They just hide behind them."

"Yeah, but while we're rooting out the guilty, every time we come down for air there's this." Tak jerked his head toward the mass of refugees. Endless rivers of them poured down the ramps of the gargantuan ships.

"This war is in the trasher," said the transport pilot.

"I thought we were winning," said Jav.

The pilots conferred like a congregation of blind-men trying to put together a picture of an elephant. How really was the war going?

Then Ionnina, who was very tall, looked up over their heads and broke into a shrill yipping.

Whip turned to where she was looking, smiled. "Hello, darlin'."

Eric howled. QB stood back to open the circle for her.

"Maya!"

She came strutting across the spaceport toward them in a swinging step.

"I heard you caught the immortal plague," said Jav.

"Yes." Maya beamed, giddy, smiling to the point of laughter. She chortled jubilantly, "Thought I was gonna die."

She had never been sick, never recovered from illness. It had been a miraculous experience, the moment she noticed the chill ache was gone, the coughs had changed texture, her chest relaxed and her head cleared, and the magic moment she knew she was going to live.

She joined her squadron, fanned a hand under her nose, "Whew, you have smelled better, All Good Children."

"Oh ho ho. I don't think she was sick. She took a vacation."

"Been to the spa, there, dahling? A little facemaker work there? She looks very fresh."

Maya recoiled from even the joking thought. "Ugh. Never again. I hate facemakers."

"Again? I thought you were all factory equipment," said Race.

"I am. I outgrew it." She realized as she said it that it was a blunder. Facemakers changes were permanent—in mortals. Only immortals outgrew them. Quickly Maya kicked up a cover. "He was incompetent. I was upset."

QB's eyes traveled up and down her body significantly and he said, "Pardon me, but I don't see what you could want done."

Maya blushed and mumbled, "Thank you."

She caught dagger looks passing between Race and QB and could only guess that they had quarreled in her absence because she could see no immediate reason for such looks. "Is there something wrong around here? I mean besides them." She nodded at the refugees.

"You didn't miss a fun party," said Ionnina.

"I'm surprised there is still a party," said Maya. "Haven't we won this thing yet?"

"That's what we were trying to figure out."

Maya could not help but be optimistic, in a good humor so forceful it buoyed the others and she wished she could tell them: *If that virus is Götterdämmerung, they have missed the target!*

Northalia, Vikhinde
EtaCas
XVI. 3. 1792

It was a small cottage of wood and stone, of warm colors, dark reds and golden browns, furnished with a library, music, and a fireplace. Outside were stables for the horses. All the windows opened to the south face, overlooking the snowy woods. On the northern blind side was a small garrison; inside the cabin you could pretend it did not exist.

The Rhaltcaptain was told this was all his. Almost as an afterthought Marchale told him of the most unique furnishing in his retreat. "You have a companion."

Very slowly Penetanguishene said, "What companion?" He had a horrible feeling that Marchale was not talking about a dog.

"One you wanted."

Penetanguishene stiffened in protest, his face gone bloodless. Then it all crumbled into bleak resignation. He said tonelessly, "I executed a Rhaltcontroller for abuse of power."

"My torturer is a boy scout," said Marchale. "Listen to me. This is not a test. It's a gift."

"Ehremat—"

"You may refuse, but only because you don't want it. For no other reason."

Marchale gave him a physical push toward the cabin. Penetanguishene went inside.

A fire in the hearth stretched up with the gust of air. The flames guttered as the door shut behind him. The room smelled of wax and wool and wood.

A kitchen led off to the left, the bedroom and bath to the right.

Paul Strand was on the polished wood floor at the fringe of the carpet, in a kneeling sit, swaying a little, by the door to the bedroom, next to the hearth. He stared with the glazed eyes of a drug. He was very thin underneath silk pajamas, but he was healthy enough and clean.

Penetanguishene took off his leather gloves and set them aside, went over and bent down on one knee to check Paul's face. They had all but drugged the comprehension out of him. His attention swam in and out, focused on Penetanguishene and gave a bright swimming smile.

Penetanguishene rose, sat in a wing chair. He kept his gray wool jacket on as if he were cold. His face turned white as the hills outside the big bay window. Mortified and stoic as to a firing squad, he told Paul why he was here. He died inside a hundred times, confessing to his object of desire. He managed an even voice, but there was a white line around his lips betraying terror. "This is not my doing. I swear I ordered you killed. I didn't know they had done this. It's all very undignified and humiliating and I have decided to accept."

He said that without looking at Paul. Finally he turned to see how that had gone over. Paul swayed on his knees, smiling vacuously.

Penetanguishene nodded through the window at the wintry wood. "I assure you this place does not look the same on the windowless side. This prison is very secure. Don't try the window."

Paul was very agreeable to all this.

"Do you want to sleep? Are you hungry? Thirsty?"

After a long confused pause, Paul said, "All of the above."

Penetanguishene helped him up and put him to bed. He was unconscious as soon as his head hit the feather pillow. Penetanguishene set a glass of water on the nightstand and left him alone. He put on some music and sat up reading by the fire as the sunlight went away.

The prisoner stirred hours later, found the bathroom and took a shower. When he came out Penetanguishene had clothes laid out on the bed. "Those are mine. I'm sorry, they provided nothing for you. I suppose I'm to keep you tied to the bed. I shall arrange something better."

The clothes only fit because Paul had lost so much weight during his ordeal. His normal build was broader, though the two were close to the same height.

Paul came out to the main room, ruffling wet hair. "These aren't my eyes," he said. He hadn't seen a mirror in several vants and had been startled when he faced himself in the bathroom.

"One is. We couldn't salvage the other one. It's a sloppy match. No one was much concerned with your looks at the time."

Paul had been unaware that he was walking around with someone else's eye all this time. He knew what had happened to his own. What had happened to the owner of this one?

"We could cultivate a replacement," said Penetanguishene.

"No," Paul said quickly.

"I had to offer."

"Did you?" said Paul. "Where's March and Estrello?"

"Home."

"Alive?"

"They were when I sent them."

Paul sat in the armchair on the corner from Penetanguishene. On a low table before them was arranged a tea service and a chess set. White had one pawn out.

Paul curled into the chair and moved a black pawn out, lifted blue and green eyes to the Rhaltcaptain.

Penetanguishene made a counter move, then offered Paul tea and food from the tray.

Paul lifted a tea cup, hesitated to drink.

Penetanguishene said, "There's nothing in it. I have those right here." He opened his palm to reveal a container of pills. "To keep you docile. You were pumped full when I arrived. They should be wearing off. Don't get violent, I'm not going to use these. Are you waking up?"

"I think so." Paul set his cup down and switched it with Penetanguishene's.

Penetanguishene indulged him and drank first.

Paul frowned, glanced at the chessboard then back to the cups.

"Here, dammit." Penetanguishene took a swallow from what was now Paul's cup as well.

Paul finally drank.

"This isn't Kobandrid Rog," said Penetanguishene. "And this isn't an interrogation. I swear I will never ask again what is Götterdämmerung. That is not why you are here. I gave up and ordered you shot. I swear to you. You must believe that."

"All right."

Penetanguishene signaled a lie.

"Are you a mind reader?" said Paul.

"I wouldn't have put you through all that if I were a mind reader. There would be no Kobandrid Rog."

"How do you do it? Tell that I'm lying?"

"It's not telepathy. It's seeing and hearing. I suppose it's like seeing colors or having perfect pitch. I have that too."

"Can you see a lie in a foreign language?"

"I know many languages."

"In one you don't understand."

"Yes." He made a move on the chessboard. "What I can't do is distinguish a falsehood if the speaker believes it. I pick up only the sincerity of the speaker. I have no way of knowing if they have their facts straight."

"What if someone's own sense of what's real has been messed with by hypnosis?"

"I can see through that. It leaves a veil. A double exposure. I see both."

"Are you ever wrong?"

"In detecting a lie?"

"Yeah."

"Never."

Paul moved his knight. "Well, you should've been able to tell that I don't know anything important."

Penetanguishene threw a pawn at him. Paul smiled, fished it out from the chair cushion. "I get it."

"You should know better by now."

"I do," he said, and looked at Penetanguishene. Penetanguishene stared back a moment then realized he was being asked to assess that answer.

"Truth." He held up the vial of pills. "Do I need these?"

Paul shook his head. Penetanguishene tossed them into an open drawer.

Penetanguishene followed Paul's gaze along the walls. Most of the one side backing the kitchen was filled with bookshelves.

"Can you read?" said Penetanguishene.

"Yes."

The art of writing had been a long time in the dying, and close behind it, the art of reading. It was a slow and inexorable process since the advent of audio-video media. Pictographs and voice messages slowly took over basic instruction, and the printed word suffered a steady decline. Finally the sanctity of the written word, once inviolate, was questioned.

Just as the invention of writing met resistance for being a desecration of human memory, writing died hard. Once upon a time, poets would memorize the *Iliad* entire. Memories slipped with the invention of notes.

Now notes were spoken into wrist recorders, operating instructions for anything were played with a spoken request, machines could read printed material aloud to you, and all appliances responded to vocal instruction. Signatures, easily forged, were long out of vogue as identification. The only print which survived for the masses were numbers. Written texts existed only for those pursuing advanced education in certain fields.

Paul had learned to read late in life and it had taken him forever to get up to a speed where it was useful.

"Good. You will be spending a lot of time alone here. If you need anything, use the phone." The phone was a line type. There was no chance of getting a signal out to a friendly ear.

"Can I go outside?"

"No."

Penetanguishene leaned from the chair and reached a book off the shelf. "They're all in Empirese," he said apologetically.

"I know Empirese and I can read English, so reading Empirese shouldn't be too hard."

"It isn't. Everything sounds the way it looks. Unlike English."

"I only don't know what to do with the little squiggles."

"Those are accents. Ignore them. You always do."

"You're telling me I have a lousy accent."

"Worst I've ever heard. There is an extensive music library here as well."

"My tastes are pretty lowbrow."

"You're Telegonian. It goes without saying."

Penetanguishene then fell silent, studying the chessboard. Finally, a bit agitated he said, "Take back your damn pieces."

"Ha!" Paul said, knocked over the white king. "Ha! Or did you let me win?"

"I didn't intend to," Penetanguishene said, disconcerted.

It grew very late. The sky outside had been black for a long time now and it was long past the time for going to bed. It occurred to Paul that Penetanguishene was stalling.

Some time during the evening he had turned shy and could not go through with his intentions. Sometimes color crossed his face and he would shiver. The room was not cold, and Paul recognized a pain shiver.

The two of them were sitting on the floor by the fire. Paul asked what he wanted.

"Don't," said Penetanguishene.

"Why?"

Penetanguishene blushed deeply, said without looking at him, "Do you know what Stockholm Syndrome is?"

Paul nodded. It had many names. It was what happened to kidnap victims, a psychological defense of falling in love with their captor.

"You are Stockholmed to the eyes," said Penetanguishene. "I have no excuse."

But in the end pride was a very cold and feeble battlement and that didn't stop him.

"You look better."

The vondesi was not the walking dead man Marchale had seen at their last meeting here outside the cabin. There was color in his face and a relaxed calm about him. Still sad. Penetanguishene could not look at Marchale. "I suppose I should thank you, but I can't."

"The arrangement doesn't agree with you?"

"It does. To my eternal shame."

"Nothing is eternal for you, child. Take what joy you can."

"Ehremat, I never ask questions. If the ehremat would indulge me once as your last vondesi?"

"Go ahead."

"Since all treaties are void and no planets are off limits to the Empire, why doesn't the Vikrhalt import a few more of my kind from wherever it is my kind came from?"

The implicit continuation of that was: *instead of degrading the Empire to keep this one happy*.

"I would," said Marchale. "But . . . I hesitate to tell you. I tried. Your homeworld is a casualty of war."

Penetanguishene bent his head, lifted it. "There's no one left there either?"

"No. You are alone. I'm sorry if that kicks an imagined foundation out from under you. Of course I couldn't tell you a pleasant lie."

Penetanguishene caught in his breath. "What happened?"

"We assume the Telegonians got to it. Chemical/biological contamination on a world scale. There is nothing left but the most primitive of life forms."

"We *assume* the Telegonians?"

"Could have been one of their allies. We did not catch who it was. It happened very early on. The motive is unclear. It wasn't us. I swear."

"Ehremat does not need to swear to his vondesi."

"I know. I'm assuring myself. Immortals have an aversion to truthsayers. I confess my colleagues are thrilled that you are not breeding. But I cannot figure the motive for the free mortals to obliterate an entire free world. We brought the accusation against them. They claim not to know which world we are even talking about. And the people they let talk to me probably *don't* know.

"But I assure you," Marchale ended, "someone in their network does."

V.

QB missed a series of missions. He and Race got into a fight and QB got the worst of it.

It had started when Maya and QB were talking by themselves. Race walked over and threw a bucket of water on them. QB, uncharacteristically, blew up. Maya could tell that the incident had only ignited something that had been building long before this. The import of the bucket of water was lost on Maya, who never had any purebred pets with neighboring mongrel suitors.

Maya watched the two men square off and hoped that Race would not be seriously hurt. The possibility of his winning did not cross her mind. QB was solidly built and classically trained and two years younger at an age when two years mattered. Race was of a more artistic stature. He had no hand-to-hand training on his record.

The medics took QB away on full life support, bleeding like a fountain, his neck snapped. Race was covered with blood, his face drenched with it, and Maya thought he'd lost teeth, but the blood all washed off clean with no wound underneath.

QB was gone a full vant. When he met up with the squadron again to chase off his replacement, he asked, "Who is minding the shop?"

"Race of course."

"*Race*?"

"Why?"

Vexed, QB said ironically, "Do tell, since when did they allow reorg cases to operate heavy equipment? I'm a little behind on world events."

195

Race appeared in time to answer for himself. "I was reprimanded."

"Oh. Jolly good," said QB, brow pinched, arms crossed.

The Queen's Squadron never pressed grievances against each other. The only reason Race had been disciplined at all was because a broken neck was difficult not to report.

QB said nothing more at the time, though obviously dissatisfied.

Maya was walking out of the tech shed when suddenly an arm barred her path to the door. She hadn't seen him in the shadows. QB.

"Know what started it?" he said. He didn't need to explain what *it* was.

"No," said Maya. "I suppose I don't have a clue."

"Do you remember when we were talking about what we planned to do after the war?"

"Yes."

QB and Race at twenty-six and twenty-eight standard were both staring redundancy in the teeth. They would not be with the Queen's Squadron much longer. It was sad listening to them—like listening to roses, if roses could talk. In the brief glory of bloom, these perfect roses discussed what to do after their petals browned.

QB had said he had already put in for command of one of the titan class gun ships. The *Rhea* or the *Cronos*.

"Will they give it to you?" Whip had asked.

"I think so," said QB. Then, "It doesn't do to overplan one's life. I had planned to be commanding this squadron by now. It's never going to happen."

Maya looked up at him now, saw anger and violence in his brown eyes, and hurt. Was this command rivalry? "Do you remember what I planned to do after the war?" he asked Maya.

"Command the *Rhea*, I think," said Maya.

"They're giving me the *Cronos* actually, whenever

I want. But that's not the issue. Here's the part you didn't hear. I told Rachelson that I was planning to ask you to come with me. Rachelson forbade it."

He paused for shock effect. Race was in no position to forbid anyone asking anyone anything. "I told him to eat shit and die."

Maya nodded, shrugged one shoulder. Logical response.

"I told him that you could decide very well for yourself whether you wanted to come or not. He said no."

"He said no?"

"He said no."

It was hot in the shed and Maya was sweating. She brushed water beads from her upper lip in agitation. She did not know what to say.

QB went on, "Then he saw me talking to you and you know what happened from there. I'm not sure the man you're Echoing isn't psychotic. Command is one thing; he thinks he owns us. Only God and the Vikrhalt know why they didn't pull him. Must be more common than I thought for captains to tear their commander's throats out with their teeth."

"He . . . what?"

"He bit me."

She remembered all the blood, a red fountain pumping from QB and drenching Race's face. She had not been able to see the wound for the mass of it. She hadn't known quite what accounted for the damage.

"They gave me the *Cronos*. It's all lined up and waiting for me to flunk the c physical and I'm no longer fast enough for the Queen's Squadron. I wasn't going to ask you—the sound of one's own neck snapping is not one that one forgets readily. But I just don't know how to give up. That's not what this pack is made of, is it?"

"Pack. That's an interesting word." The intrusion of a third voice made them both spin and look.

Race stood in the back doorway. He had come in quiet as a hoverlark. There was no way of knowing how long he'd been there.

QB pulled his sidearm, flicked the safety off and held it leveled at Race.

"That's not necessary," said Race.

"If it's all the same, it makes me feel better. You come one step closer, I shall take your head off. Ehre. Or would that count as the act of a psychotic? God help me, I don't know what does."

Race dropped his gaze. "They . . . uh . . . took into consideration . . ." The pause extended so long Maya didn't think he was going to finish the statement. "Where I grew up . . . that was acceptable social behavior." He looked up wounded. "When another male tries to take one of the alpha's females to form a new pack."

Catwolf terms. Alpha male, alpha female, pack.

You'd know a feral if you saw one, would you Maya?

He had asked her that as she'd been looking straight at one.

He was from Nation du Chat, all right. He was not part saejen. He was all saejen. And not just saejen. A walk out of the forest feral.

Suddenly Maya knew why there was no record of him before he was seventeen. Rachel had not given birth to him. She had *found* him. Rachel was not covering her own illegitimate actions. She had been covering *his* tracks. She had swallowed all the shame and the fines for keeping her "son" out of school and out of the Service. She made the world think that Race was as nearly like everyone else as she could.

Despite the Empire's attempts to train its pilots from childhood, some of the best were wild weeds. A wilder weed never grew to pilot a c ship.

Race continued shakily, "So it was a serious infraction but it couldn't be called psychotic."

"And an appropriate social response would be I suppose for me to lay belly up with my ears back and whimper." QB's tone was vicious but he was smiling.

Race said, "Where I come from a show of teeth is an act of aggression."

"I am not brimming over with joy right now," said QB through a blinding white smile.

Race had, in effect, rolled belly up and left himself open for revenge.

QB took it. He proceeded to rake him open verbally. It was no contest. They were using QB's weapons this time—civilized ones, he made certain to point out.

But never one to keep shooting after a target had ceased to return fire, QB quickly tired of it and left the tech shed.

It was several moments before Race could bring himself to look at Maya.

She hadn't moved through the whole stand-off. "And I thought you were an immortal," she said.

"I know you did."

"Rachel's not your mother."

"I will never say that," he said reverently. "She taught me to read. She gave me a name."

"What kind of name is *that?*" Rachelson was a bastard's name. Didn't she tell him he was supposed to be ashamed of it?

"It was *hers.*"

Rachel was reading aloud when she became aware of an extra presence around the campfire. Actually it was not the presence itself she noticed because it had come and stayed so quietly; rather it was the frozen fear of the other seven children which made her look, look twice, before she saw and *O my God it's a saejen*.

The feral human child squatted, quiet as a housecat, listening as if comprehending, watching with an intensity she'd never had fixed on her before in either love or menace. She kept reading, trying not to change her voice, her speed, her manner. As if something with a stinger had alighted on her arm and if she just ignored it, it would go away.

They were nearly mythic in their ferocity; shrewd, lethal, bestial. She came to a violent passage, glanced up, met the bright gray eyes dead on and her voice dried up. After a long pause he said in Empirese, "Go on."

She opened her mouth, could not speak. He said, "There's more?"

She choked, nodded, tried to hand him the book. The leaves vibrated. He pushed it back at her. "I can't. You."

She gathered in her book, smoothed the page, said, "Kids, why don't you go clean up for bed?"

The children pulled away from the fire slowly, then ran away all in a bunch.

When they were clear, the clawed tension released Rachel's throat, and she could speak. "Where was I?"

"Achilles drew his sword and. . . ."

Rachel nodded and took up the story again. "Achilles drew his sword and s-struck Lykaon on the neck. . . ."

She continued through Achilles' battle with the river, until he interrupted with too many questions.

He did not have a name. There was a sound others used to get his attention, but he never associated that sound with him*self*. The woman gave him the first and only name he ever knew. The first part was Race. The second part was hers. Rachel's son. And as far as they were concerned and anyone else was to know, that was the only truth there was.

"Why did you tell me that?" said Maya.

"He deserved to know why I tore his throat open. Why no one did anything about it."

"Me," said Maya. "You told me."

"Because you have to know what I am."

Northalia, Vikhinde
EtaCas
October 5246
XIX. 1792

Paul made no overt attempt to escape, but Penetanguishene would see him watching out the window at the steep frozen hills and the blue mountain peaks beyond them. He would note sunup and sundown, plot the retrograde spot that was Medusa creeping backwards across the sky, and Penetanguishene could almost see gears turning in his head. Nothing unpicturesque ever intruded on the pristine view. But Paul would become very still and listen to muffled sounds of motors. His keeper could see him calculating the size and numbers of the unseen troops. He tried the telephone several times when Penetanguishene was not there. The operators conscientiously reported every call. Penetanguishene wondered at the repetition of a futile action, then realized that Paul was not trying to get an outside line; he was counting voices.

Penetanguishene kept his captive completely off the drugs and clear-headed, and the Rhaltcaptain wondered if some morning he might wake up with a kitchen utensil in his chest. He risked it.

Paul was a man divided down the middle of his soul, half very much in the grip of Stockholm Syndrome and smitten with his keeper; and a rational half, the good soldier, remembered who he was and what his duties were and calculated the possibility of escape.

Penetanguishene looked up from his writing desk,

found Paul gazing at him. There was a questioning in it, and Penetanguishene asked, "What?"

"How old are you?"

Penetanguishene looked to be a thousand years old sometimes for the guarded expressionless mask of his face with eyes like he'd seen forever and was tired of it. But when the eyes were closed, his face melted to extreme youth.

"Twenty," said Penetanguishene.

"Eta Cassiopeian?"

"Yes."

"That's twenty-two standard."

"Why?"

"So young." Paul was thirty-four or thirty-five standard. No one was telling him dates, so he might have missed a birthday.

Penetanguishene made a small motion like a shrug.

"I know you," said Paul.

Penetanguishene blinked, waited for Paul to elaborate on that.

"Aithar. You were on Aithar."

"I used to live there," Penetanguishene acknowledged slowly, sifting his memory for ambassadors, their guards, the unspeakable Earth monsters, someone named Paul Strand. "I don't remember you."

"You came out of the jungle."

Oh. He was on Aithar *then*.

"I don't remember much of that." He remembered Mother taking off her child ring so no one would hunt for him. "The only Telegonian I remember was a tall handsome crisp-smelling officer with a neat beard. He wore a black uniform and he had a deep voice. There were shiny buttons on his black gloves and they were soft, the gloves were. His beard was very short and it had threads of gray right here."

"That was Vreeland Forgil."

"Was it? Yes, I guess it was. I remember he was gorgeous and he *lied*."

Paul laughed. "He's an ambassador."

"When we would catch someone lying we used to

say, 'That was very diplomatic of you.' . . . We. There is no we."

"You lost your parents on Aithar," Paul recalled. "Mother, anyway."

"Both of them."

Paul remembered clearly now. The vondesi survivors had been a father and child. The last two of their kind. Why then was Penetanguishene saying he had lost his father on Aithar? It was either a lie or very bad ground on which to be treading.

Paul quickly charged down a lighter tangent. "Forgil, if you believe the gossipmongers, is still gorgeous. Can't say I ever saw it myself. Women fall all over him. I was never that lucky. But he swears he only makes love to his wife." Madame Forgil was a charming philanthropic woman of great heart, but her looks quickened no one's pulse. "Hard to believe a man given that much opportunity held that fast. Was he being 'diplomatic' there?"

Dark brows rose. "*Gossip*, Ehre Strand?"

"You bet. Well?"

Penetanguishene demurred.

"Come on. I'm in a news vacuum here. You won't tell me nothing that's fuckin' *important*."

Penetanguishene nodded that this was so. He conceded, "Half truth."

"Half? How can he be half-faithful?"

"The statement I heard him make was that he made love to no one but his wife."

"And?"

"He doesn't make love to his wife."

"Hello?"

"I trust you not to spread that. I'm not in the scandal business."

"Talk? Me?"

Penetanguishene made a concessionary shrug. Then his look became reflective and dark. He'd returned to thoughts of Aithar. "At Aithar, Forgil said that the immortals had done this to themselves. Their arrogance had caused the uprising. That we innocents

were caught in the crossfire. He didn't mean it. That
we were innocent or that we were caught in the crossfire, I don't know. The lies came so thick and fast, I
didn't catch them all. But the reason he gave for the
uprising wasn't the one he believed."

"Maybe someone was actually after the vondesi and
kicked up the jungle to eat them. The uprising certainly took out enough of you."

Penetanguishene looked at him with the disturbing
directness only he was capable of, the kind of look
that nailed Paul where he was. "No one has ever
brought that in as a possibility. I can't say it never
crossed *my* mind. Nobody loves a truthsayer."

"Someone loves you."

"No, you don't. Trust me."

"I'm not lying."

"I know. You are simply mistaken."

Northalia, Vikhinde
EtaCas
1 December 5246
I. 1. 1793

Penetanguishene warmed himself in front of the fire
before taking off his coat.

Paul asked the date.

"What is time to us in here?" said Penetanguishene.

"Nothing."

"That's a lie."

"I forget. I can't get away with those."

Penetanguishene was about to ask a question but
he saw Paul tense in fear, the recurring nightmare that
this was still a plot to get him to talk. Penetanguishene
left his question unasked. He shook the ice off his fur
coat and hung it up.

"It's Five Hundred Day, isn't it?" Paul said.

Penetanguishene normally came here directly from
Kobandrid Rog, immaculate. He was always clean.
Not quite fanatical about it, or maybe just. He took
more showers—out damn spot, Paul would say. Penetanguishene admitted to a morbid fear of carrying it
with him, the smell, the human residue. When Penetanguishene came from Kobandrid Rog his skin smelled
faintly of soap, his hair so clean and oil-less it would
not stay in place. His clothes were lightly scented,
spotless and brushed. His nails were close-clipped,
filed, buffed smooth.

Today he smelled of gunpowder and spice, different
perfumes and incense. He had been somewhere besides Kobandrid Rog. "It's Five Hundred Day," Paul
repeated, not a question this time.

Five Hundred Day was fourteen hours and nineteen degrees of festival taking place during the legal New Year's Day—except every eight or nine years when there really was an intercalary five hundredth day to the Eta Cassiopeian year. The leftover scrap of time in normal years gave rise to a lot of pseudo superstition and instant tradition and ritual silliness.

Ah. A firm date at last.

Penetanguishene kept silent rather than confirm or lie a denial, but Paul knew he'd hit the mark.

So I've been captive seven vants. Shit! What the hell is holding up Götterdämmerung?

Or has it been tried and failed already? Do they think I talked? That was not a possibility he wanted to consider. Not that he could do anything about it here and now.

Penetanguishene was looking at him hard. Paul said, "Been to a party?"

"Grand Hall," said Penetanguishene. He let himself fall into the wing chair and kicked off his shoes. "Vancina's maiden flight into opera landed with a resounding crash. Or rather a splat as hugish eggs will."

Paul chuckled.

"What?"

"You're a stitch."

"There was a reception afterward on the roof of the Karylanton. I didn't stay."

"Why not?"

"I'd rather be here. Ilu, I wish I could take you to these things." He rolled his head to the side to face Paul. "When the war is over I'll show you Beltava. The opera. The gardens. It is the most beautiful cultured elegant city in the known universe."

"I'm sorry. I would find them horrible." Paul envisioned its foundation built on piled bodies. "I know what it cost."

"Only because you attribute a positive worth to the kind of scum we assess in negative value."

"All life is precious."

"It is not."

"Through these lenses it is."

"You're not seeing the world, Paul. You're looking in a mirror."

"All life, especially human life, is precious if you believe in an interested Creator."

"Which I do not."

"I do."

"Do you? Still. That is interesting."

"And I think the Vikrhalt's breeding and weeding methods are cold-blooded and ruthless."

"Nothing is more ruthless than Nature. If you find order disturbing, try randomness. And democracy is nothing but the rule of the lowest common denominator. I don't want to talk about this." He got up and found a bottle in one of the cabinets, blew the meager dust out of two steins.

He set the bottle between them. Xylan. A traditional Five Hundred Day drink. The Rhaltcaptain poured himself a toast to ring in Empire year 1793. "Forever live the King and Queen."

He did not make Paul join him in that toast.

"Where is the King anyway?" said Paul.

Penetanguishene kept silent. Forbidden question.

Unknown to most of the Empire, the King and Queen were the same immortal. She changed faces from time to time to keep happy the mortals who identified so with their own gender.

" 'Kay," said Paul in the stubborn silence. He picked up the bottle. "You know, I knew the champion xylan drinker of the universe. He could down this whole thing and stay standing." He set the bottle down and added, "For about two seconds."

"The only thing that can contain that and stay upright is the bottle. Your friend is a liar."

"He was my father."

Paul saw Penetanguishene looking for a way to extricate his foot from his mouth. Paul added, "But he was a champion liar, too."

A look that passed for a smile crossed Penetanguishene's face. He refilled his own stein, poised the bottle over the second stein. "Hit?"

"No thanks."

"Your file says you drink to excess."

"I do, I did. Kind of forcibly quit. I don't miss it."

They moved to the chessboard.

"What is Penetanguishene?"

"What do you mean?"

"Your name. What's it mean?"

"It is where Marchale's thumb came down on a map of Earth. A place of shipwrecks."

"They can just name you like that?"

"Why not?"

"Don't immortals ever go bad?" said Paul.

"One. Selqarth, called the Deceiver. He lived by lies and he killed many of my kind. He killed his own kind. Anyone who got in his way. That was hundreds of years ago. He was taken care of."

"He was taken care of. You sound like a fucking I.I.N. spook."

"He was assassinated."

"Thank you." Paul appreciated plain speech. "So if immortals aren't perfect, why aren't you allowed to question anything they say?"

"I don't know. I told them you were dangerous. I wish they had believed me."

"Do you really?" That would mean he wished Paul were dead.

"No. Of course not. But they'll regret doing this. Checkmate."

"You can't do that."

"Why—?" he began, then saw.

"You can't put yourself in check like that."

Penetanguishene withdrew his man.

"A bit overanxious on the kill there."

"Here." Penetanguishene fished out the pill bottle and slapped it in front of Paul along with the xylan bottle. Joke, Penetanguishene style.

Paul cackled wickedly as Penetanguishene studied the board in mounting distress. Finally Penetanguishene threw his prisoner men on the board and said, "Take back your damn pieces."

The war was everywhere, dragging on forever when everyone said that modern war would be measured in degrees, and battles in ticks. The Queen's Squadron rushed from point to point, putting out fires that blazed in all places at once. The pilots did not play tag anymore. They slept, grabbing rest and quiet while they could. Their music was played very softly or not at all. No one counted days that weren't days in the Elsewhere. They only received distress calls and answered them, and knew that a defensive fight never wins.

Bases safe enough to put a c ship down on were hard to find. They lived inside their ships. Every planet in the Empire, with the exception of EtaCas and Valhalla, was in dire circumstance.

And more and more citizens of the Empire called Telegonia by the name it gave itself, New Earth. Whip swore you could tell when someone was about to surrender by the name they used for the enemy.

The Vikrhalt's tactics had been to hit the enemy's military installations, to break their armed forces in their nests and to control the stargates, and to constrict trade in and out of Telegonia.

The tactics of Telegonia and its free mortal allies had been the tactics of terror. They occupied towns, hit industry, civilian and military alike. They rained fire on civilians until whole planets surrendered and gave them the military installations, just to stop the terror.

"We forgot to account for the unthinkable. There is no tactic too low for the Telegonians. We play by rules which we have made, and some idealistic ass-brain *assumed* Telegonia would too. Unthinkable to us is jolly thinkable to them, otherwise we wouldn't have this war to begin with!" QB summed it up for all of them and spoke what no one else dared. "And which is why we seem to be, against all odds, losing it."

PART THREE

GÖTTER-
DÄMMERUNG

Northalia, Vikhinde
EtaCas
13 December 5246
I. 15. 1793

I.

Penetanguishene stared out the bay window at the falling snow. Paul was shocked to see a tear fall. Penetanguishene spoke facing the window, "There is to be a prisoner exchange. The Empire needed a high card to offer. I volunteered you. The Telegonians haven't said yet, but I know they'll accept."

Paul was numb. He took a deep breath, asked, "Who are you getting for me?"

"Kingsmen. A half cadre of them."

Penetanguishene waited a long time by the window before he spoke again. "Your happiness has become indispensable to my life."

"I'm happy here."

"The world outside has changed."

"Are you going to explain that?"

"No. You'll see when you get out."

"You're losing the war."

Penetanguishene said nothing, and Paul knew suddenly that he was right. *We're winning!* It was hardly possible, yet he knew that New Earth was winning against its superior foe. It would be over soon and Penetanguishene wanted Paul out of this cozy prison when it happened.

"I don't want to go home," said Paul.

Penetanguishene flicked his finger to signal imaginary guards as he had in Kobandrid Rog. He was calling Paul a liar.

"I get it," said Paul.

"How stupid can you be?" Penetanguishene scolded. "Why would you even try that with me?"

"I didn't want to hurt your feelings."

"Idiot."

"Yeah, sometimes."

The Rhaltcaptain wore his black dress uniform when he came to collect his prisoner.

"It's a little difficult," Penetanguishene said, pale as death and moving robotically. "You were reported dead. The circumstances of your captivity are known to no one."

"I will have to tell them everything," said Paul.

"I know this. I should warn you, you were awarded the Diamond Star five vants ago."

"Oh shit."

"You're also a short colonel."

This set Paul to laughing. "No, that's impossible. That requires infinite energy "

"Pardon?"

"Inside joke."

"You have to get changed."

Penetanguishene had brought coarse prison dress for him. Paul's clothes in the cabin were all comfortable and the best quality. Paul held up the rough smock. "Who's this supposed to fool?"

"Your grandmother. I don't know," Penetanguishene snapped.

Paul dressed. "It's not a requirement, not a written one leastwise, for you to be dead to receive a Diamond Star, but the recipients always have been. They're all going to be quite put out that they've given it to a live cocksucker."

"Unless your trying to get revenge, please shut up. I've been retching all morning."

"No, I'm not trying to get revenge. How do I look?"

"They want your head shaved."

"Oh, please."

"To hell with it. Let's go."

Penetanguishene led him out, took his time crossing the grounds, allowing Paul to see the garrison and count the forces that guarded the little cabin to assure him that he had been held against his will. His de- briefing officers would be sure to ask why he had not escaped.

During the exchange, Penetanguishene looked like he would pass out. At the moment of parting he gave Paul a small box. "For love, for honor." And he turned his back and marched out.

Paul's homecoming was a quiet, hushed, even grim affair.

The box was confiscated as soon as Paul was in allied hands, along with the clothes he was wearing, and he himself was run through an analyzer, scanned for bugs and bombs and phony parts, and given a thorough ident, then debriefed for days on end, physically painless but as intense and psychically grinding as Kobandrid Rog. The military men squirmed at the detailed account of where he had been, what he had been doing, as if it might come off on their hands. It did not occur to Paul to try to lie, and it did not occur to him that his own people might not believe him.

Why did he get himself captured? Why didn't he escape? Why didn't he commit suicide? And they asked over and over, did he talk? Paul assured them he had not. They asked, how not?

Paul had considered the possibility that Götterdämmerung had already been launched and failed. He was getting the idea now that they had not tried it yet, and were very worried that Paul had leaked it.

"Nobody gets through Kobandrid Rog without either talking or dying."

"I did."

"*You?* Why did they reward you with your nice little shack in Northalia?"

"Wasn't my reward. I wasn't the good dog. I was the bone."

They asked him why Penetanguishene had given him the box.

"I haven't the vaguest. You didn't let me see it."

They showed him. They were buttons. He guessed they were from his uniform jacket, the one he'd been wearing when he'd been captured. They had not been cleaned. A few blood and chemical soiled threads clung to them. The jacket itself had dissolved. The buttons were all that was left.

"Why did he want you to have these?"

Paul shrugged. "They're mine?"

He bet Penetanguishene didn't account for this, that the torture, the brainwashing, all meant nothing to these people. Stockholm Syndrome might not exist for all these officers seemed to care. There was the lingering suspicion that you asked for it. Here is the second half of rape. The idea that it's your own fault.

Didn't know that, did you, Penetanguishene.

Or maybe he did. And Paul suddenly knew why Penetanguishene had given him the buttons. He knew they would be confiscated and analyzed. The buttons would tell where he had been; they carried the residue of things done to him.

But all the blood on those buttons you thought would salvage my honor don't mean shit to these tiny brains. They see only Northalia. But thank you for trying.

Ah well. I have survived worse than this.

Keep telling yourself that, Paul.

Finally allowed free, Paul went to see the two crew members from his ship who had survived. Penetanguishene had released them as promised, but only one was still alive. One had suicided from survivor guilt shortly after coming home. The other refused to see Paul.

Paul went to see Trevor. He could not say that it never crossed his mind that, should something happen to Bristol, Paul would be left to comfort Trevor.

Always serious, she was somber now, all animation gone. She was bone slender. She woodenly let Paul kiss her cheek.

Paul hesitated. "Did you have the baby?"

She nodded.

"Boy or girl?"

"Boy," she said. Slit lips let that out and pursed again. There was a long pause before she said, "Bristol wanted to name him Paul. I named him Carver Luther."

"Good name," said Paul.

"Better than Paul."

"I get it."

He let himself out.

The only warm reception Paul received was from Vreeland Forgil. Leave it to an ambassador. He sent flowers and a note praising his valor, then followed it with a personal call. Forgil asked how in the world he had done it.

"Done what?"

"Hold fast in the face of hell?"

"I don't know. I wouldn't do it again. Then again if you'da asked me if I could do it the first time I'd've said hell no."

Forgil confided, "I am hesitant to tell you and ashamed to admit that there was talk of hitting you ourselves in Kobandrid Rog. I appealed for us to stand by our own."

"That's all right, ambassador. I'd've been rat happy to see a hit man at the time."

As Forgil was leaving, Paul said, "Oh, and Mr. Ambassador."

"Yes, sir?"

"I'm not as easy as you think I am. I know you only came here to verify my story. I like your approach better than the I.I.N.'s though."

Forgil paused, then said, "You're quite right. But I do believe you and I am grateful. More than you can know."

Paul had been assigned a therapist. He went only in hope that the man would certify him fit for duty.

The therapist was concerned with his trying to get back into society.

"Screw society. I want to get back to fucking work!' Paul shouted. "Last time I looked out there was a war on!"

He was told to see the medic first.

Paul stalked over directly. The first thing he noticed were sealed clear pouches containing his buttons on the white desktop.

The medic picked up one of the pouches. "Your buttons, especially the threads were very informative. They said quite a lot about where you've been."

Paul kept his hands buried in his pockets. "Yeah?"

"They confirm your story of Kobandrid Rog."

"Well, hell. Now tell me something I don't know."

To his surprise there actually was something. "The metal resonates of a cyn exposure. You were on the receiving end of a toxic exposure of cyn gas. You have accumulated a critical dose."

Paul remembered the choking orange haze of truth gas. "What does that mean?"

"Sudden death. Your cells will disintegrate all at once with massive hemorrhaging. The tissues will just give out. It should be quick. Though honestly not entirely painless. And I imagine frightening."

Paul had trouble absorbing this. The information only got as far as the intellect and stalled there. He felt nothing.

"When?"

"Don't know."

"Well Jesus, put it in the ball park."

"I guarantee you won't see sixty. But then again you might not see thirty-five either."

"My birthday is tomorrow." He would be thirty-five.

"I know."

Numb, Paul mumbled something like, "I see."

"Will you be all right?" the doctor asked as Paul headed for the door.

"Hell no," said Paul.

The doctor meant did he want an antianxiety agent. Paul did not.

He found a public car. He didn't remember the trip home; he was suddenly there.

Alone in his flat he started to shake. He hugged himself but could not hold down the tremors. Before he knew he was about to cry, a sob was already in his throat and tears were splashing down his cheeks. "Shit." He grit his teeth. The shaking only became worse, the tears a flood. "Shit, shit shit shit."

A lid on his endless possibilities. Death might hit anyone at any time, but not to see the lid was the trick. What was suddenly missing from Paul's future was the possibility of long life. That card was out of his deck. Never mind that he might not have drawn it anyway, the impossibility made the difference.

And the doctor! *Oh, you're so bloody clever, you are! You won't see sixty. Then again you might not see thirty-five.*

My birthday is tomorrow.

I know.

You knew. You knew. It wasn't so much the news— well, yes, it was the news—but the breaking of it had been so abominably glib. *Jesus Christ, what a way to tell a man he's about to die any second. You might not see thirty-five and you KNEW that was tomorrow. Damn you damn you damn you!*

He was slapping the wall.

"SHIT!"

You chose that way to tell me. I could kill you for that! And Penetanguishene.

"You didn't tell me." His voice rasped from his clogged throat.

He didn't know how Penetanguishene was supposed to have told him: By the way, besides all the other things I did to you, cut your fingers off, put a nail through your ball, sliced your eyes, boiled you alive, killed your men, made the woman you love hate you, ruined your name, I also in effect planted a time bomb in you. You don't have the rest of your life like you think you do.

You might have told me, you goddamned coward.

You murdered me, goddamn you and you didn't tell
me! *Son of a bitch. Son of a bitch.*

He beat the wall, split the skin on his knuckles,
slapped the bloody smudges with his palms till they
stung. *God! God! God!*

He slid down against the wall into a fetal crouch
hugging himself again, feeling small and more alone
than he'd ever felt in his shortened life, in or out of
Kobandrid Rog.

Blind-sided.

Anything in Kobandrid Rog had been expected.
After Bristol was shot, there was nothing Penetanguishene could do to shock him. It was *fair* in that one
expected to be taken apart piece by piece in Kobandrid Rog.

This. This was after he'd gone home and hollered,
"Ollie ollie in free!" And the worst of it was, Penetanguishene wasn't asking him questions. The game was
over and there was no one to fight and this pain was
all for no purpose whatsoever.

Penetanguishene had wondered where Paul's breaking point was.

It's here. It's right here.

Fort Ujiji, New Earth
EtaCas
1 January 5247
II. 14. 1793

Fleet operations summoned Paul from his home just after midnight. A military car collected him, and MPs admitted him from the quiet night to the glaring tense operations room. Holomaps glowed at every turn.

Paul hadn't taken off his scarf and no one had greeted him when someone said, "They moved your friend into a field command. We need you to tell us what the hell he thinks he's doing."

Paul paused to orient himself and untangle what he was being told obliquely. "Your friend," spoken so snidely, had to be Penetanguishene. The rest of it was impenetrable. Feeling put upon, Paul said silkily, barely audible, "I am not a mind reader."

"He's moving troops during the holiday truce. He's replaced General Kayir."

"Who's got Kobandrid Rog?"

"They dozed it. Your friend had to get a real job."

Details of the current maneuvers were slapped before Paul, with a sector map of Aithar.

"Aithar? They gave him a command on Aithar?"

"Here's the setup," said the officer, ignoring Paul's surprise. "The Vikhens were getting their tails whipped. Cease-fire came just in time for us not to push them off the planet. Then they shitcan Kayir and bring in Penetanguishene—"

"To Aithar?"

"Why not. He knows the terrain."

Knows the terrain? He was just a kid! "I'll tell you why not—"

"First thing your buddy does is re-take all this territory during the cease-fire. He's halfway across the continent. Probably farther now, the transmissions just haven't arrived yet. The stop order never got to him. Vikrhalt insists he knows there's a cease-fire. Of course he knows there's a cease-fire. It's on the news. But no officer takes orders from the news. Here's the odd part. He's not covering his butt. As if walking over the land makes it his. He's not leaving any troops to hold it. We have a landing force ready to come down at truce's end and just take it all back. Fact is," he glanced at his chronometer, checked Aithar time, "they're doing it now."

"No. You don't want to do that. He's setting detonators. He'll wait till you're down and then devastate the continent."

"He can't. Scorched earth isn't a Vikhen tactic. This whole thing started over our right to cut our own forests."

"You're not dealing with the Vikrhalt. They've washed their hands. The orders didn't get through on purpose. The Vikrhalt wants that stargate back and the planet is expendable. They've sent Penetanguishene in to spend it."

"No, no. He's still a soldier of the Vikrhalt."

"Absolutely," said Paul. "And without orders, they're expecting him to make the foul choice and take the fall for it himself. It's a trap."

"That is not the Vikhen way."

"Oh, yes it is. They know what he'll do, and he knows what they want him to do—what they want but can't order. The Vikrhalt is coming unglued here and they're going to take the New Terran 4th and 85th invasion Fleets with them if you don't get them the hell out of there NOW."

"That can't be right."

"Then why the fuck did you ask me?"

"Thank you Lieutenant Colonel. That will be all."

They didn't want his input. They wanted an echo.

Paul made for the door. He did not need to collect his things, he'd never taken them off. Then there was a consternation among the controllers. Their monitors all snowed over. Transmissions from the tachyon repeater to Aithar ceased.

"What happened? We lost contact with the invasion

force." The controllers re-checked the chronometers. "What time is it on Aithar?" They tried all channels, all machines, trying to raise the ships in the area. It would be a long wait before the signal could make the round trip.

"What's going on?"

Into the barrage of questions, Paul offered the obvious answer, "I guess he torched the planet."

"No, no. He couldn't do that," the intelligence officer was saying, but Paul had already left the room.

Some of the officers dogged him out, insisting to his back, "It can't be. It's not Vikhen. They just destroyed a unique habitat."

Paul spun and was shouting in their faces before they could stop, and they almost walked into him. "Doesn't it ever give you even a moment's pause to fight such a discriminating enemy? They confine their targets to us, the military. We don't even need to waste ships defending defenseless cities because their defenselessness protects them from the Vikrhalt. The same mentality that scorns individual rights, when faced with a city is suddenly all protective. We hack and slash and hit anywhere. We who hold the individual sacred can justify bombing civilian centers. And a unique habitat. What the hell is that to us—unless the Vikrhalt bombs it. Suddenly the Vikrhalt is fighting the way we do and we're appalled."

"Aren't you? Appalled?"

"Disappointed. There used to be something to admire about the Vikrhalt. Now they're just like us."

"Go home, Paul. You're still brainwashed. You don't even talk like you anymore."

Paul, he was now. Like a prisoner in Kobandrid Rog. What happened to *Lieutenant Colonel Strand?*

"So are you. Did any of you jingoistic parrots ever once have a thought that was wholly your own?" Hadn't he asked Penetanguishene that once? The two sides had become indistinguishable.

"Someone call a medic."

A voice echoed over a speaker, "Dr. Hannof. Dr. Hannof to ops."

"I'm going," said Paul, and walked to the car.

Fort Arctica
Aithar
II. 15. 1793

All Good Children go to Aithar. Commander Rachelson relieve current commander and take command of invasion force until replacement can be organized.

The c ships came down in a blizzard of their own making. The winds of Fort Arctica were calm and the ice crystals quickly settled again around the c ships like a scene in a glass bubble that has been shaken.

Penetanguishene came out to meet his replacement and saluted, arm across his chest. His face was as unreadable as ever. The expressions of the troops behind him, which he handed obediently over to Race, were hostile. If Penetanguishene felt anything about being relieved of command, he showed none of it. His troops did. Race had thought they would welcome the arrival of a sane commander. No such thing.

Penetanguishene had never held a field command before. Race, who had commanded for a long time, picked up immediately the sense from the fighting men, the fanatical loyalty to the Rhaltcaptain.

"How long have you had this command, ehre?" Race asked.

"Thirteen days," said Penetanguishene.

How had he done it? Instilled that much loyalty in so little time. Maybe the vondesi did have mind control.

Before Penetanguishene the troops had been under command of a general who spent their lives like loose change. Into this Penetanguishene had come like a dark angel. The troops knew what he was, the monster of Kobandrid Rog, but God, he was on their side and he was getting them out of there. And letting them win. They had greeted the new commander with relief approaching adoration. He was the tough and dirty tactician they had been longing for all through this dismal war. For his first order, he'd sent the old CO, the general, to fill a position which promised the life expectancy of a gnat. He'd been killed immediately, and all the men and women who had been dreading that assignment cheered.

From there he had been so calm, so fearless, his orders so marvelously defiant of the truce which served only New Earth, that they followed eagerly.

And the enemy, so accustomed to the Empire having its hands tied behind its back, had walked into the trap like beasts into a slaughterhouse.

The celebration of that victory ran all night long, as the Vikhinden troops watched the continent burn.

They had withdrawn to the arctic wasteland and were now told that their savage savior was being recalled in disgrace. They were to follow the ace Race Rachelson—a hero who never saw his enemy's face— while they waited for a new general.

They glared at their interim CO with murderous resentful eyes.

After reviewing the troops, Race turned to Penetanguishene in puzzlement. "Your people would follow you to hell."

Dark eyes looked far away. The Rhaltcaptain started back to his transport.

"Very convenient, considering where I am bound."

Fort Arctica
Aithar
II. 21. 1793

Outside, ground crews were moving equipment. A woman passing the window of the chalet which served as headquarters looked in. She lowered her hood and lifted her goggles and smiled at the handsome commander inside.

"You're being paged," said Maya at Race's side.

Despite his reputation, Maya had never seen him with anyone. The war had kept them all busy. After the war he would make up lost ground no doubt.

Race shook his head.

"I can hold the fort," Maya offered.

"When have I ever settled for second?" said Race, and he turned his head and looked down at her.

She missed it, or pretended to. She gathered in her concentration. She was not going to run this time. She had practiced for hundreds of years how to mesmerize and control a mortal's attention. but she fumbled her thoughts and pieces scattered all ways. His gaze remained steady and deep. Outdone, she looked away.

He said, "Come with me." He extended a hand, palm up, waiting for hers with seductive insistence.

She avoided his compelling gaze. "No, ehre." She felt she was drowning, intimacy like a physical presence pushing all the air out of the room.

"It's an ultimatum, Maya," he said, tender and threatening.

"You don't know what you're asking."

"I'm not asking."

"I would choose to face anything else."

"I am sorry. This is an order."

She laughed, tried to. It came out a dry, spent bark. "On what authority?"

"Didn't anyone ever tell you? Rules don't apply to people in love."

"People is plural, Race."

"I know."

"I have not said that I love you."

"I noticed."

I don't. I can't. I don't know how and don't get it into your beautiful thick head that you're going to teach me, you cocky feral bastard.

As if he had read her mind he said, "You look at me differently since I told you."

"No, I don't."

"You see me as some kind of beast."

"Race, I always saw you as some kind of beast." She heard her mistake as soon as she said it. But she was getting the idea that she was betraying nothing. *He knows.*

She looked up at him and again tried to cloud his mind. He was absolutely beyond her control. His gray eyes were as clear as ever and she wondered if he hadn't got a hold of *her*.

"You don't know what I am," she whispered.

"Yes, I do. Who we were is not who we are."

Was this the beast from the wilderness telling her that he wasn't a beast? *Or does he know I used to kill worms at a whim and forgives me now that I know they are more than worms?*

Her lower lip trembled, voice shook. She was trying desperately not to cry in front of him. "Race, you're going to die." *Did you hear what I just said?*

"Must everything be forever?"

"Yes." She yanked out of his draw. She misunderstood his question and she found a shield in indignation. *I am not this evening's entertainment!*

He only repeated the command: "Come with me."

She backed against the wall. "What do you want from me?"

After a long thought he gave a hesitant questioning answer as if to ask: Is this too much? "Love?"

Heart hammered; mouth prickled. Panic like she had never felt in the cockpit gripped her inside. "You cannot love me, I am a god."

There it was.

And Race of all things, snorted and gave a wry smile in patient benign scorn. "When you begin in a world whose only time is right now, and go from there to bouncing in and out of reality and see just how enormous and complex and ordered the universe— and the Elsewhere—is, you people lose a little of your wonder. You're not a god. You just live a long time."

Close enough to feel the heat in the space between them, she was about to say, "I am not part of your feral right now. I am tomorrow," but he cut her off.

"Shut up, Maya, I'm on a sundive here. I have never been so afraid as I am in this moment and don't say anything I have to finish this all at once or I'll lose my nerve again, something I'm not used to doing except around you and it really pisses me off what you do to me but I can't help it and I've tried to stay away from you and I can't even do that so here it is: The moment I saw you— She walks in, this incredible snot and all the mere mortals pale in her shadow and I suddenly know she isn't. I haven't looked at anyone since I saw you; I haven't even noticed if anyone was there. I know I can lose my life just for asking but it's yours anyway and I don't give a shit. I don't have forever, I can only offer all my tomorrows and as many of yours as I can fill, Maya will you marry me?"

She'd had a retort ready, but for the wrong question. She'd been braced for the usual: This moment is all that is real and we might not have tomorrow. Come up and spend the night with me.

She tensed to rigidity, felt the blood flee her head, leaving her dizzy and pale. She thought she was about to faint, and she stood motionless as stone until the spell passed. Panic was strangling her. She forced the choking fear to loosen its grip. *If I don't do anything stupid, I won't even remember this one thousand years from now.*

Blood rushed to her face and made it burn. She spoke slowly, as if the words themselves were trying to keep their balance on a tightrope, "You're out of your goddam mind."

She exited the headquarters and walked away across the snow field.

Fort Ujiji, New Earth
EtaCas
7 January 5247

Word reached the Interstellar Intelligence Network
that Penetanguishene was back on EtaCas. "So what
is he doing now?" the I.I.N. agent demanded.

"Why don't you ask him," said Paul. He turned to
an Army video phone and said, "Intercontinental."

"Country?" the machine voice inquired.

"Vikhinde."

There was a pause for the request to go through a
labyrinth of clearances. In a second the machine said,
"City?"

"Beltava."

"What are you doing?" said the intelligence officer.

"Calling him up."

Paul thought it ought to be difficult, ringing up an
enemy commander in war time, but it was as simple
as doing it. In a moment Penetanguishene's face appeared on the screen. On seeing who was calling, he
showed as much surprise as he ever allowed in public.
He did not give a greeting or ask questions. He
waited.

"What are you doing?" said Paul.

There was a disgruntled humph behind him from an
I.I.N. agent who thought Paul was playing with them.

After a long pause Penetanguishene said, "Take
back your damn pieces." And the image went blank.

Paul turned off the phone, stunned.

The I.I.N. agents were all over him. "What did he
say? What did that mean? Is that code?"

Paul nodded dully. "The war is lost."

"Can they be that far ahead?"

"No. Them. Us. He said he's lost. Vikhinde's lost to us."

"You believe that?"

"He does. He can't lie."

"Maybe he just learned how. To fox you."

"No, it fits. It's why they dozed Kobandrid Rog. It's a preamble to invasion—invasion of Vikhinde. They don't want to get caught holding that card at game's end. And it's why they took the Aithar stargate. Something to bargain with. This is the end game."

"You don't think a lie is a possibility?"

"I suppose I should, as remote as it seems."

"You really think him a man of honor?"

"Oh hell, it goes way past honor. Obsession is more like it. But I also know there's nothing he wouldn't do for the Empire. Lying included. But really, in light of everything else, I'm beginning to wonder if we need to use Götterdämmerung."

"Perhaps you're right."

The quickness of it brought Paul to silence. *They're humoring me.*

Perhaps you're right.

There was a lie even he could hear.

Perhaps I'm right. Perhaps I'm right. Bullshit, perhaps I'm right!

Paul knew he'd already begun to talk like Penetanguishene. Maybe he could hear like him as well. Such a transparent *lie*.

These officers would not for a moment consider not using Götterdämmerung. Because they did not simply want the Empire broken—it already was. They wanted Vikhinde itself.

Paul at once knew what this was all about.

Unless somebody stops Götterdämmerung, we are going to obliterate a beaten Empire.

II.

Even before war had been declared, the Vikrhalt had built an arsenal of doubles of Telegonian officials. They were called doppelgängers, spies molded and trained to pass for high ranking Telegonians.

Empire Intelligence intercepted an order for Lt. Colonel Paul Strand to report to a secure room at Fleet HQ prepared to divulge what he knew of operation Götterdämmerung to Admiral Bertrand Krestly. Strand's orders gave him twenty-four hours lead time in which to assure the validity of the orders. But the delay also gave the Vikrhalt time to get their Krestly doppelgänger into position.

It was necessary for the real Krestly to be stopped from making the appointment. Assassination was an option, but it turned out to be easier just to stall him on Telegonia's infamous traffic grid for two hours. By then the doppelgänger had met with Paul Strand, collected Götterdämmerung and returned to Beltava. Let Telegonia choke on the deception when they discovered it.

It was done smoothly. The Krestly doppelgänger returned to command central to report his success.

Among his superiors were two new faces. One he knew from news vids and scandal sheets to be the vondesi Penetanguishene. The other was a woman he had never seen before, not in this guise anyway.

She was short for a modern woman, not impressively beautiful, more like a stern and pretty nurse than a regal figure. The deference of all around her was the most noteworthy thing about her. The spy suddenly knew who she was. He was about to drop before her on one knee, but with a motion of her dark eyes—a quick sideways flick—she belayed that and she gave the Rhalt sign for him to proceed. "How do they mean to tear down our empire? What is Götterdämmerung?"

The man gave the Queen a quick bow of his head, cleared his throat in Krestly fashion as had become his second nature. "Ehremat." And he told them what Paul Strand had told him.

Götterdämmerung was a two-headed monster. One part was a diversionary assault on the Hydrus Base. It was a strategic target and the assault would be sufficiently devastating that the Empire could not afford to ignore it.

This attack would cover the launching of a fleet of innocuous-looking cargo and trader and supply ships from a secret base located beyond the Cygnus stargate. The ships would be carrying the immortal virus. They would disperse and approach EtaCas by widely divergent routes. Once they left the factory and passed through the stargate, there would be no tracking them all.

"When?" said the Queen.

"Imminent," said the spy. "Strand doesn't know the exact date and time."

"Where is our squadron right now?" said the Queen.

Penetanguishene pointed up. The Queen's Squadron had been called from Aithar to orbit EtaCas on standby.

"If we send our squadron to the factory and the reserves to Hydrus, who is within twenty-nine hours of Valhalla?"

"Both of them, ehremat. On the margins."

She turned back to the officers. "Send them at once to take out this factory. Send a conventional force after them to back them up. Yes?"

She checked all the faces for objections. Her vondesi looked troubled. "Yes?" she said.

"A question for the doppelgänger," said Penetanguishene.

The Queen motioned him to proceed.

"Did Lieutenant Colonel Strand identify himself to you?" Penetanguishene asked the spy.

"Thoroughly."

"How thoroughly."

"Completely."

"Why?"

"What do you mean, why?"

"Why would he go through elaborate lengths to establish his identity to you, when you were the one receiving secret information? You were in a secure room."

The Krestly double-cleared his throat. "We weren't in the secure room."

There was a stirring of the other officers.

"Why not?" said the Rhaltcaptain.

"Strand was nervous. At the last minute he decided not to go in. He was rather paranoid about giving information in a place where he was expected to. We ended up in a children's petting zoo."

"A what?"

"He was trying to be unpredictable. He wanted a place no one would monitor us."

"That is what a secure room is for."

"He preferred the zoo."

"Where he identified himself to you, point for point on all the recognition flags in our files, I am certain."

The double grew uncomfortable. It was as if the vondesi had been walking in his footsteps. "So he identified himself as Lieutenant Colonel Paul Strand. What is wrong with that?"

"He was not."

"Well, it wasn't one of *ours*, so who do you suppose it was, ehre, and for what purpose?"

"I have no idea."

The intelligence officers had enough of this. The ranking officer broke in impatiently, "It pleases me to say that you are slipping, Rhaltcaptain. I have never liked you." The truthsayer would know that he meant that wholeheartedly. "Suppose they did sniff out our ruse. If they were to give us false information, they could have

used the real Paul Strand to do it. What purpose would
using a double serve? It makes no sense."

"Nothing much does anymore," said Penetanguishene. "I think it would be a mistake to suppose that
just because it makes no apparent sense, that it isn't
happening."

"You are delaying a vital mission. I would advise
you keep any other groundless objections to yourself."

"No," the Queen intervened. They were all startled
to hear her voice. They hushed to let her speak. "The
vondesi has been our loyal and efficient servant in
these worst of times. We shall listen to you."

"Don't go to Valhalla, ehremat."

An explosion of sputtering surrounded them. The
intelligence officer broke in despite himself. "What?
EtaCas is about to be besieged with a lethal virus and
you say don't go to Valhalla!"

"For Götterdämmerung to be the killing stroke that its
name implies, it would need to reach all the immortals in
one stroke. The immortals are much safer scattered."

"But immortals should not be made to play the odds.
They all ought to be free to go to where it is safe."

"Is there such a place? The Telegonians are making
us stake everything on Valhalla."

"Then indulge them. We can defend Valhalla
against anything so long as we have faster than light
ships and they don't."

"Then I would assume that they do," Penetanguishene said quietly.

"Penetanguishene, your value to this empire is as a
truthsayer. You are not, never were, and never will
be a strategist."

"What is the Cygnus Gate?"

"That," said the doppelgänger. "Now that gave me
the only tense moment in my masquerade. I'd never
heard of it. I soon gathered that I wasn't supposed to
have heard of it and my lack of inquiry gave Strand
some alarm. He said: 'Aren't you going to ask me what
Cygnus is?' I very quickly said: 'Listen to me, you little
shit. I'm getting real tired of you trying to get behind

me with your I've got a secret shit. If you're waiting for me to beg you to tell me what I'm supposed to be hearing, you'll wait till hell freezes over. Are we straight on that, Strand? Get on with your job.' "

"Very Krestly. We're all impressed. So what did he tell you? What is Cygnus Gate?"

"It's property of Alpha Centauri, Earth's oldest ally since their war of independence. The gate leads to a worthless location, remote and not very hospitable. Good place for setting up a factory no one wants around civilization."

"But where exactly?"

"I don't know. He doesn't know and it's irrelevant. The gate leads there. You want to know if it's farther than twenty-nine hours for a c ship without the gate. I'd say probably."

"We are meant to send c ships blind through a stargate that we don't know where leads? I don't like it."

"One seriously doubts you were meant to."

Penetanguishene deferred to the Queen. "Ehremat?"

"Dispatch our squadron at once," she said. She turned toward the door. They all saluted her exit.

The Krestly double-muttered, "So much for Ambassador Forgil's assurances that Telegonia would never use the virus."

Penetanguishene said, "The ambassador's promises were quite sincere. He has a genuine horror of germ warfare. If there is a plague, he has been out-maneuvered."

"What do you mean if there is a plague? What have we just been talking about?"

"I would be suspect of information so easily had."

"Yes, you would. You like to pull their balls off first. You ought to get some lessons in subtlety. Kobandrid Rog was a waste of real estate. I brought home Götterdämmerung and you can't stand it and that's all there is."

"That wasn't Lieutenant Colonel Strand."

"Just because you couldn't get it out of him."

Penetanguishene quit the chamber.

That wasn't Paul.

Fleet HQ, New Earth
EtaCas
9 January 5247
II. 23. 1793

Paul sat in detention, elbows resting on his knees,
his head bowed over his loosely clasped hands. Admiral Krestly had stalked out and sealed the room two
hours ago.

Paul waited.

The door opened again at last. The officer found
him as the admiral had left him, sitting docilely, hanging his head. Paul did not look up when the door
finally opened again. He knew it would be a military
investigator. The officer said nothing and Paul finally
lifted his head to see who it was. " 'Lo, Luke." They'd
sent his brother.

Luke Strand gazed down, stern and gray as an iron
ship. His buzz cut hair made his head look as flat as
an old aircraft carrier. He shook his head, if one could
call the slow grim side to side motion a shake. "You
always were a dickhead."

Paul had nothing to say. He had not seen Luke
since before his captivity.

Luke unbuttoned his boxy coat. He did not come
straight to business. He said what had been on his
mind. "Why the hell did you go public with all that
shit?"

Paul felt a moment's umbrage. *Welcome home, kid.
Good to see you in one somewhat pared down piece.
Glad you're alive. How are you, kid? Why the hell did
you go public with all that shit?*

"Same old Luke," Paul muttered, then answered,

238

"Better than to pile it in a closet until the stack of bones tumbles out of its own weight."

"Didn't you think about how Mom must feel?"

"Mom is doing just fine; why didn't you ask her? Don't hide behind Mom if you've got a problem. You're the one who's squirming, brasshole. You must know I have been conditioned to zero tolerance for deception these past months."

"You've been conditioned to talk funny," said Luke, inspecting him critically. "What happened to your eyes?"

"Well," said Paul. Stupid question.

"Shitty match," said Luke.

"It works."

Luke's attention had already dropped to Paul's chest. "I wouldn't wear that if I were you."

He meant the medal pinned to Paul's green jacket, the D.S., Diamond Star. Paul called it his Deep Shit. The government had made the mistake of awarding it; Paul should have the grace not to pretend he had earned it.

"You would never be me, Luke, and you'll never have one, so don't bother yourself deciding what you'd do."

Luke Strand was too prosaic, too straight-line by-the-book. You had to be a raving maniac to win a D.S. And being dead helped.

"You would think after that business in Northalia—"

"Oh, bugger Northalia!"

"There's been enough buggering in Northalia."

There hadn't been any, but this was totally beside any point, and Paul refused to answer to it or explain personal details. And he had more important things to worry about. "Get off Northalia! I would do it again. What no one addresses is the man I lost as a direct result of my own blunder and no one gives a shit. Bristol Derrah died because I was stupid and I didn't believe in vondesi. That's my sin—my only sin, and if you don't count that, then I'll wear this medal, damn you. Now get on with what you came for!"

Luke sat, opened the case he had brought. "I've been sent to ident you." There was a load of elaborate equipment in the case.

Paul shrugged for him to go ahead. "What do you think?"

"Oh, it's you," said Luke taking out a DNA blood gauge. "I knew that the moment I walked in."

Paul suddenly lost all anger. *You may be a brass plated dildo, but you're all right, Luke.*

Luke set the blood gauge to zero. "Why didn't you tell Operation Götterdämmerung to Admiral Krestly? Arm."

Paul rolled up his sleeve in silence, shook his head.

Paul had been stuck in a balky public car when he was supposed to be here reporting to Admiral Krestly. By the time Paul arrived, thoroughly late, he expected Krestly to be hours gone and MPs waiting for Paul. He found instead a recently arrived Krestly, furious, but not at Paul. Krestly had been delayed himself on the traffic grid. He was relieved to see Paul here, because someone had told him that Paul had been here earlier and left—with Admiral Krestly, someone else said. "Idiots," Krestly had grumbled.

The two officers entered the secure room and went through the I.I.N.'s elaborate clearance procedures.

Krestly had sat where Luke was now, smug with his new clearance, and waiting to receive New Earth's ultimate secret.

"What is Götterdämmerung?"

Paul had opened his mouth.

And his throat constricted so that he could not talk. Could not breathe. He sat in panic, not breathing. A calm detached part of his brain held aloof thinking: This is interesting. I have to breathe.

And Krestly had to call parameds when Paul passed out.

They had pulled Paul off the floor, revived him and left. Krestly resecured the room and started again. Paul sat there blinking and breathing, looking at the admiral. Finally he'd said, "No, sir."

He'd watched the admiral turn all imaginable shades of red and purple. Krestly ordered, demanded, threatened, and eventually stormed out.

Paul hadn't tried the door, knew it would be sealed. He hadn't left the bench until Luke arrived.

Luke withdrew the gauge from Paul's arm, checked random cells for DNA makeup. He glanced aside to Paul to answer the question. "Well? Why didn't you tell him?"

Paul tried to answer why, but he did not know. His eyes had gone unaccountably liquid. He blinked, shook his head, mumbled, "Just couldn't."

He physically couldn't. He had buried the secret so deep that even he could not get it back out.

Fort Ujiji, New Earth
EtaCas
9 January 5247
II. 23. 1793

Paul returned to his office at the Army base. Later in the afternoon his door opened and MPs tramped in, took positions on his flanks, and crossed their arms in waiting. They did not explain themselves.

Paul glanced at his watch, at the calendar. He guessed it must be starting. Götterdämmerung. These men were waiting to see if he was a traitor.

No, they were waiting to *prove* he was a traitor. They already thought they knew.

"Can I ask what you're waiting for?" said Paul.

The two heraldically placed gargoyles did not move.

Paul started for the door. A beam rifle angled out to block the way.

" 'Kay," said Paul turning back in. He sat down. "What's going on?"

His blocks of stone would not reply.

Götterdämmerung is in motion.

If something went wrong—and a lot could go wrong—they would assume that it was because Paul had talked.

O Jesus.

At length one of the gargoyles moved. He glanced at his wrist chronometer, exchanged glances with his companion. They lifted beam rifles in readiness.

Ah. Dead time.

The MPs moved in to arrest Paul. Each one seized an arm and hauled him to his feet.

Suddenly one paused to touch his ear to listen to his com.

In the next moment they dropped Paul and charged out of the room.

Alone in his office, Paul knew what they must have heard to let him go.

The Valhalla resonator had gone dead.

His legs went spongy beneath him. He sank to the floor and sat, shaking.

Valhalla

The immortal Kveta leaned against the balustrade of the tower in the Spring Quarter, feeling the breeze off of the crystal lake, watching trees drop white blossoms into the water.

The sudden explosion sent her crouching and clutching for the railing as the tower rattled and the whole world shook. With a shattering roar from above, the fleeting image of a c ship gashed the artificial sky, its weapons blazing.

The c ships were not supposed to be here.

Ilu! Ilu! Why have they turned on us?

A bright flash and a mushroom cloud blossomed from the Winter Quarter.

A rumble in the ground and a torrid wind.

The tower swayed. Kveta held tight, then with a shrieking crack, the tower broke and in slow motion at first, quicker at the end, she was falling. It was so surreal and she had been alive for so long, that the immortal never quite believed she was plunging to her death.

The Queen's Squadron emerged on the other side of the Cygnus stargate into a firestorm. They had expected guardian ships. They had not expected there to be so many and so ready for them.

Suddenly the c ships were flying through a gauntlet of enemy fighters. Maya hammered the accelerator to full to get out of the swarm of them. Her wings flickered with glancing shots sliding off her reflectors.

The other c ships had done the same. It was instinctive by now. When in trouble, fly flat out for the sun.

But worse than the ready ambush was the sun itself.

Ionnina shouted as they streaked toward the red wall which filled their forward vision. "Red Death! We've been had!"

Eric cried: "It's Betel-fucking-guese!"

Betelguese. Nightmare of nightmares. Betelguese was so huge it could hardly be called a sun. It was a fiery *region* of blazing near-vacuum, less dense than breathable air, a pulsing diameter of between 480 and 800 million miles of red vagueness. The star itself was bigger than some solar *systems*. Betelguese was nearly one light hour across. Its mass was twenty times Sol, but its volume was equal to 160 *million* Sols. It hadn't the density to catapult the c ships into the Elsewhere.

QB: "There's no laboratory here, Rachelson. This is a kill jar."

Race: "Queen's Knight to Queen's Squadron. Shake these fighters and go to high ground. Are you with me, kits?"

He was on the shortest course into the red gas vastness that was Betelguese.

Maya hit the confirm beacon and fell in with him, weaving an evasive pattern. Ahead of her was nothing but red. Behind her one pursuer crinkled suddenly into a cinder.

Maya: "Temperature?"

"Watch your gauges," Race sent, his signal breaking up. "Remember to account for the return through the corona. Best, kits."

Transmissions ended as Betelguese took over the radio.

Maya's ship met the corona rushing out like a wave to meet her. She speared through its tenuous heat shroud at top acceleration. Even this 3100-degree gasball had a hellish corona. The pursuers veered off behind her. She caught fragments of their alarmed transmissions as the Queen's Squadron plunged into the furnace.

Weird and nightmarish to dive into a sun and not come out Elsewhere.

Her sensors were overwhelmed and washed out, reading only vacuous heat and red oblivion. Flying blind, she could not even see who was around her.

She switched to computer pilot, letting the machine figure the best guess for avoiding collision based on its last reading of relative positions, and pre-planned emergency flight paths. If everyone in the squadron was on computer pilot, they would not collide. Probably.

Her viewports showed her nothing but red blaze. She checked her working instruments. Temperature gauge. That was working. Creeping up.

Slippery as the c ships were, they were not designed to fly through millions of klicks of solar furnace. She could not afford to maintain this path. She needed to risk a blind turn.

She was heating up so that she need not look at the gauges. This was not from friction; it was the sustained heat of the sun with nowhere to dissipate. And millions more kilometers of it ahead.

She punched in a turn command, blind emergency mode. The ship veered up steeply on a path no one was supposed to cross.

Nearing the surface, she could see a gradation in the redness. She caught herself holding her breath as if she were underwater. The red swirling thinned. She was growing very hot in the cockpit. Sweat rolled down her sides. *Ilu!* And still the corona to go.

And in the midst of it, the resonator kicked in. A pulsing alarm signaled on her resonator receiver.

Her heart shuddered. She almost grabbed the stick and executed a racking turn. She thought someone in the squadron was sending this signal, the only kind that could penetrate the sun, warning her that she was on collision course.

She kept herself from the panic move, remembering: *If I can't see him, he can't see me. No one knows if we're about to collide or not.*

And c ships could not send; they could only receive on the resonator.

So who was signaling?

Valhalla.

Valhalla is under attack and I am trapped inside Red Death. Ilu! Ilu! This isn't happening.

Temperature crept off the instruments. Her breath came hot in her mask. She thought something had to be about to melt or burst into flames.

The resonator signal gave twenty-nine hours warning. Any attacker coming through Valhalla's stargate still had twenty-nine light hours to travel before coming into firing range of Valhalla.

The Queen's Squadron was still twenty-seven hours from Valhalla *if* they could get to FTL. *And we CAN'T!*

Outside temperature shot up. The corona. Maya held her breath, sweat streaming into her eyes, her vision swirling with the gaseous cloud.

Get me through this.

Clear!

Maya gasped. The coolant system kicked in, washed through the cockpit.

There were no fighters in visual range. Her sensors picked up other c ships surfacing within several kilometers. None of them were beyond the horizon. The horizon was too distant for anyone to have traveled beyond it.

The c ships came streaking out, pulling gas trails behind them. They were scattered over 30 light seconds of each other. Maya moved in to regroup.

She had located the positions of the enemy fighters. None of them were closing in. They were all milling back at the stargate, with no further attempt to come after the c ships.

As if they knew that the c ships must come to them.

"QB to squadron. Anyone notice that the *pursuit* ships *aren't*?"

Jav: "They know we're bottled."

Tak: "Who's on the resonator?"

QB: "Valhalla."

The squadron needed to get back through that stargate. Without it or a dense star they were 520 years away from EtaCas like any other spaceship. The Telegonians had learned their Achilles heel and had hung them up by it.

"Queen's Knight to squadron. Regroup. I see seven. Who's not here?"

Tak: "Whip. Where's Whip?"

Ionnina: "There." She shot a course into Tak's locator.

The eighth c ship, Queen's Castle, was just emerging from the sun, pulling a long red wake, itself glowing red-white. Just as they were thinking he had made it clear, a wing flaked off as if made of soggy cardboard, and the ship spun out in a wild whirling course, spraying off pieces of itself and coughing out a Kingsman pod along the way.

"Queen's Knight to Queen's Castle Echo. Tak, get that pod. I'll cover. QB take the squadron. I think the gate guardians are going to move."

And sure enough, the fighters blocking the stargate edged away from their position of advantage, lured by the prospect of capturing a crippled c ship.

QB: "Hold back, Squadron. Let them hang themselves. Ion, Maya, ready on the button with me."

Several of the sublight fighters peeled off from their posts and moved in on Whip's ship. As a number of them closed, QB ordered, "Now."

QB, Maya, and Ionnina sent a destruct message to Whip's ship. That part of the vessel was still functioning, and it annihilated itself, taking the nearest enemy scavengers with it.

Maya picked off another fighter who had strayed wide of the gate.

By then Tak had Whip's pod in his hold and the Queen's Squadron was ready to make a rush at the more lightly guarded stargate.

They shot through the gauntlet back into known space to orbit around a substantial sun.

Jav: "How's our time?"

Race: "We're all right. Twenty-seven hours to Valhalla. The resonator started eleven degrees ago. We have over an hour margin."

As he said so, the resonator's pulse quit.

After a confused silence, Eric asked if he were having problems with his resonator chamber.

"No. They quit sending."

Valhalla had two resonators at the stargate and one at the fortress itself, for backup and fail-safe. It could not be accident that all three were silent. Whatever caused it to go silent had just happened. The resonators had nothing to do with time or travel, only with the event. Its pulse was instantaneous everywhere at once.

Eric: "Did they call off the alert?"

Tak: "The reserve squadron must have taken care of it."

QB: "The reserve squadron wasn't that close."

Jav: "What are we going to do about the plague lab back there?"

"There is no plague lab," said Race.

Jav: "Then where is it?"

Maya: "Jav, there's no plague." There was not even an attempt at one. "We were set up."

With the alarm gone silent they were not sure what they were supposed to do. Race decided: "Queen's Squadron to Valhalla. *Yesterday*."

The Queen's Squadron dove into the sun. In the Elsewhere they accelerated until their engines shut down, leaving them only enough energy to decelerate into spacetime.

"Tak, how's Whip?"

"I think he's dead, Race."

"Go look. We have time."

There was no conversation, no music, no transmissions between ships while Tak crawled back from his cockpit and checked the Kingsman pod.

The next message was from Tak: "Race, he's dead."

"Can you preserve him till we get to hospital?"

"No. It was radiation. Must've picked up a scratch in his skin before we dove. He's so hot I could power the ship off him. I don't know how he got himself into the pod."

After a few hours someone turned on the music, loud. Even the blaring strains sounded hollow and could not dispel the invasive emptiness.

The Queen's Squadron sublighted at Mu Cas A, refueled, and blazed out the .6 astronomical units to Valhalla's world.

Maya remembered her first sight of the Queen's Squadron had been here. She had been in hiding in this safe fortress as it came under attack, and these formidable machines had frightened her in their rescue.

They skimmed low over the planet.

The planet was bald.

Eric: "It's hot."

They skimmed a full orbit. The radiation counter went wild over a surface pocked with deep craters.

Finally Jav spoke: *"I can't find Valhalla."*

Maya needed to consult the computer navigator to find where it was supposed to have been.

They had flown over it. It was gone. Utterly gone.

The Queen's Squadron climbed into helpless orbit, watching and scanning the surrounding space for what force had done this. Slowly they became aware that the Queen's Squadron was alone in the system.

The Queen's Squadron. Of what Queen?

PART FOUR

GIANT KILLER

I.

A deferential path cleared for Lt. Colonel Paul Strand as he moved through the operations room. It put a damper on Admiral Krestly's victorious glee to be required to salute this person.

Paul was in foul humor. "Why did we even use Götterdämmerung? Without it we could have negotiated peace with a very deflated Empire."

"Didn't anyone ever tell you, Strand? In any infestation, you need to kill the Queen."

"We did that all right," Paul said dryly.

"We need to be careful now," another admiral advised. "Even now the isolated country of Vikhinde has the technological edge and it could turn mean. We've shot the head off. We need to contain the writhing body quickly. Wounded things are most dangerous. The Empire is lashing about with no head. If it decides to turn vicious, we could have a whole new war on our hands."

"You mean if they decide to fight like we've been fighting," said Paul.

He could tell that they wanted to order him out. But the missing fingers, the mismatched eyes, the Diamond Star and the success of Götterdämmerung checked them.

Bertrand Krestly would mutter in private that as hell holes went, Kobandrid Rog was overrated.

"The Vikhindens still have two operational c squadrons," said the admiral.

"We have a c ship," said Admiral Krestly confidently.

253

"They have sixteen, with sixteen or more veteran pilots. And who are they answering to anyway?"

Someone else suggested, "Can't we count on some kind of ground swell from the common people now that we've overthrown the immortal tyrants?"

Paul snorted. "Face it, the people who were unhappy with this empire were not its subjects. It was us. Now we've got the subjects rat pissed off and unhappy, and holding Vikhinde is gonna be like holding a wet cat that don't want to be held.

"It's a headless serpent rat all right, but it wants a head so bad it'll latch onto the first likely dictator to come along. Any stray immortal out there is fair game for crowning."

"We'll just have to mop up the strays and exterminate those too."

"You're talking genocide," said Paul.

The whole lot of them fell to a startled pause. Finally one said, "I wouldn't call it that."

"No, you wouldn't, 'cause it's a bad word. You'll call it something else. It's still genocide."

Ignoring him, the officers conferred among themselves, "Who is known to be alive?"

"Marchale for one."

Suddenly the building shook as if from an earth tremor. Fleet Headquarters were nowhere near a fault zone.

Alarms sounded. The building shook and rattled.

"What the hell?"

"I think we're under attack."

Krestly repeated, "They can't do this!" over and over. "They can't do this!"

"How stupid are they?"

"Not at all," said Paul, nodding as if to acknowledge a nice move on a chess board.

"They'll bring Sebastionique into it!"

"No shit," said Paul. "Wouldn't you? Now they can surrender to Sebastionique instead of to us or to Earth. They know what we'll do to them if we get our hands on them. Sebastionique will just absorb them."

A quick consultation of satellites confirmed that all bridges to Sebastionique were open and that Vikhinde was welcoming Sebastionique troops in—hastening them in fact. Empire troops surrendered in battalions.

Admiral Krestly shouted, "No!" He turned from the monitors. "They can't get away with it that easy!" Krestly had cherished all through the war a vision of himself riding an armored vehicle through the Empire's capital city. "I want Beltava!"

Another man frowned, said to Paul, "You may have done it all for nothing, Colonel Strand."

"Right now that's actually a comforting thought," said Paul, wishing there was some way he could help the Vikhindens across the bridges, and wondering if he was his nation's greatest hero or this millennium's greatest fool.

Valhalla

The Queen's Squadron circled in impotent orbit of dead Valhalla when shots came out of nowhere. Suddenly there were ships—c ships, firing at them. The Queen's Squadron returned fire. The attackers were not painted in Telegonian colors. They looked like the reserve squadron.

Unfamiliar voices sounded on Maya's com, "Careful, there's only seven of them. Where's eight? I want to know where eight is. I can't find the Queen's Castle."

"He's neither here nor there, you bloody selqarth!" Tak cried returning fire at the traitors.

"They've come for us, like they did Valhalla!"

Maya would have nodded at that, but the wrong voice was saying it. That was the Queen's Squadron's line, but it was a reservist talking.

And cries of "Traitor!" were flying both ways.

The Queen's Squadron did more dodging than shooting, hesitant to fire upon their own, loathe to believe that the reserves had turned on them. Salvos of words fired with the shots.

"Wait! Wait! We didn't!"

"Who else could?"

"What hit Valhalla was a Telegonian c ship!"

"No such thing!"

"There is now!"

"Yes, and I've got it in my sights!"

"Who do you think did this?"

"I found who did this!"

"Stop shooting at each other! The Telegonians must have a c ship!"

"Yeah, because someone gave them one of his engines four years ago!"

"I can't believe it. And I flew with you people."

"Then don't believe it!"

Finally Race sent: "Queen's Knight to Squadron. Take out hostiles."

"Aye aye."

The skirmish escalated to a full battle, the Queen's Squadron firing in earnest now. Beams slashed the vacuum without visible track. Their trajectories showed on Maya's canopy, making the starfield look like a woven cage of red-laced fire.

The Queen's Squadron destroyed two before the reserve squadron escaped into the sun. Race called off the pursuit. He warned, "Keep an eye out in case they come around again."

Eric: "Do you think they did it?"

Race: "Not really, no. Maybe one of them. *Some*body sold out. God knows who. They all think it's me. Dieu, and I trained those mutts."

QB: "Then why did we engage them?"

Race: "Because they wouldn't stop shooting at us!"

Jav: "Where do you think they've gone?"

Race: "Where we should go. EtaCas. To look for someone to take orders from."

When the Queen's Squadron entered Eta Cassiopeian space they immediately picked up a transmission not intended for them, alerting all forces that the Queen's Knight was a fifth columnist.

Then that order was belayed when general orders were broadcast on all channels to all armed forces: All fighters, all units, were to surrender to Sebastionique. The Queen's Squadron was to surrender with weapons deactivated or risk being fired upon.

A closed transmission entered Maya's receiver. "WE DON'T KNOW THAT! Hide fox and all after. Yesterday."

Race's ship streaked into the sun, the Queen's Squadron after him.

Once they were all on the other side of reality, Race said, "We didn't hear that order. We're still in the Elsewhere."

"How long do you intend to keep up this charade?" said QB. "If this is a mutiny, I am going back right now. Killing you first, of course."

"Red rover," Race sent. Red rover was a summons for someone to come into his ship in person.

QB: "Would you mind specifying red rover?"

Race: "Everyone."

QB: "We won't fit."

Race: "We will if we love each other. Get in here. I need to see your faces."

It was always an eerie sensation spacewalking in the Elsewhere. It was not even spacewalking. The total nothingness of the Elsewhere was utterly bizarre, like nothing in existence. Because it wasn't.

Maya sealed her suit, took a breath for courage, and opened her canopy.

She steadied herself against the vertiginous sense of motionlessness when she knew they were traveling at thousands of kilometers per tick—for whatever a tick was worth Out Here. How slender was her safety line in the face of eternity. She pushed over the abyss to Race's craft, and crawled into the hold with the others. Race closed the hatch once they were all pressed inside.

The hold pressurized and Race took off his helmet. Maya took off hers. They crushed together with a jostling of helmets and shrugging of shoulders in the confined space that was quickly growing stuffy, the seven of them overwhelming the purification system.

They settled into silence, exchanging looks.

Race said, "Thank you for coming. This is borderline mutiny."

"Borderline?" said QB.

"Anyone who wants to go back, go. This is really my battle. It's the only battle left. The Vikrhalt is lost." He lifted his brows at QB. "Take anyone else who's not with me. Only leave me alive if you don't mind."

"I'm waiting to hear your alternative proposal," said QB.

"According to what anyone knows, we haven't heard the surrender order yet. The moment we sublight again, we're in mutiny. But if we surrender now, Götterdämmerung will have Rachelson written all over it. And worse, whoever actually is responsible will get away with it. I will suffer anything for the Empire. My taking the fall for a traitor does not serve the Empire."

"What can we do that hasn't been done?" said Jav.

"One of us has to bring back that stray engine to Beltava while Beltava still stands!" Eric declared.

"That's it," said Race.

The pilots exchanged glances.

"Can it be done?" said Tak.

"No," said QB.

"I have to try," said Race. "It's my engine. I lost it. I'll bring it back."

"You're free to die trying," said QB.

"Help me find it?" said Race.

"I can do that," said QB.

"Well," said Eric. "If Race and QB agree, that can only mean—"

"That can only mean that I have to rethink my position," said QB.

"Well?' said Race. "We haven't a whole lot of time here."

"I've rethought."

"And?"

"My position remains curiously the same. There are no alternatives. But you're right. We have no time. If our troops are surrendering, then the fall of Beltava is impendent."

"I'm going to get my engine," said Race. "By myself if I have to. I release you from my command."

"In," said Ionnina.

"I'm in," said Jav.

They were all still with him, "Under the Queen. Under God. To the immortal Empire. To my death. For glory."

They took the ritual oath and put their helmets back on.

QB, still unhelmeted, elbowed over to Race and restrained him from putting on his helmet. He said something Maya could not overhear, her head closed in its bubble.

Race suddenly burst into tears and kissed him. QB put his helmet on. When Race had his sealed, he opened the hatch.

The pilots returned to their ships.

The first voice on the com was Eric's. "Okay, Race, where did you put it?"

"I lost it right around here. So give it four years at cruising velocity."

"Hell, it's out of the galaxy."

"Which way did it go?"

"And you had best be exact. We will either find it right away or not at all, in which case I shall content myself with something do-able. Needles in haystacks come to mind."

The engine had left a precise pointer in a trail of stray atoms in the nothingness, heading out toward a destination of nowhere.

The Queen's Squadron blazed out after it at full acceleration, burning up the light years.

Errors expanded to enormity at this distance and, as they must, they found it immediately. There had been nothing Out Here to throw it off course.

They turned it around and headed back with it in tow. The long journey was spent figuring out how to attach it for a passage back to realtime.

They were running different ideas through the simulation program, when Race thought to ask it if he had enough energy to decelerate the extra mass to the speed necessary to make the crossing.

Negative.

"What if I sublight and refuel and come back to the Elsewhere, will I have enough?"

Negative.

"What if I refuel from the other ships so that I am fully loaded. Will that be enough?"

Negative.

"Dammit! Dammit! Dammit!"

"Race." That was Eric.

"What."

"Fire up the engine."

"The—?"

"You're crossing with three engines. Why not use all three?"

"Does it still work?" Tak cut in.

"I'll look," said Race. He was already reaching for his helmet.

He climbed outside and checked it over. It seemed undamaged, and its fuel feed was intact. He could tank it up from the other ships.

He climbed back into his cockpit and asked the simulator now, "Would I have sufficient energy?"

Yes.

"Can I do it?"

Insufficient data.

There was a whole battery of considerations and unknowns, with no means or time to test them.

"Nothing efficient or stable about it," said Jav. "Even if we can rig it to work on this side, the instant you cross and the momentum reverses, the inertia will yank that thing right off."

"As long as it waits till I'm on the other side," said Race. "All I have to do is get through the wall, and who cares what happens to it there? It can break off. I just have to get it through."

"It could blow up under you," said QB.

"Yes, well, don't get behind me," said Race.

When they arrived back at Eta Cassiopeia, Race sent his squadron ahead through the wall two by two. QB and Eric went first. Ion and Jav next.

Maya looked back at Race's jury-rigged ship. She wanted to say something to him. There was no time and this was no place at all. Later. She did not know what she wanted to say, but Race had been moving like a man with a wound ever since she had walked away from him. She ought to say something.

"Tak and Maya, go."

They decelerated through the wall. And there was EtaCas.

She looked back where she expected Race to appear.

Ticks passed.

Eric, who had sublighted first, sent: "Where is he?"

Ionnina: "Should we go back and look?"

Tak: "Isn't he here? Where did he come out?"

Waiting.

QB: "If he's smart, he's running."

Eric: "Race wouldn't do that."

QB: "Race is not the smartest man I ever met."

A light like a sudden sun flashed in the blackness of space and grew, the nova blaze of matter annihilation.

QB: "There."

All the viewports darkened with the sudden light. When the brightness diminished to nothing, Maya lowered her head to rest on the control panel.

He didn't make it.

II.

Into the stricken silence came QB's comforting dry voice: "Hide fox and all after."

He steered into the sun, and what was left of the Queen's Squadron followed without question.

When they came out in the Elsewhere, they replayed the red rover meeting, in QB's ship. As they gathered in the hold, Maya noticed grimly that there was more room this time.

Maya took off her helmet, shook out her damp hair which drifted up and out with the lack of gravity. She was too stunned for tears. She did not believe what she had just seen.

The normally voluble group was somberly quiet. Jav said, "We really must surrender this time." The orders had come from the surviving Vikrhalt.

Mumbled misgivings circled round. QB said, "I would propose one of us hold back."

It was not the suggestion so much as the speaker of it—they all gaped, and Ionnina said, "Mutiny?"

"Yes," said QB. "Not all of us. Only one is required to stay free until he can gather proof enough for an interstellar court. I suspect our testimonies won't be enough. Rachelson managed truly to lose the evidence this time."

Silent ascent met him from all around.

"Well, then. For honor. For the Queen," said QB.

"For Rachelson," said Eric.

"If you must."

Jav took hold of QB's arm and demanded, "QB, what did you say to him?"

QB tried to ignore the question but the squadron was looking at him hard. QB had had the last face-to-face words with Race.

QB paused. "I told him I didn't expect to see him again."

"You said something else."

QB looked around, as if there were something to see, then he faced forward looking at no one, and said flatly, "I told him what I thought of him."

Maya felt her eyes stinging. The last thing she had said to his face was, "You're out of your goddamned mind."

QB had been in the Service a long time, an old warrior who had lost enough comrades to know the ways of war and that each parting might be the last. Suddenly Race was gone and QB, of all people, was the only one with things not left unsaid.

The others all volunteered to be the rogue.

"Ion," said QB.

"Io!" Ionnina answered eagerly.

"Take the Squadron home and turn yourselves in."

"No!" Ionnina cried. That was not the order she was expecting. She proposed drawing lots.

QB said with gentle mockery, "You're having delusions, Ion. Since when do you people live in a democracy? I am the ranking officer here and the issue is decided."

Maya spoke. Her voice came out sandy. "Correct on all counts except who is ranking." All the stares turned her way. She tried to clear her throat. "It is decided. All of you go now and surrender."

"Pardon me, *Lieutenant*," QB rebuked her with her rank.

"You're outgunned here, Tristram, trust me."

He stared at his junior officer; then it twigged, "You *are* Rhalt. You lied."

"I am not, and I did not lie, you *worm*."

Stunned looks surrounded her. This was not a slow group. Everyone caught what she had said, what it meant. They were only having difficulty swallowing it.

"There is no discussion here," Maya pressed on. "You vowed to serve the Vikrhalt. So shut up and surrender. Anyway, I am the only one here who *cannot* commit treason, so you see it must be me."

Eyes rounded as credence was catching up, none rounder than Tak's who looked precisely like a man who had just learned he had run—stomped—across a minefield. QB looked like he was standing on one. He'd gone chalky white. He touched his midriff as if suddenly ill. Then he broke into a bright graveyard smile and chuckled very softly. "My my, Maya."

Entering deathrow made Paul queasy. Walking through a prison gave him a feeling that he ought, being on the outside of the bars, to be running for it. He clutched his visitor pass and security clearance tight in the two fingers of his left hand. The hand looked like a talon. He had come to see the one who had done this to him.

These last days—had they been only days?—were a blurred shambles. The universe was in upheaval.

It had been one of those wars of which the ending only sets up the beginning of the next one. Vreeland Forgil was hard at it trying to settle all sides into harmony. He was asking the conquering nations for emergency power and a new position from which he could try to contain the violence. The people of the Empire were accustomed to dictatorship. They needed a strong hand to guide them through this interim chaos.

The council of planet-nations was considering it. Paul thought everything was being done so much faster than it ought. He needed to move fast with them or be run over.

There had been a melee for Beltava as war's end turned into a feeding frenzy, with New Earth vying for part of the territory being carved up for the feast.

Penetanguishene had been party to stalling New Earth's occupation of Beltava, which allowed the capital to fall to Sebastionique instead. Admiral Krestly was livid over the stolen thunder.

Allied forces caught up with both Penetanguishene

and the immortal Marchale at the landbridge to Sebastionique. They had not been trying to escape. They loaded civilians onto the last train out of Vikhinde and sent it on its way, then themselves walked directly into New Earth hands.

New Terran troops captured Marchale with the intention of bringing him to trial. They needed an immortal to accuse and execute publicly for the crimes of all the others who were out of reach of slow vengeance. Marchale had dodged that humiliation by provoking one of his guards into killing him outright. The incident was preserved on recorder. Paul had viewed it. It was frightening. Marchale told the man to his face what he was doing, and pulled it off anyway.

Marchale gave a chilling speech: "There was a perfectly marvellous useful word that has dropped out of the language. Hubris. It's an old word. I remember it from my childhood. It is translated as pride, but that's not right. Arrogance is closer, but imprecise. The sin of pride—what sort of sin is pride? It is not. Hubris is peculiar only to those in power. It is a privileged flaw. You wouldn't know about it. A sense of invincibility. Beyond reproach, check or accountability. That is what fells empires. Every time. And I'll be dammed if we didn't step in it again. Eye-deep in our own hubris. Oh, I know you haven't understood a word, you sullen ox. You are so easily maneuvered, we should have been able to avoid all this. How did we become so oversure of ourselves? Just because it is ridiculous, doesn't mean it can't hurt you. Ah, the fixed bovine stare. I can still get a ring through your nose."

And he'd proceeded to do just that—a variation on "Please don't throw me in the briar patch, Brer Fox. Anything but the briar patch."

His captors told him he would be tried and executed, and Marchale smiled brightly, "Ah, the famed Telegonian legal system!" He sounded delighted, as if he *wanted* a trial. He seemed so sure that once in legal hands he would be safe, that his captors started to believe it. And he was in such mockingly high spirits that there was only one way to bring him down and make him believe they could kill him.

They killed him.

One shot in the chest. Marchale had smiled in triumph, and died breathing his wife's name.

The recording ended. It left Paul troubled. Immortals were such expert manipulators, how *had* they lost control and gone to war?

Penetanguishene had been the opposite of Marchale. He had walked straight to his doom and let them kick his ribs in. He had not uttered a sound.

They say he offered no defense at his trial. Here he was, in blistering time, tried and sentenced, with only a half deck left until his execution.

Walking through the prison's stark white corridors filled Paul with creeping paranoia, even if it smelled better than Kobandrid Rog. Only the tips of barrels of the computer guards' weapons protruded through the slits in the walls. His skin crawled up Paul's scarred back as he passed them.

Emotions ran a roller coaster as he arrived at Penetanguishene's cell. His steps slowed, mouth dried, throat tightened, pulse quickened.

Rage boiled. He meant to say, "By the way, why didn't you tell me that you murdered me?"

He had rehearsed it a thousand times when he'd envisioned this scene.

The forcefield lifted, bars parted.

Dark head lifted, dark eyes met his.

Paul's thoughts scattered to the sixteen winds. The neat figure on the cot looked a bit fragile, his broken bones newly knit. He sat gingerly erect; only his head had been bowed. When he looked up with obsidian eyes, the only expression to leak out might have been resignation.

Paul's breath caught, and one inane syllable sprang to his lips. "Hi."

"Paul."

"My headshrinker told me not to come. It would undo everything they'd done."

"Did it?"

"Immediately. My heart leapt."

"I'm sorry. I was hoping you had rejoined the mainstream."

"Can't. There's no mainstream after a war. I just keep going through motions hoping eventually the power of inertia will take over." He sat across from Penetanguishene. "I appealed your case."

"You didn't."

"You weren't just railroaded. You were tried and sentenced at light speed."

"So?"

"Another case came down same time as yours. One of our men. A popular hero. He was charged with smuggling the seized Vikhinden funds from New Earth banks and using them to fund a compassionate space-lift of refugees whom we've been derelict in assisting. It was a moral obligation. He broke our laws to keep a promise that was being shirked. He overrode our government and now we've got a shitload of refugees no one wants on our doorstep. Your trials were real close together."

"They should convict him."

"They did. They also convicted you. They can't convict both of you. One is guilty of following his conscience against orders and the other of obeying orders against their idea of conscience. They can't convict both of you."

"They did."

"One of you has to be innocent. They can't have it both ways. He defied the law for what he thought was right. You didn't defy the law for what they thought was wrong."

"Different juries."

"Truth can't hang on some jury's idea of debatable right."

"You should have been Vikhen."

"No. It's simple justice and logic. Which one of you did the right thing?"

"Consistency has never been a byword of humanity."

"It must be a byword of Law or *our* empire is built on sand."

"It is."

"I can't accept that."

"Damned if you do and damned if you don't is as old as the first codified human law. Are you familiar with Hammurabi's law on witchcraft?"

"Can't whistle that tune offhand."

"The trial of the river. If the river accepts the accused, he is innocent. If the river rejects him, he is put to death. The problem is, if the river accepts him, that means he drowned. The accused is equally dead either way. One way he happens to be right, the other wrong. But this is mortal law. Don't concern yourself, Paul. I've been ready to die for a very long time."

"I know and it drives me piss ass crazy. I want to live."

"I realize that and I am sorry."

Paul fell silent. That was so quickly done and followed none of the scenarios he had rehearsed. An admission and an apology and there was nothing else to be had out of him, for Penetanguishene could not give Paul his lifespan back.

Penetanguishene regarded Paul's D.S. "I've never seen one."

"That's 'cause it's usually worn by a tombstone."

"I'm glad they didn't do any political waltzing to take it away from you."

"Oh, they were ready," said Paul. "My nightmare has been for these past vants that the engineers fubbed it and something happened to that ship, and it wasn't going to show and everyone would assume it was because I talked when really it was lost someplace where no one would ever find it. You see, I knew what a bastard that ship was. Lot of people jolly eager to take my D.S. away. And they're real pissed now that I get to keep it. Drives 'em fuckin nuts. It's almost worth it."

"How did you get c tech?"

"Remember that c ship Rachelson crashed four years ago? He lost an engine. We found it."

"No."

"What do you mean, no?"

"I know you're not lying. You're simply wrong."

"How do you know that?"

"I was a c pilot once."

"I didn't know that."

"It's one of the things I couldn't tell you. You don't have Rachelson's engine. Whoever told you that was also misinformed or he lied."

"Then where *did* we get c tech from? A traitor?"

"I don't know."

"Rachelson's name keeps coming up," said Paul.

"No."

"You're sure."

"I adored Rachelson. Anyone who knew him did. There was not a venal cell in the man's body."

"He's dead, you know. Blew up on re-entry."

"Which makes me wonder what he was carrying."

"Weird you should say that. You have no way of knowing, but the rest of the Queen's Squadron claims he was carrying that stray engine."

"That sounds like Rachelson."

"Trouble is, the computer records of the c ships themselves don't back up their pilots' stories."

"Who has the ships?"

"They're in international custody."

"Their memories have been tampered with."

"By who?" It didn't seem awfully likely.

"Paul, why did you give your own Admiral Krestly a false plan for Götterdämmerung?"

Paul gave a quizzical look. "I didn't tell Admiral Krestly nothing."

"I knew that wasn't you."

"What wasn't me?"

Penetanguishene explained that the Empire had sent in a doppelgänger Krestly to receive the secret information, and that someone posing as Paul had led them far astray.

"This makes no sense," said Paul.

"The truth, especially as it concerns human endeavors, is not always logical."

"Well shit, how many sides are there in this war?"

Revelation came in a blindingly bright instant. "Three. There are three." *It's not a war, it's a coup.*

"What?"

"We were so busy looking at each other, we neglected to account for a third."

"Sebastionique?" said Paul incredulously.

"No, not Sebastionique. A third. Is this a war between nations or . . . Dammit Paul, there is someone *else*. We've been set up."

"We the Empire?"

"We, you and me. Empire and Telegonia. We. Do you know the story of Jack the Giant Killer?"

"No."

"The three players in this tale are two giants and our despicable hero Jack. This is an Earth tale, naturally."

"Naturally."

"Jack, your basic free mortal, happens upon two giants sleeping. The giants have bags of gold, as giants always do. Jack tosses a pebble at one giant, who wakes up and gruffly demands to know why giant number two struck him. Giant number two says that he didn't. They go back to sleep. Jack tosses another stone. Replay the scene. And again. Soon the giants are fighting and accusing each other, and they do each other in, and Jack scampers off with the gold. Mortals think this is a clever story. We are a pair of dumb giants."

Paul nodded. "When equal opposites clash, it's the guy in third place who gets the pizza."

"Yes, I suppose that's what I said."

"Not Sebastionique?"

"Not necessarily Sebastionique."

"Lord, some more vondesi would be helpful right about now."

"There are none. Someone destroyed my homeworld."

"I didn't know that."

"Perhaps Jack did it."

"Busy boy. 'Kay. Suspect codenamed: Jack. Who is he?"

"It's too late."

"It's too late for your empire, but it's not too late for all its mortal subjects."

All the nonsense was falling into place. Pieces that didn't fit slid into a pattern easily on the premise that the two superpowers had been pitted against each other for the benefit of a third. Paul realized he had fought for the wrong reasons.

He didn't know he was speaking aloud till Penetanguishene said, "I don't believe that any war is ever fought for the reasons given to the warriors. Does a democracy ever know why it fights? You are given reasons to fight, but are they the real ones? Who makes the agenda and decides why you fight? Or is the decision made to fight and then reasons created to give you. You are simply manipulated rather than outright and honestly conscripted. We use a lash; you make up a tasty-looking carrot and hang it out. But it's not a carrot, it's lies and hidden motivations. So how much more free choice had your deluded volunteer soldier than our conscript?"

"I have my own agenda now. Find Jack."

Penetanguishene gave a halfhearted nod. "Our only lead seems to be a false one."

" 'Kay. What fake Götterdämmerung did this fake me tell your fake Krestly?"

"We were told of an armada of plague ships."

"No. That wasn't any part of Götterdämmerung."

"Part of the diversion for it. It kept the Queen's Squadron busy."

"No. No part at all. We were real surprised when the Queen's Squadron didn't show up. I figured it was Rachelson's doing."

"No. Someone told us of a plague."

"There was no plague ship. As far as I know, no plague."

"I thought so. Vreeland Forgil insisted there was no plague."

"That doesn't mean anything. Forgil had no way of knowing for certain one way or the other. He doesn't have red card clearance."

"He knew Götterdämmerung."

"What makes you think that?"

"He said he didn't. And he was lying."

"But he really *didn't* know."

"He did say also that he was not made privy to any such plan, and that statement was true. I can't reconcile the two statements."

"I can," said Paul.

"How? They're mutually exclusive."

"No they're not. He wasn't *told* Götterdämmerung. He *devised* it."

"Ambassador Forgil?"

"He's not ambassador anymore. They're creating a new position for him with near dictatorial powers. Reconciler, I think they're calling it. Ever hear of a fireman who lights fires so he can put them out?"

"I believe I just have."

"The putting-out-fires-with-gasoline school of diplomacy. That man was in the thick of every crisis leading up to war. Who else was in a position to orchestrate all this?"

"I think you just named Jack."

And prelude to all of it was Aithar. Forgil needed first to get rid of the truthsayers so he could do the rest. Forgil had been at Aithar.

Penetanguishene remembered an attractive man lying.

"He couldn't have done all this with several hundred vondesi alive to call him a liar at every turn."

Paul nodded, "Such a nice guy."

"Remember this always. Evil is attractive."

Paul stared at him. "You and I were never meant to be enemies."

"We were never meant to be lovers either, but someone has warped the universe past all natural order."

"Penetanguishene," Paul said with a sudden thought.

Penetanguishene lifted his brows to invite the rest of it.

"Forgil oversaw the surrender of the c ships."

"No wonder the machine minds don't back up their pilots."

"There's still one c ship left at large. Everyone's real anxious about it. Christ! How can one man work so much evil? He's all but wiped out two species, and seems to be getting away with it." He had tentacles everywhere, anticipating everything, and leaving such a slender trail, Paul was sure he would erase that soon also.

"Who is the pilot of the missing c ship?" Penetanguishene asked.

"Can't remember."

"Maya of the Timberlines."

"That's it. Why? Who is she?"

Footsteps approached from the corridor and the cell opened.

"I didn't call for you," said Paul to the guards.

The guards ordered Paul out now. "No one is allowed access to the prisoner. It's time for his execution."

"No, it's not. And there's an appeal in."

"Appeal's been decided. Execution's been moved up. Sorry, sir, you have to leave now. We're not to let anyone in."

"Whose order?"

"Oh, guess!" said Penetanguishene peevishly.

The guards would not say.

Tentacles everywhere.

"Don't bother about me," said Penetanguishene. "Whatever regime comes out on top, I'm done. A man who cuts off limbs and eyes earns no one's sympathy. I'm ready to go."

"I—"

Penetanguishene hissed at him as the guards pulled him toward the door. "Just cover your ass and get Jack. Paul, you were never here. If he finds out we've made contact already, you'll be marked. Anyone asks, do me a favor: for Gods' sake *lie*."

Paul was getting angry. It was time to rip the ring from his nose, the tentacle from his throat, and take the offensive.

Funny, he thought, Penetanguishene may actually have prolonged his life instead of cutting it short. Paul said, "There's a better way to get out from under a death mandate."

Penetanguishene shook his head, confused.

Paul gave a wry smile and answered as the barrier closed between them, "Drop dead first."

The death notice for the war criminal Penetanguishene crossed Vreeland Forgil's desk with an addendum. The record spoke: "The executioner certified death at 1007 hours. At 1008 hours Colonel Paul Strand, D.S., died of heart failure precipitated by a fatal cyn dose received at Kobandrid Rog."

Forgil nodded in satisfaction, set the record bubble aside. *Two birds.* Always a good feeling. He was one step away from home free.

"Any word on that rogue c ship?" he asked his aide.

"No, sir."

He would like to believe she ran away. But that was not what c pilots were made of, especially not the Queen's Squadron. The longer she remained at large, the more damage she could wreak.

She. Who was she?

He rang up the file on the missing pilot. Her name was Maya of the Timberlines. Her position was Queen's Knight Echo.

Rachelson's Echo. Not good.

The file said she had no surviving family.

No levers there. Damnation.

Aggressive, said the file. Fearless. No vices.

Reaction time, recognition, execution, all superior.

Leadership and working with others, borderline, but improving.

She had the profile of a classic lone wolf, but no, he had no illusions that she might have run away.

Damnation, where could she be?

Alpha Base
14 January 5247

III.

Maya had assumed that the first thing the conquerors would do after destroying Valhalla would be to hasten to the Empire's remote c ship factory at Alpha Base and claim it. But when she sublighted there, she found she was ahead of them. Four full days after the fall of Valhalla.

It's still here! Why is it still here?

She was able to approach the base undetected, because there were no scanners turned skyward. This place was approachable only by c ship, and until now, all c ships had been friendly.

She set down a few kilometers from the base and hiked in.

Did Telegonia have more than one c ship and were they on their way here now?

Why hadn't the traitor who gave them c technology given them the location of this base as well? Was the traitor reserving this information for himself? Or did he even know about it?

Traitor. There had to be a traitor. But who, how, why, and why wasn't he here now?

Evidently the pilots who surrendered were being uninformative. The traitor must not be among them, unless he was one of the two reservists killed in the skirmish with the Queen's Squadron at Valhalla.

Or maybe the Telegonians did know about this place and this was a trap set for Maya. She walked into the compound. The factory workers were busy destroying the machinery and records. No one had surrendered here yet.

Then Maya saw her—someone in charge. Maya had

never seen her before, not wearing this face. She was directing the scuttling of Alpha Base. A short woman with a full figure, dark blunt cut hair and brown eyes. There was something more about her—outwardly young, but with a cloak of age and authority. Maya called, "Ehremat."

The woman turned.

Maya's words deserted her. The woman who answered to ehremat beckoned to Maya. "Who are you, child?"

Child indeed. Maya took a leap of faith, "I was Ashata. Who are you?" *Child.*

"I am the Queen. Get me out of here."

Maya's c ship waited out in the flat. The Queen stopped before it, said to Maya, "Are you our Brutus? *Kai su, teknon?*"

"No. We were ordered to surrender. I exempted myself."

"So did we."

"Ehremat, everyone thinks you were at Valhalla. How did you get here?"

"When Götterdämmerung was imminent, our vondesi told us not to go to Valhalla. So we came to the most remote place we know. We came here on a reserve ship. We have been stranded here since."

That meant that the reservists hadn't talked. The traitor was not in the reserve squadron. He wasn't in the Queen's Squadron. So who and where was he?

Maya said, "I don't understand why this planet wasn't hit right after Valhalla. Someone didn't tell the Telegonians everything."

"Because he is dead, too," said the Queen. "Rachelson did this to us."

"No!" Maya's screech took the Queen aback. More quietly, firmly, Maya said again, "No."

"The machines themselves say so."

"*Mine* doesn't! Mine is the only one untouched by Telegonian hands. Someone has made the other machines lie."

The Queen spoke like a sigh, "Ilu Ilu, can you find our vondesi? We need him more than ever."

"He's dead."

"We shall never cut through this murk now. All is fog. Someone rid us of our vondesi well and truly. He finished what Selqarth started. Another hater of light and truth."

"I am beginning to think this was not a simple betrayal in war," said Maya, "but the cause of the war itself. In hindsight this smells like a long, patiently plotted campaign. What if all those things the Telegonians did to provoke us and then denied they did—what if they really didn't do them? Someone who could live long enough to set it up and live long enough to reap his feast of fallout. Someone who can do all this and leave no track. There is only one sort of being who can move through our system without a trace. Someone who knows of c ships and someone who can wait."

"You are saying it was one of us."

"Has to be," said Maya.

"It horrifies us to admit your suspicion has merit. But what of the virus? An immortal plague is not a weapon which one of us would use."

"There was no virus. It's a rumor. That's all it ever was."

"How can you ever be sure about a rumor?"

"Ehremat, I caught it. It was a cold. Corinda died because she thought she would. One of us would never use a virus, but we could use the *rumor* of it. Makes for a nice terror tactic."

"But there is still the matter of this secret base," said the Queen. "An immortal would know about this base."

"*I* didn't know about this place until I became a c pilot!"

"That is because you were not at the meeting when we made the decision to move the factory. You were never at meetings, Ashata."

The name made her wince, a twisting thorn in

sinew. She hated ever having been such a creature as Ashata.

"You could have found this place had you known to look for it."

"Who else wasn't at the meeting?" said Maya.

"Someone comes to mind immediately. But we killed him five hundred years ago. He was not there because he was dead."

"So is Ashata."

The Queen lifted her brows speculatively.

To imagine oneself the originator of a new thought was a human conceit, to imagine oneself unique. If Maya had died and come back as a mortal, what made her think she was the first and only? That it had not been done before?

The trouble with annihilation was you never quite knew where all the bodies were buried.

"Selqarth is alive."

The Queen spoke aloud to herself, "And didn't we just say someone finished what Selqarth started with the purge of the vondesi? Selqarth finished what Selqarth started. What face could he be wearing these days?"

"Since he has access to the c ships' memories, he must be working from the other side," said Maya.

"Who has been taking the surrender of the c ships?"

"The intermediary," said Maya. "The man everyone trusts. Vreeland Forgil the Peacemaker."

"Look no further. We see him now."

"I never liked that man."

"We liked him too well. We don't know why we did not recognize him before. In the pre-war years, Forgil was credited with saving Telegonia from the wrath of the Empire. All those incendiary incidents he settled were his doing. The Deceiver lives. This time he calls himself Vreeland Forgil. Well." She faced Maya, eyes alive again, her chin high. "Knowledge is power. We see him and he does not see us." She patted the side of the c ship. "Beam us up, Scotty."

"Ehremat?"

"Old joke. Just how young are you, child?"

"A thousand years."

"Ilu, Ilu, too young to be flirting with mortality. What makes a young child dance this close to death?"

"If I had been hiding where it was *safe*, I would be dead now." Maya opened her ship's side hatch.

"This is so."

Maya climbed into the small hold and opened a Kingsman pod for the Queen. She turned. "I don't even know what to call you. Something besides Ehremat."

"So many names. When we were young and our name was Isis, we needed titles. Yards and yards of them. In the thousands of years it became a bore. We are Isis, no more, no less."

Thousands of years. Not *the* Isis! The god with the longest worship in human history.

A smile ghosted on the Queen's lips. "Later, when Christianity eclipsed our worship, you just look at the early depictions of the Madonna and child and tell me that is not We and the infant Horus. People do not give up their gods quickly."

"We're not gods. We just live a long time," Maya murmured. Her eyes misted.

The Queen abruptly dropped her royal plurals. "There is much cause for crying right now, but I have lived a long time and these tears sound like a broken heart. Were you in love?"

A strange question between immortals, but so direct and to the heart, there was no embarrassment. "Just a mortal," said Maya. "He died."

"Yes. They do that. Poor child, you have succeeded in becoming human." The Queen placed a hand on her head. "Stay with divinity, child. It is much easier."

Maya sniffled, wiped her eyes. "You'd better get in the pod, Ehremat. There's no such thing as safe space anymore. Selqarth will find this base sooner or later. Where can I take you?"

"Where are you going?"

"If there can be one rogue immortal, there can be two. I neglected to account for him, and he for *me*."

"We could always rely on our Squadron. Get him, Maya."

Her name. That was her name.

"Where do you want to go? Beltava?"

"No. Beltava has fallen. Leave us on the Far Worlds and then forget you ever saw us. Three can play this game. The Queen died at Valhalla. We shall be back. People do not give up their gods so quickly." She started into the pod, turned with a final thought. "Do you know who is your mother, child?"

Maya blushed. That was a delicate topic. "No."

"It may be me. I was not named for a chess piece. I was named for a bee. Do you know what Götter-dämmerung means?"

"Twilight of the Gods."

The Queen slid into the Kingsman pod, spoke before she sealed it. "Remember, child, twilight comes at dusk, but it is also twilight at dawn. The immortal Empire is not dead. It only sleeps through another dark night. We can wait a very long time."

Get Selqarth.

Maya stood before the mirror, tied the leather thong around her head, arranged the feathers and cat-wolf fangs so they fell down behind her ear with a thin braid of coarse dark hair. Her smoky brown eyes seemed sunken, smoldering in angry depths.

How? I can't get near him.

She put on her necklace of catwolf teeth. She shook her head. The teeth rattled.

Make him come to me.

She put on her dress uniform jacket, the one with no unit badge on the sleeve. If you're not Queen's Squadron, you're not anyone.

I have something he wants. The last witness that can call him a liar. He will want to come aboard alone without witnesses.

She brought out a twig she had kept from a visit to

EtaCas, and she fixed it in her headdress. It was a brittle monarch sprig Race had broken off a tree named Rachel.

Dressed for a final battle, Maya strapped herself into the cockpit, ran up the mammoth engines.

Very well. Come and get it, Selqarth.

Fort Ujiji, New Earth
EtaCas
15 January 5247

Paul checked into Penetanguishene's claim that the c ship's memories had been altered to contradict their pilots. He found no trace of overwrite.

None.

None?

He checked again. There was not a sign of tampering.

He had been so sure.

Was it possible that one man could do so much damage without leaving the smallest clue?

That Forgil had done it, Paul was convinced, even in the face of non-evidence.

Then he started questioning Forgil's humanity.

How had Forgil got hold of c tech? Easy, if he was immortal. Immortals had access to absolutely anything in the Empire, if they knew what questions to ask the Net.

Paul wondered if there weren't a reason, besides public face as a humanitarian, that Forgil so violently opposed the idea of an immortal virus.

An immortal would be able to alter a c ship's memory without leaving a trace.

Forgil is one of them.

There had to be another way to check the story of the c pilots. Something to contradict Forgil's false witnesses.

Paul went to see an old friend.

Trevor's brown eyes flew wide. "Paul!"

"Rumors of my death—" He shrugged to say they had been greatly exaggerated.

Her long arms went round his neck. She had forgiven him for being alive.

"But don't let anyone else hear it, 'kay?"

Trevor yanked herself back, sensing something odd afoot. " 'Kay, Paul," she mumbled distrustfully.

"Trevor, sweetness, I want you to take a reading and make as many copies as you can. In case I exit suddenly, I want this on record."

"What do you need?"

"The energy output when Rachelson reentered spacetime. Did the big ears make a recording of that?"

"Absolutely."

"Then calculate the mass involved in that cataclysm."

"Why?"

"Call it paranoia," Paul said cheerfully.

"You know what they say," said Trevor. "It's only paranoia until it happens."

Paul nodded, "They're pretty smart for once."

"Who's they?"

"Thems that says those things. Come on, reading, woman. I'm on the clock here, the big one."

Trevor frowned, turned to her instruments. "I guess I don't see what harm it could do."

Until the answer came up to a sum equaling well over one loaded c ship. The mass was equivalent to one c ship plus over 2000 kilos. "Hell of a payload." Trevor shook her head.

"That's the mass of a c engine," said Paul.

Which seconded the pilots' story and contradicted the machine minds which claimed Rachelson had been carrying nothing unusual.

"What does this mean, Paul?"

"Means take out a huge life insurance policy."

"Oh, thank you very much, Paul!" Trevor cried. She threw down a record bubble. No sooner was he back in her life than he was ripping it apart again. He left before she could scream at him to get out. "I don't blame you for hating me," he said on his way out.

She shrieked after him, "I could never hate you, you jerk! I refuse to love you! I'd sooner marry a grenade; it's less painful!"

I'm doing it now, he thought. *Using people like pawns.*

It was still left to prove that the extra 2000+ kilos was a c ship engine. It could be a load of turnip chips for all he could prove right now.

Suddenly a continental alert sounded.

"Shit!" Paul said in the middle of the corridor to no one in particular.

He took a jet tube to Fleet HQ and buffaloed his way into operations. "What's going on?"

"Missing c ship." The controller nodded at the tracking screen.

"She surrender?"

"Not really. It's unmanned right now. They're letting it land."

"Unmanned?"

"We think so. A Kingsman pod ejected a few minutes ago. All indications are the pilot ejected. The ship is under robot power now."

Paul saw a plot on the monitor making slowly for a landing in Arctica.

"What happened to the Kingsman pod?" Paul didn't see a tracking for that on the screen.

"It wouldn't acknowledge."

"What happened to the fucking pod?"

"It refused to acknowledge transmissions."

They were telling Paul that they shot the son of a bitch out of the sky. "Did you shoot the c ship too?"

"*No*, sir!"

The equipment was too valuable. I see. "Was the pilot in the pod?"

"We think so."

Christ. "Where's the ship landing?"

"That's restricted, sir."

"Remember who you're talking to."

"It's not even red card level, sir. It's on a need to know level."

"I need to know."

"Sorry, sir."

"Who's taking possession of the ship?"

"That would be Vreeland Forgil, sir."

"Why him?"

"In case anyone is aboard. He's a peacemaker, you know. Last thing they want is you up there to create an incident."

"Just tell me where it's coming down."

"I can't. No one is allowed."

"Right. Of course." Paul started out. "By the by, my being alive is on a need to know basis, and fucking nobody needs to know. Got that?"

"Yes, sir."

Paul withdrew to a travel computer to plot two hundred courses across Arctica by private shuttle. The courses he selected cross-hatched the continent. The ones that rejected or re-routed drew him a picture of a forbidden zone. They'd cordoned off a 100 kilometer-wide circle. At the center would be the c ship.

Paul shut off the computer. He waited to see if anyone rang up his terminal and replayed the activity. Nothing happened.

He got up slowly and walked out of the building at what he hoped was a casual gait. Tentacles everywhere. He expected one to realize Paul Strand was still alive and seize him any next instant.

He passed up two public cars, took the third one to a public transport station. He rented a vehicle, went out to the hangar, found it in bay 306.

He felt his heart pound in his chest. Careful. The story that he had died suddenly was such a horribly likely one, it could come true at any second.

He listened to his heart ticking like a speeded up time bomb.

He approached the flyer in bay 306.

Pain.

He dropped to his knees, hanging onto the flyer's wing.

Pain in his chest, under his ribs. He winced.

It passed. He belched. *Is this death or is it last night's pizza?*

God. The fate of the known universe hangs on a pizza.

He laughed, his heart still speeding.

You're holding too tight, Paul. Let it go. Let it go.

Long ago, early man in his ego had the planets, sun and stars all revolving around himself. Since then humanity had grown used to the idea of being rather ordinary, middle weight, middle aged and at the edge of things. He forgot that something had to be at the hub, and Paul was startled to find it was he. Civilization at this moment revolved around Paul Strand—proof positive that God had a sense of humor. "And if I may say so, sir, it's a sick one." Paul clawed his way up the wing to stand. "Wait. I take that back. Jesus, I don't get it."

He took long breaths to calm his heart. *Let it flow. Let it flow.* He boarded the flyer and put it on manual control. Do what you can, the outcome is in God's hands. He cast his own fate to the unknown.

Paul fed in no course, afraid to turn on automatic anything, lest a tentacle writhe out and take over.

He flew, manual all the way, to Arctica.

He knew better than to underestimate his adversary. The way had to be fraught with fail-safes and detectors, mine programs for impudent worms like Paul Strand who thought they could battle an ageless force of towering evil—a deceptive craft of thousands of years, powerful enough to fell an empire without it knowing who struck the blow. A master in this game of chess. Paul looked for hidden moves and unaccounted for pawns. Going alone was folly. Calling for help would only trip a snare.

He did not know how he could hope to win.

Arctica, Sebastionique
EtaCas
15 January 5247

The Presence waited inert and shrouded in mist on the icefield. His last enemy.

Vreeland Forgil stepped down from his transport and approached it.

There was an tendency to anthropomorphize these things. Selqarth actually had a greater regard for these machines than he had for anthropoids. He felt a kinship with these powerful ships and their ability to break free of the bonds of spacetime itself.

And you are the only one left who can hurt me.

He pulled his immortal disk from a hidden pocket and made the c ship's hatch open to his command.

The ramp slid out in welcome.

Forgil climbed in the rear hatchway into the small hold.

A sudden barrage of beamfire blazed all around him like a burning cloak, a fiery corona around his screen. He'd had sense enough not to walk in unshielded. This was, as he thought it might be, a trap.

When the firestorm cleared, he met an enraged brown-eyed gaze lurking in the crawlway. A savage she-beast decorated in teeth and feathers. He tried to stare her down. Thousands of years of practice gave him the ability to subdue lesser minds with a look.

But suddenly this one was rushing at him with a flying kick.

He pivoted, flicked her foot over in mid-air, twisted her into an awkward landing. In his thousands of years, he'd had time to hone many skills.

She bounced back as expertly as he himself might have. He took his peace staff and cracked her across the face with it. Blood gushed from her long haughty nose.

He could have finished her then with his projectile weapon, but he enjoyed kicking the hell out of this well-trained worm. It was nice to know he could still compete with the worm elite. He had not lost his edge during his long masquerade as a man of peace.

But this battle was not easy. For a mere she-worm she put up a formidable fight. This was a much tougher breed of she-worm than he remembered.

When she was down and beaten, he stepped back and produced his projectile gun. It was a less accurate weapon than the beam guns, but it would go through the energy screens. He considered how best to kill her. Make up a story of self-defense? No, he had expertly bruised her past belief. One brown eye swelled shut, the other glared at him with a knowing fury. Her full lips were split and puffed up with coloring bruises. She was a raw bestial thing. He needed to destroy her body, and he had to make up a likely story of what he was doing with a weapon with which to do it.

For a moment his mind wandered, forgot what he was about. As if the mortal thing had the power to confuse in the way immortals did.

He snapped back to his senses when, impossibly, footsteps sounded outside, climbing up the ship's ramp. The she-worm looked in the direction of the sound, also startled.

No one was supposed to be here.

Damnation!

He called out hastily, "I said: No backup!"

A man appeared in the hatchway, pushed back his arctic hood. "I'm not your fucking backup."

"Strand!"

"I didn't know peacemakers carried guns," said Paul.

He did not know they wore beam shields either.

Jesus, how am I to kill him? He had hoped his arrival would give whoever had been battling Forgil in here time to do something, but he now saw that Maya of the Timberlines was doubled over on the deck. And Paul had just walked in holding a useless weapon.

Forgil was off balanced, but only for a moment. He said conversationally, "I see reports of your death were premature."

"So were yours."

Forgil lifted his brows to say he was unaware that he been reported dead.

And Paul addressed him, "Ashata."

Forgil gave a look a confusion, then burst into laughter.

Paul pressed on. "You altered these c ships' memories. You know how to get in and out of the Vikhen system without leaving a trace—because *you* are Vikhen. And I gave you the means! I can't believe I did that. The immortal disk I picked up in the c ship crash—that was yours."

Forgil just kept laughing and shaking his head.

"And I gave it back to you. No? I'll bet money you have it on you right now."

"You win that one. How much money did you wager?" Forgil said amiably and produced the disk.

He dialed up execution mode and grabbed Paul's arm.

Paul jolted back convulsively. But in the next instant realized he was still breathing and that absolutely nothing had happened except that Forgil was laughing at him.

The disk had fallen to the deck when Paul jumped. The pilot Maya was reaching for it when Forgil retrieved it. He tossed it up and caught it like a coin, offered it to Paul. "You may have it."

Paul took it gingerly, passed his thumb over it. It certainly looked like the one he had salvaged from the c ship crash. It should have killed him. If this were the disk. If that were Ashata. He had been so sure. This must not be the real disk. He set it on the console.

Forgil said, "I'm so glad you're already logged as dead. It saves me the trouble of explaining what is about to happen to you."

"Shit, you think I'd step in here if it was that easy for you? I left a trail," said Paul.

"There are always rumors of conspiracy any time a hero dies." He lifted his weapon, took aim at Paul's face, but the corner of his eye caught a movement at his feet—Maya was reaching up with fluttering hands as if to find a grip on the console to drag herself up. Her hand groped over the top. Forgil pushed her down with his foot. As her hands swept over the console top, something slid, skittered and rolled across the deck toward the hatch. It was Ashata's disk. It rolled partway down the ramp, tipped and spun itself to a stop.

Maya bent over coughing, hawked up blood and spat out a piece of tooth. Her eyes flooded with pain tears. She could not see where the disk had gone. She heard it spinning out on the ramp. *Life is short. Honor is long. Dishonor is longer.*

Forgil's attention had returned to Paul, to the glitter at his chest. "Your D.S. is not on your hero's grave, Lieutenant Colonel?"

"Colonel," said Paul. "You'll have a tougher time accounting for this than you will for me."

"I don't need to account for it."

"I told you I left a trail."

"Twice now. You're becoming too insistent here. I don't care what breadcrumbs you think you scattered after you. You have a rude surprise coming, Hansel. Please tell me, what do you think you could possibly have done that I can't overcome?"

"You *are* worried or you'd have fired by now instead of standing here chatting. And I won't be tricked into telling you. I've been with tougher interrogators than you."

"What? Your pretty vondesi? I always wondered, who got to be on top?"

A flash of anger overtook his composure. Paul had

been hearing comments like that ever since he got home and he was getting very tired of it. He spoke to himself aloud, "Steady, Strand, consider the source. If it comes out of an asshole, it's just a fart."

Forgil was distracted again by Maya creeping out the hatch to the ramp. "Now, now. I don't know where you think you're going, dear." He hit the control. The ramp lifted, pushing Maya back inside. The disk rolled in past her grasping hand, and the hatch snapped shut. The disk rolled to a stop against Forgil's foot.

Forgil put a hand to his side where Maya had landed a lucky blow. It was starting to ache. "Tough worm," he commented. "And you were an extraordinary worm, Strand. I am almost sorry."

"At the risk of sounding like a real bad vid, do you mind telling me what *was* the fucking point?"

"Something you could never understand," said Forgil. "Life is too long to be wasted as a pawn when you know you're a god."

Maya maneuvered herself to lay at Forgil's feet. The disk was within reach. *Keep him talking, Strand. Keep him talking.* Slowly she inched her hand toward it, touched it. Closed shaky fingers around it. *Got it!*

Forgil's heel came down on her forearm, hard, forced her hand to open.

"What have we here?"

Forgil bent down and plucked the disk from her hand. He held it up between his finger and thumb. "This? Is this what you've been after? And what do you think you're going to do with this?" He laughed at her. "Why, you silly little worm. In the hands of anyone but its owner this is an inert plastic lump. And Ashata is dead." He pocketed the disk, smiled down at her.

Maya died inside. She'd had it in her hand. Gone. Gone. He was up there laughing. Hope shredded away into despair. Her broken teeth throbbed.

Then in a miraculous moment, Forgil's hand came out of his pocket with the disk. He gave a cruel grin and dropped the disk into her hand.

She seized his ankle—and he let her. He thought it a joke and he expected to be laughing. She pressed the disk to him, rasped, "Nobody's dead around here but you, Selqarth."

She doubted he even heard her.

Paul dodged the crumbling body in the cramped confines of the hold. "Jesus Christ!" He gaped at the fallen Forgil, then at the bruised bleeding c pilot, Maya of the Timberlines. "If you're . . . ? Who's he?"

"Selqarth." She spat blood on him.

Paul knew the name from history, but he had slept through that chapter. "Who's Selqarth?"

She spoke more to herself. "A monster who has destroyed all that was good in the world. I have lost the only man I will ever love."

Paul quirked a smile. "Me too."

She knew him now. Strand, Paul Strand. That had been a scandal. "You are Penetanguishene's prisoner," she said. "You could die any tick."

"Yeah, I know."

"How do you live?" She asked as if earnestly needing to know.

"I take what I have. None of us knows how long they have."

"You know how long you haven't."

He shrugged. "All I know is I'm breathing now."

"I should have let him kill you first, but since I didn't, you must let me go."

"Ehremat—"

"No *mat*." She dragged herself along the console, opened the hatch. "I am Maya." She hurled Ashata's immortal disk out the hatch into the snow. She coughed. Ribs blazed with every inhalation. "You must have the ship. It's the only one whose memory is not poisoned by Selqarth. Retrieve our names."

She pulled her silver survival bag from the ship's tiny storage compartment and she stumbled down the ramp.

Paul watched her stagger and crawl over the ice. He ought to take her prisoner. She was Vikrhalt.

She fell, picked herself up, lurched ahead.

He could always rationalize that she might not make it.

Wind swirled around her in an icy veil.

Letting her go was not militarily a good idea. It was probably treason. But this day had shaken his faith in the military the way Kobandrid Rog could not. The world was now in shades of gray. In Kobandrid Rog he had known he was right and the fires of hell had only tempered his resolve. There had been a right and there had been a wrong and he had known which side he was on.

He returned to Fleet HQ with the c ship and the dead Forgil. "Good God, Strand! What killed him?"

"Stepped in some hubris."

"Wh—?"

The immortal plague, Paul thought.

Forgil's immortal disk and an autopsy scan would reveal to the world the true nature of the peacemaker.

While Paul was being debriefed on the incident, he was about to report Maya's existence, but what came out of his mouth instead was, "I miss Kobandrid Rog."

The officer recording his testimony paused. "You mean Northalia, sir."

"No. I miss Kobandrid Rog."

For men may come and men may go,
But I go on forever.

—Tennyson, *The Brook*

Alone in a dark room at the edge of Arctica the woman ached, in agony she could not bear. She had not decided what her name was now, or even if she could live.

The tooth enamel had regrown thinly over the exposed nerve; her ribs knit. The swelling had gone down from the bruises around her eyes. She was out of danger and out of the worst of the physical pain.

Its passing left her to face worse, with nothing tormenting from the outside to balance the pain that was tearing at her from inside.

What about me?

The grief was overwhelming, and she had nothing to keep her mind from it. She writhed alone on the floor, thought her heart would never heal.

God, if I could do it over again. She would not have walked away.

Suddenly she wanted a child and the only man she could even bear tentatively to imagine touching her was gone.

Race, a part of you could have lived forever.

It was cosmically unfair. *No one is dead but you, Selqarth.* Out of all the people supposedly dead who weren't—the Queen, Paul Strand, Ashata, not to mention Maya—why wasn't one of them Race? Nobody's dead but . . .

She sat up suddenly, lifted tear-tracked face from the floor and blinked puffy eyes into the dark.

Nobody's dead but . . .

The trouble with annihilation is . . .

She turned on a light, checked the date and tried to remember how much air was in a Kingsman pod.

*   *   *

Paul woke, aware that someone else was in his room. He heard nothing but he could tell. He almost called out a name but the owner was dead. He reached for a light.

"Don't touch it."

A hard voice. Female. He found her shape in the gloom, with a glitter of starlight on dark wet eyes and muted gleam on the beam gun. She said huskily, "You must get me a c ship." She sounded as if she had a cold. Either that or she had been crying.

"You waving that thing for exercise, ehremat? You know it doesn't matter to me. I could die any tick, remember?"

She held the weapon steady. She had been brandishing it. "I thought you would be clinging to your shreds of life."

"Not tight enough to commit treason. Otherwise I'd have a whole lot more than shreds left, 'kay?"

"A c ship. Now."

He answered her in her own language. "I guess it's characteristic of immortals to requisition top secret material and actually expect it to be forthcoming." He sounded just like the vondesi. More ghosts.

"You've activated an alarm, haven't you," she said.

"No."

"I leave here with a c ship or with you dead."

"Still whacking away with a stick. Why don't you paint me a nice carrot?"

"What?"

Paul braced himself up on an elbow and said reasonably, "Tell me why do you want a c ship."

The tone of demand slipped. It wasn't a cold; it was tears. "I need to see something . . . and I can trade information."

"What?"

"I'll show you how to use the sun reader to tell if something is in the Elsewhere."

Paul nodded conditionally. "In return for?"

"I need to see if something is in the Elsewhere."

*   *   *

The c ship escaped atmosphere without strain. Its power was seductive. Even at sublight speeds the c ship exuded invincibility and menace, and it took over the soul.

Paul momentarily forgot to let Maya out of the Kingsman pod in which he had smuggled her up.

In space near the sun, he let her out. She elbowed forward in the crawlway. "Any trouble?"

"No." Paul was a general now, and his country was making up awards for him since it had already given him its highest. Anything he wanted, he received. Take a c ship up? Go ahead, sir. There were not many people outranking him now to say he could not.

Maya pointed over his shoulder. "Turn on your sun reader and your magnetograph."

Paul surveyed the display of information, temperatures at altitudes, rotational velocity, predicted flares. "Now what?"

"Pick up those sunspots and ask for one with no polarity."

"How?"

"Search!" Maya called over his shoulder. "For a sunspot having no polarity."

The reader flashed red in answer. Negative information.

"Do a partial orbit and get this field," Maya ordered.

Paul tried it. Again he received a red flash. Negative information. "What am I looking for?"

"A sunspot that is not a sunspot."

He searched the sun over, received nothing but red flashes.

"Ehremat, that's all the big ones."

"We want a little one. It will be a little one."

If it's here.

There were none.

"That's all of them, ehremat."

Can't be. She tried something else. "Search. For an unpolarized region within a larger polarized sunspot.

The region measuring one ten millionth plus or minus fifty percent."

"A spot within a spot?" said Paul.

"Yes."

"Race dove into a sunspot?"

"No. It will be a recent one. He wouldn't have dived into a sunspot, but one could have formed after he went in."

Within degrees the sunreader said, "Isolated." Green flash highlighted a small spot within a spot.

"Mass!" Maya demanded.

"150 kilograms," said the machine voice.

"Ilu," Maya breathed.

"Mass of what?" said Paul.

"There are 150 kilos that went into the Elsewhere here and haven't come out."

"Don't cry in here, ehremat. Those tears become bullets under acceleration."

He could hear her sniffling behind him. The more contained they are, the more disturbing it was when they cried.

"It's Race."

"Um, 150 kilos doesn't have to be a Kingsman pod. It could be debris sheared off. Rachelson was bucked down once for not riding a ship down. Do you think he would bale out again after what happened the last time?"

She had thought of that. Over and over and over on the way here. She remembered him saying, "Had I to do it again, I wouldn't."

After what happened last time.

"Nothing happened last time!" The last time Race abandoned a c ship, it supposedly took out an immortal. It hadn't. *I'm right here.*

There was only one way to know for certain.

Paul would have to give her the controls and let her take the ship into the Elsewhere.

So surprised when she didn't kill him.

When the Kingsman pod opened again, Paul knew

that the immortal hadn't popped him out with the space junk while she took the ship and fled to parts yet unimagined.

He was not sure why she didn't, or why he had given her the chance. These were bad strategic moves on both their parts.

Paul wormed out of the pod into the c ship's tight hold. As he emerged he saw that she *had* popped out a Kingsman pod.

And replaced it with another one. "Race Rachelson, I presume," he said to the sealed pod.

That pod remained shut tight.

Paul floated forward to the crawlway and tapped on the firewall. Maya opened the access. He spoke over her shoulder. "Is he all right?"

"I—I haven't checked. I have to concentrate here."

She was having difficulty containing herself. She had the pod monitors switched off. She was afraid to turn it on.

If Rachelson was not on suspended animation, then he was decks gone.

They could be bringing home a corpse.

Paul looked ahead through the viewer. "Shit."

Presented with the awesome blank of the Elsewhere, he clutched at Maya's shoulder.

She recovered enough to say with disdain, "Grounder."

Paul was lost in wonder and dread.

"What is it?"

"Nothing," she said easily. "Perfect nothing. It doesn't even exist."

His unnerve had a calming effect on Maya.

Good, she had to hold together to get them back.

" 'Kay, let's head home," he managed to whisper.

"We *are* heading home," said Maya. "At a half million klicks per tick."

That couldn't be. The ship did not seem to be moving at all.

Maya moved the stick to turn a tight circle. Paul clutched at the back of her seat, but the expected centripetal lurch was not forthcoming.

"We're at EtaCas," Maya announced.

The computer showed their exact location in Galactic coordinates.

Maya sent Paul back into the pod for deceleration. He was sure she would kill him this time.

But she ferried him back to spacetime, and he was more shocked still when she surrendered the controls at sublight speed.

"Now you must let me go," said Maya.

"Yeah," said Paul.

Her thick brows converged. She hadn't expected such ready agreement and she did not trust it. "Why?"

"Because I'm allergic to genocide. Why didn't you kill me?"

She gave her head a slow side to side. She could not say. When had worms acquired an individual worth?

"Doesn't matter," he said. "Go forth and multiply. I never saw you. Where should I put you?"

She moved back to the pods. "Set us down somewhere where . . . if he's dead . . . I can bury him." *And if he's not . . . he can walk away.*

Before she closed the lid on her pod Paul called back, "Hey."

She looked forward.

"I peeked. He's alive. S.A." Suspended animation.

She sealed her pod with pounding heart. *He's alive. He's alive.*

Will he be happy to see me?

She kept a crouched vigil a hundred paces from the Kingsman pod, waiting for the occupant to revive from suspended animation. She held her arms around her bent knees, sometimes tugged at blades of scrub grass. She squinted at the westering sun. They were at the edge of a forest on the Alquon highlands.

A catwolf yowled somewhere in its depths. From the treetops came the rusty metal flute of a peridot bird's evensong.

The pod rested on the bank of a rippling watercourse. The stream had carved a winding path through soft shale leaving jagged stone shelves. A violetta splashing in the water fluttered up, perched on the pod, shook the droplets off its wings and sailed into the forest.

Maya lost sense of time. It could have been degrees, could have been hours. How long had she been waiting there listening to her heart break?

The Kingsman pod opened. Race emerged and leapt clear of the pod, and crouched into battle posture. He spun a 384 and then straightened up. There was no one around but Maya.

He gazed into the forest, spoke with his eyes directed somewhere inside it. "Is the war over?"

"It's over."

"Who won?"

"They did."

"You're still free."

"I'm dead. So are you. Your name is clear."

"Where's my squadron?"

"In Beltava. Making trouble for the new regime. Trying out their free mortals' rights."

"Where's your ship?"

"I traded it for your name."

"What's the date?" he said, then waved that question away. "It doesn't matter."

He started walking toward the woods.

So that was it. She watched him go, heard herself call without intending to. "Race!"

He stopped, took a long time deciding to turn around. Finally he walked toward her. She stood up to meet him, brushed grass and dust from her hands.

The gray eyes that saw clear through her raked her up and down. She completely forgot what she wanted to say, if she had ever known at all, confronted by the kind of fury only a wound ignites.

He spoke. "You hurt me. You worse than hurt me. What in hell makes you think I would open myself up to that kind of pain again?"

She shook her head and started to go.

He was not done. He said at her back, "But God knows there are things stronger than pride or pain."

She turned. He was waiting, and of all things he looked scared. Vulnerable as a quick-lived rose.

She whispered because she could not find her voice. "This is impossible. I am forever and you are a moment."

"It's *my* moment and I want you in it. I never intended to ask twice: Will you marry me?"

Where did all these tears come from and how long had she been crying? "I have to," she said. "I love you more than life." It came out a wail, as if entirely against her will.

From her, he took it.

He put his arms around her. His mouth on hers frightened her and made her as embarrassed as a child. Another part of her wanted to be here like this always, or for as much of always as there was for them.

When they parted Maya realized she had been gripping his uniform with her fists. She loosed her hold. And he started to walk, his arm around her waist, guiding her toward the woods.

She said, "I need a new name."

"Yes, but don't pick one. Let them choose it. Something they can pronounce. Until it's safe to come out again."

She peered into the forest that was impenetrable to unaccustomed eyes, a solid screen of green and brown. She heard calls and cries; she had not learned to sort them. It was all unknown, confused and harboring dread. She realized where they were going and whispered, "Ilu."

She must have looked frightened because he said, "Consider it advanced survival training. You're used to mixing with the lower brutes."

She straightened her posture, squared her shoulders. "Nothing lesser beings haven't done before me."

"That's my Maya."

They stepped into the woodland fringe as the sun was sinking low, its rays slanting long, and monarch tree shadows reached far into the forest with the fading twilight.

Eta Cassiopeian Timekeeping

There are 499.12 Eta Cassiopeian days in an Eta Cassiopeian year. It is a long year, equal to 415 Earth days.

An Eta Cassiopeian day is short and measures in Earth units, 19 hours 58 minutes and 5 seconds. The Eta Cassiopeians divide their day into 16 units which they call local hours. A local hour equals 74.88 Earth minutes.

Eta Cassiopeians ascribe 384 degrees to a circle. The Eta Cassiopeian time unit known as a *degree* equals the time it takes EtaCas to rotate through one Eta Cassiopeian degree of arc. A degree equals 3.12 Earth minutes. There are 24 degrees in a local hour. Further subdivisions are called *ticks* (or skinny seconds by the Telegonians). There are 192 ticks in a degree.

Eta Cassiopeian moons are of little consequence for timekeeping or for anything else. The year is divided arbitrarily into twentieths, *vants*, of 25 days each. Vants are rather short since the days are short, so the most common unit in the business world is the *doublevant*, 50 local days, which has the virtue of dividing evenly into 5 *decks*. A *deck*, 10 days, is the Eta Cassiopeian answer to the week. The unit of five days, a *halfdeck*, is little used and exists to describe how many decks are in a vant (two and half).